K*I*Smet

Chris Calder

HEDDON PUBLISHING

Second edition published in 2019 by Heddon Publishing.

Copyright © Chris Calder 2019, all rights reserved.
No part of this book may be reproduced, adapted, stored in a retrieval system or transmitted by any means, electronic, photocopying, or otherwise without prior permission of the author.

ISBN 978-1-913166-20-5

Cover design by Catherine Clarke

This is a work of fiction. Names, characters, businesses, places, events and incidents are either the products of the author's imagination or used in a fictitious manner. Any resemblance to actual persons, living or dead, or actual events is purely coincidental.

Book design and layout by Katharine Smith, Heddon Publishing.

www.heddonpublishing.com
www.facebook.com/heddonpublishing
@PublishHeddon

After ten happy years in rural France, Chris Calder has returned to England. He came late to writing novels, and now has four published with two more on the way.

Chris says that he tries never to forget that readers of fiction expect to be diverted and entertained. He loves feedback and always responds to emails from readers. He believes passionately that taking on board what readers want is the best way to improve what he does.

For Elise –

With thanks –

Chris

August 2020.

This book is dedicated to the memory of Lance Callaghan, whose wise counsel, generous help and continuous encouragement fuelled and sustained my writing ambitions. He leaves a vacuum that cannot be filled.

For their advice and support I am also indebted to Karen Davies, Laura Lawrie and my long-suffering spouse Joan. My grateful thanks to you all, and to Elise !!

Chris Calder

CHAPTER ONE

THEY ARE GOING TO KILL ME. NO ONE WILL LISTEN. YOU MUST HELP ME.

The words jumped off the page. They were crudely handwritten in block capitals, like the rest of the letter that Edmund Lafitte, Member of Parliament for Somerford was holding in his hand. It had arrived the previous day, asking for an interview. Why a letter? Surely a simple phone call would have sufficed? He read it again and that sentence stood out. A hoax? Possibly. A crank? More likely. But if it was genuine, another matter altogether. He glanced at his watch. Ten to twelve. If the man was coming, he was cutting it fine.

Edmund attended his constituency office on most Saturdays, from nine until noon. The last visitor had just left. If the man did not appear in the next few minutes, the letter was probably not genuine.

A soft knock on the door and his secretary Rosie entered, holding a notepad.

"Has he turned up?" Edmund asked.

"He's just come in. Mr Khan."

"Do we know him?"

"I don't think he's been before. I asked what it was about

but he wouldn't say. He hardly spoke at all. Scared out of his wits, if you ask me."

"Better wheel him in."

"Right. Oh, and you've had two calls; Beth Stanway and Amir. They said you're not answering your mobile. I told them you've mislaid it and you'd call back."

Lafitte checked his watch again and picked up his desk phone. "I'll do that now. Can you give me five minutes, then bring Mr Khan in? Whatever he wants, I'll have to keep it short, I'm meeting Stella for lunch."

At just under six feet tall, slim, fit and still only thirty-eight, the man who had been called the most eligible bachelor in the House of Commons was sitting at a cheap pine desk in a room at the back of the rented premises. Formerly a grocery store, the place had been vacant when he took on the lease after being elected to the House of Commons seven years earlier. Edmund lived in London but spent most weekends in Somerford with his partner Stella.

Rosie asked, "Do you want me to stay on?"

"No, it's OK, you go on home, I'll lock up." Edmund drew forward the pad on his desk.

Rosie paused at the door. "I've searched reception and your mobile's definitely not there."

"OK, no sweat. It's probably somewhere at Stella's, or in her car."

Rosie nodded and left. Edmund decided to call Beth Stanway first. She answered immediately.

"Elizabeth Stanway."

"Hello, Beth. Ed Lafitte. You OK?"

"Hello Edmund, I'm fine." She sounded breathless and stressed, the words tumbling out. "What's the latest? In *The*

Globe this morning it says that the situation with Peter and the other hostages may be improving. Have you heard anything from the Foreign Office?"

"I haven't, but they're not on full staff at weekends."

"Oh." She sounded disappointed. "Nothing new since the last meeting?"

"Negotiations take time, Beth. I'm sure that if something had happened they'd have told me. But I'll be back in Westminster on Monday. I'll see what I can find out and get back to you."

"Surely there's someone at the Foreign Office today who'd know if there's any news?"

"If there was, I'd have been told, I'm sure. What does it say in the paper?"

"It's about the Red Cross in Syria. It says they're expecting some news about the hostages."

"Nothing specific, then. Sometimes the papers have to be a bit vague. Why don't you call the news desk? *The Globe's* been badgering the FO ever since Peter was taken. They look after their own, especially war reporters. They'll know if there's anything going on."

"Will they take my call? I mean..."

"Just tell them you're his mother."

"OK, I'll call them. Can you get back to me on Monday anyway?"

Edmund confirmed that he would and they ended the call. He did not think that there was any new development in the Stanway case but he would check, just to be sure. With the war on the ground now going against Islamic State, news was unreliable and sketchy.

He glanced at his watch and picked up the handset again.

There was just enough time to give Amir Hakim a call.

Hakim was his constituency agent, the man most responsible for Edmund's success in winning his Somerford parliamentary seat seven years earlier. He had overturned the sizeable majority that his opponent, a prominent Labour Party politician, had enjoyed for two decades. The call was answered moments later. Hakim's distinctive voice, normally high-pitched, was almost falsetto.

"Hello, Ed. I've been trying to get you."

"Yeah, sorry. I can't find my mobile, but it'll turn up. Everything OK?"

"Fine, nothing serious. I just wanted you to tell you that I can't make it on the twentieth. My cousin's over from Canada for a few days." Hakim called in to the constituency office regularly, usually on one of the Saturdays when Edmund was there.

"Don't worry, I'm sure we'll manage."

"I'll catch up with you next time."

"OK. I'll check with Rosie and call you back to confirm."

"You'll have to find your phone first."

"Very funny. See you." Edmund rang off.

A minute later, Rosie returned, ushering in the last visitor. "Mr Khan," she announced.

Khan was wearing clean, casual khaki jeans and a blue padded anorak. He came forward and Edmund gestured towards the chair on the other side of the desk.

"Please take a seat, Mr Khan."

Rosie was right, the man was nervous. His thin brown face wore an anxious expression beneath the dark hair neatly parted on one side. His eyes flicked around, moving constantly.

"Thank you," he murmured.

Edmund looked up. "How can I help you?"

"I – I don't know what to do. Me and my family..." Apparently in some distress, Khan shook his head mutely.

"What about your family? What's the problem?"

"They – some people are going to harm them or kill me if I don't pay."

"You're being threatened with violence? Surely that's a matter for the police?"

Khan's mouth turned down. "I went to them but it was no good."

"Why not?"

"They don't want to help."

"Really? Who've you spoken to? I know all the senior officers in the constituency. Who refused to help?"

Khan shook his head again. "Not here, I live in Donfield."

Donfield? Clearly, Rosie hadn't checked the envelope that the letter had arrived in. Edmund made a show of looking at his wristwatch. "Mr Khan, I'm sorry but I have an appointment in the town. Perhaps you should take the matter up with your own MP? I really don't know why you've come all the way from Yorkshire to see me."

Khan looked up. "On the news it said you negotiate with Islamic State. That's why I came."

"The Foreign Office does that. All I'm doing is trying to help a journalist who's being held hostage. He lives in this constituency."

"You can't help?"

Edmund stalled. Why get involved? After a few moments his curiosity prevailed. He had enough time for a question or two.

"Are you telling me that you and your family are being threatened by the Islamic State?"

Khan spoke again, more softly. "They have men everywhere. They're called the Brotherhood. The Yorkshire group's in Donfield and they take money from Muslim businesses."

"Extortion, you mean?"

"They call it tax. We have to give them twenty per cent of our income every month, in cash."

"Twenty per cent? Incredible. What's your business?"

"Take-away food. Used to be a restaurant but we closed, it was losing money. Now it's only take-out."

"And if you don't pay?"

"They do something bad."

"Like what?"

"A friend of mine is a halal butcher. He didn't pay and they hurt his son, broke his arm. The boy is only ten." Khan was visibly distressed. "Then they said if he still didn't pay, his son would die."

Lafitte stared at the man for a few seconds, then picked up a biro and flipped open his notepad. "Can the incident be verified? Did the father go to the police?"

"No, he was afraid. The boy was taken to hospital, Donfield General. I can get the date if you want, but the father is saying it was an accident. They're afraid to tell the truth, it was not an accident."

"If the victim says it was an accident, Mr Khan, I don't see what can be done."

"But you *must* help," Khan pleaded. "There's nowhere else I can go."

Edmund felt sorry for the man. "Do you attend your

mosque? I mean, are you a practising Muslim?"

"Yes."

"Why don't you go to your Imam? He should be able to help, or he may know someone who can."

Instantly, Khan's demeanour changed. He shook his head in rapid, emphatic movements. "No, no, I can't do that. Definitely not."

"Why not?"

"He's – I think he's their leader."

"What, the Imam?"

Khan's nodded, his face grim. "Yes."

"Let me get this straight. You're saying that your Imam's responsible for extortion?" Edmund put his biro down. "I'm sorry, but I find that hard to believe."

"I am not lying, Mr Lafitte."

"I didn't say that. But it's hardly likely, is it?"

The man's face hardened. "You don't understand. He's mad, crazy. He wants to kill non-Muslims."

"What?"

"Mad, he's mad. You have to believe me. He's crazy and he's got men who'll do anything he tells them. Anything!" This was a near rant. Khan had raised his voice and was breathing heavily. "All are frightened and no one is listening. That's the problem. You have to do something."

Edmund waited a few moments. "Tell me, have you spoken to your own MP?"

"No."

"Why not?"

"He's a friend of the Imam. The MP is Javid Nasir."

"I've met him. You think he's connected with this Brotherhood?"

"Most likely. I can't risk it." Khan licked his lips. "If they know I'm talking to you, they'll kill me for sure."

So that's why he sent the letter. Edmund looked steadily at his visitor. The man genuinely believed that his life was being threatened. After a few long moments, Edmund spoke. "If what you say is true – and I'm not saying it isn't – this really is a matter for the police. Extortion is a serious crime. You say they're not helping, so I'll tell you what I'll do. Let me make some enquiries." He opened a drawer in the desk, took out a business card and handed it across. "In the meantime, take this. Give me a call in a week or so." He stood up. "Now, if you don't mind, I must..."

Khan interrupted. "There's something else." Edmund remained standing.

Khan said, "Two men have already been killed by these people. One of them was my cousin Mansoor, drowned in the canal. They said it was suicide because his taxi business was doing badly. And there was a note to say sorry. He was paying, then stopped because he couldn't pay any more. I'm telling you, Mr Lafitte, Mansoor would never have killed himself. Impossible."

Edmund sank back onto his chair. "What about the note?"

"Not even his handwriting. His wife told the police, but they wouldn't listen. It was worse for her when the coroner said he took his life himself. It was in the *Donfield Echo*."

Lafitte wrote down the name of the newspaper. "When was this?"

"Last week."

"What was his full name?"

"Mansoor Ali Khan. He was only thirty-six. He was a family man; he would never have killed himself."

Edmund was making notes.

"You said there were two. Who was the other?"

"Gulam Hussein, he came from Uganda in the 1970s. His father bought a paper shop and built it up. Gulam took over when his father retired. I didn't know him personally but he refused to pay the Brotherhood."

"What happened to him?"

"Hit and run. The car was stolen and they never found the driver."

Edmund was still writing. Without looking up he asked, "When did that happen?"

"About three months ago."

"What makes you think that the Brotherhood did it?"

"He made a big mistake. He made fun of them. He said he would never give in to them."

"That hardly proves anything."

"Mr Lafitte, we are peaceful people. In this kind of situation we mostly keep quiet and pay up. When we can't, they don't believe us and they call us enemies of Islam."

"What do you mean?"

"The Imam says he's God's messenger and some people believe him. They're extremists who say anyone getting in their way must be punished."

"Can you name any of these people?"

Khan seemed about to answer, but checked himself. "No, sorry."

"You don't seem sure."

"I can't name anyone, Mr Lafitte."

"You can't? Or you won't?"

"I can't, I just can't." The man's face was a picture of misery. He lowered his head and mumbled, "I'm sorry."

Then he looked up again. "But the police know who they are. For sure."

The man is too afraid to say more. Edmund closed his notepad and put it aside. "All right. Leave it with me and I'll see what I can do."

Ten minutes later, Edmund was hurrying towards Bridge Street in the town centre, a few minutes' walk away. He was late, but he knew that Stella would forgive him. She always did. Holding his tablet in its case and with his raincoat folded over his arm, he bounded up the steps into the Three Feathers Hotel, strode past the bar and on through the arched doorway that led to the restaurant.

The manager, a dapper man clutching a clipboard in the crook of his arm, smiled. "Good afternoon, Mr Lafitte. Let me take your coat."

"Thank you, Oliver."

"Mrs Tudor is already here. Your usual table."

Edmund eased his way between tables of diners to the corner where Stella sat at the table that had been set for them, complete with a basket of bread rolls and a bottle of red wine. She was holding a nearly-full glass, looking cool and composed in her navy blue suit and crisp white blouse, its wide collar a contrast to her auburn shoulder-length hair. She tilted her head and he bent to kiss her proffered cheek.

"Sorry to keep you, sweetie, I was held up." He straightened, adding, "You're looking gorgeous."

Stella's mouth twisted into a smile. "And you're trying to bullshit me. You're late."

"It's that blue suit, my favourite."

"I know." She reached down for her handbag. "You left

your mobile on the bedside table."

"Ah, I wondered where it was."

Stella passed the phone to him. "Four or five missed calls."

Edmund glanced at the display. "Six, actually." He was about to tap the phone when a waiter arrived to take their order.

Stella leaned forward. In a loud whisper she said, "Don't even think about it. We're here for lunch, not business."

He raised his eyebrows. "OK, no probs."

They placed their orders and the waiter left. Edmund picked up the bottle of wine and poured some into his glass. "Sorry, that was thoughtless. It's been a rough morning." He looked across. "You?"

She shrugged. "Um, the usual Saturday. Neighbour disputes, a divorce and an unfair dismissal. So much for having one in three Saturdays off, it's ages since the last one. Hector says junior partners have to work harder. The sod." She was referring to Hector Walford, a senior partner in the legal firm that she worked for.

"Why am I not surprised? They're stringing you along, dangling the carrot."

"I've waited long enough. They keep talking about it but I still have to see it in writing."

"That's the trouble with law firms, they're slow. You're wasted there."

"I like my job. Most of the time it's OK." She lifted her glass, took a sip and placed it back on the table. "One thing for sure, I'd rather be a lawyer than a politician."

The waiter brought over their first course plates of soup. He placed the dishes before them and left.

Stella reached for a bread roll. "What was the problem this morning?"

"Some guy who says he's being threatened by people from Islamic State. Could be nasty, if it's true."

She tore the roll in half. "Anything to do with the Stanway case?"

"Not directly. He knew I've been trying to get Peter Stanway back, so he thought I could help." He picked up his spoon. "Not much chance of that. We'll see, I'll make a few calls."

CHAPTER TWO

When his mobile rang at a quarter to one in the morning, Imam Zulfikar Ali Mahmud was sitting quietly, meditating in his darkened living room in the city of Donfield. The call was earlier than expected. He switched on the table light, put on his wire-framed spectacles. He glanced at the display briefly and took the call.

"Yes?"

"There's a problem."

"What?" *An anxious moment.* "Have you done it?"

"Yes, all finished. I cleared out his pockets, like you said."

"What's the problem?"

"There was a business card in his jacket, the MP's. What do you want me to do with it?"

"Throw it away," the Imam snapped, then immediately changed his mind. "No. Wait, let me think." He heard the other man's heavy breathing for a few moments. Finally he spoke. "You took out everything else?"

"Yes."

"What was there?"

"Car keys, his mobile, a biro, and some loose change. Also, some paper tissues and some money. Thirty pounds, in notes."

"Put the card back."

"Put it back?"

"Yes. Put it back in his pocket and make sure it can't fall out."

"What about the other things?"

"No, only the card. Get rid of the rest, especially the phone. Remember what I told you to do with your mobile? Do the same with his."

"It seems a waste."

"Listen," the Imam hissed, "this is important. Do what I said. Get away from there and use your phone one more time to call me when it's finished. Then smash up the mobiles and throw away the pieces. Scatter them."

"As you wish."

"Make sure you do it." The Imam ended the call, thinking about what might happen when the MP's card would be the only thing found on the body. Yes, he nodded to himself in satisfaction, he had done the right thing and it felt good. He put the mobile down. He would wait for the last call, after which he would destroy it.

A few hours later, on the other side of the city, Detective Chief Inspector Charles Royce of Donfield CID was in an unmarked police car, being driven by his sergeant Colin Brody at a steady pace along a main road out of the city. Royce was peering through the early morning mist when they were overtaken at speed by a red sports saloon that disappeared into the murk ahead.

"Idiot!" Royce exclaimed.

"Pity we can't get after him," Brody said. "It's his lucky day."

Royce wiped his face with his hands. "I really, *really*

didn't want to get out of bed. Crack of dawn on a Sunday, for Christ's sake."

"Could have been better timed, sir."

"For sure. The victim's a male, beheaded. Unbelievable." Royce was peering ahead. "You know where it is?"

Brody raised his chin. "About a mile on, off the next lay-by."

"Must be where the killer parked up, then. The body's off a pathway through Milford Park. Not far from the road."

"Who found him?"

"Early morning jogger." Royce snorted. "Must've stopped him in his tracks, no mistake. They're holding him there."

A minute later, the lay-by came into sight. Two patrol cars, an unmarked police van, and a white Corsa saloon were parked there. A silver Mercedes estate stood on the grass verge alongside. There were two men in the back of one of the police cars.

"Lay-by's full," Royce observed. "Looks like they're all here."

"Doc Granger, too. That's his Merc, I'll pull up there." Brody slowed the car. "Not often he gets to a scene before us."

"I'm guessing Poulter pressed a few buttons." Royce was referring to Sergeant Jimmy Poulter, who had been on duty when the call came in. "Nasty business; the doc must've been told to get on with it."

Brody eased the car onto the grass verge. "He'll not be best pleased, then, Sunday morning and all."

They stepped out and a young uniformed policeman came forward.

"Morning, sir." He indicated towards Royce's right. "Down the path, about a hundred yards on the left." He pointed at the lay-by. "Sergeant Bates is with the man who found the body. He's in a bad way, so the Sarge took him to wait in the car. And there's an ambulance on the way."

Royce nodded. "Thank you, Constable…"

"Stokes, sir."

"Constable Stokes. Tell the sergeant we'll be back to talk to the man after we've had a look around. Who's there at the moment?"

"The full team, also Doc Granger."

A few minutes later, the two detectives reached a cordoned-off area in a clearing in the wood. Two uniformed constables were standing by the tapes. Inside the enclosure a photographer's camera shutter clicked in rapid staccato bursts. The pathologist was on his knees, examining the torso of the victim. His assistant, a young woman, stood alongside. All three were wearing white coveralls. One of the uniformed policemen came forward.

"Morning, sir. Sergeant Stevens, Bull Street. I've got men posted on the path both sides, to keep the public out."

Royce took in the scene. "Christ! What a mess." Brody stood beside him, saying nothing. His eyes stared out of a face that had turned grey.

The pathologist looked up. "About time, Charlie. Where've you been?"

"Oh, you know, overslept," Royce drawled. "Not really. But it's not often you get to a scene first, Patrick." He lifted a section of the tape and ducked under it. Brody had not followed. He was standing still, rocking slightly on his feet.

The woman saw this and frowned. "Are you all right?"

The doctor raised his head sharply to look at Brody. "If you're going to throw up, Sergeant, stay where you are. I don't want you contaminating the scene."

Brody turned around, doubled up, heaved and was noisily sick.

Royce said nothing but the uniformed sergeant showed sympathy. "Better out than in."

The corpse was lying on its right side, knees drawn up and hands cable-tied behind its back. A metre away lay a severed head, apparently having bounced or rolled there. A considerable amount of blood had been shed and the photographer was taking close-ups of the torso and neck. Royce picked his way carefully around the corpse, observing every detail. He pointed to a spot near the shoulder of the body, where there was a damp patch of something he could not identify.

"What's that?"

Doctor Granger had been kneeling by the side of the body. He stood up. "Vomit," he said, tersely. "Could be the victim's, but possibly not. I've taken a sample and I'll let you know when I've done the PM."

"Time of death?"

"Sometime between five and seven hours ago, I'm guessing. I'll know better when we get some tests done."

"Around midnight, then. Any ID?"

"Nothing in the pockets. Except a card." He turned to his assistant. "Sheila?"

The woman held up a transparent plastic bag of the type used to preserve evidence. Inside, there appeared to be a small printed card.

Royce moved forward. "What, nothing at all?"

She answered, "The pockets were cleared out, except for this."

Royce took the bag and held it up. He peered closely at the card, turning the bag around. "A business card. Is that blood?"

"A bloody thumbprint, Inspector. I'm not swearing, it's blood."

Royce read out the name on the card. "*Edmund Lafitte, Member of Parliament*." He raised his eyebrows. "Well, now. An MP, what's that about?"

The doctor said, "I'll need to examine it in the lab."

"OK, we'll take a photo. Any suggestions whose print it is?"

"The only thing I can tell you for sure is that it isn't the victim's," he replied drily. Beside him, the woman chuckled.

Royce didn't think the gallows humour funny. He turned to speak to Brody. "Take a photo of this, Colin. You OK to do that?"

Brody's face was still pale but he seemed to have recovered. He coughed and wiped his mouth with a handkerchief. "Yes, sir." He took out his mobile. Royce held up the bag and Brody took photos of the front and back of the card.

The doctor said, "Never seen anything like this before. Barbaric."

Royce handed the card back. He was thinking aloud. "No car keys in the pocket, he must have been brought here by the killer. The way he was butchered, makes you wonder, why here?" He moved forward to take a closer look at the severed head, leaned over and said, "Poor sod. Didn't stand a chance."

"There's a car parked up in the lay-by, sir," Brody volunteered. "A Vauxhall Corsa."

Royce straightened. "So there is. Good point." He looked around. "Anyone here own the Corsa parked in the lay-by?" There was no response. He looked at the uniformed officer. "Sergeant?"

"Not one of our lot, sir."

The woman said, "Not mine, I came with the doctor."

Royce turned to Brody. "Go take the number, Colin. Then get on to Jimmy and do a trace. I'll be along in a minute to speak to the bloke who called it in."

"Yes, sir," Brody said, leaving.

Royce's mind was working to a pattern honed over years of investigations. He moved away from the immediate scene and was examining the ground between the pathway and the enclosure. Had they walked the victim to the place where they killed him, or drugged and carried him? Not drugged, because he would have been conscious if he was kneeling when the fatal blow was struck. So he had been forced to cooperate. At gunpoint? Probably. You could hardly push a man forward at the end of a sword.

The sword. It would have to be quite long. Heavy? Maybe, or maybe not. *So at least two people responsible. Interesting.*

Five minutes later, Royce was trudging back towards the lay-by. Brody was standing on the path at its closest point to the road, a few yards away from his own car. He came forward.

"We've traced the Corsa, sir. Three years old, registered to a Mr Sayeed Iqbal, Donfield address. When Jimmy called back he said that the name rang a bell, so he checked. Seems a Mrs Iqbal phoned Bull Street nick just after three o'clock this morning, saying that her husband had gone missing. She said he took a call around midnight and left the house but didn't return. And he's not answering his mobile."

"Looks likely, then. But there's no mobile here, is there? Could've been taken by the killer."

"We can get the number from the wife, sir."

"We'll go see her. And somebody needs to ID the body, but not a good idea to ask the wife. She'll have some family photos; we'll see what we can get. If it's the same bloke we'll get his GP to do it. The wife can see him later, after the doc's tidied him up."

"Should I organize a WPC to meet us there?"

"Yes, do that." Royce began walking towards the lay-by. "First things first. Have you talked to the witness?"

"Only to tell him that you'd be along. His name's Palmer. Caucasian, about thirty. Sergeant Bates is still with him."

Royce quickened his pace. "Come on, then."

They headed for the patrol car. The uniformed sergeant stepped out from the driver's side as they drew near. A heavy truck swooshed past, barely inches away. Royce thought they were too close to the road. This was no place to conduct an interview. He moved forward and spoke to the policeman.

"Sergeant Bates?"

"Sir?"

Royce lowered his voice. "How's the witness, a Mr Palmer, is it?"

"John Palmer, lives a couple of miles away. He was badly shocked, but he's calm now."

A huge transporter thundered past, the air in its wake causing Royce to wince. He raised his voice. "I'll take him to our car."

After a brief introduction, Royce felt that the witness appeared well enough to be interviewed and he and Brody led Palmer to their car. Brody opened the rear door and leaned in to retrieve his tablet and a file from the back seat. He turned to the witness.

"Please get in, Mr Palmer."

On the other side of the car, Royce had opened the rear door. He settled into the corner and turned so that he was nearly facing the witness. "Sorry we kept you, sir. It was kind of you to wait. First, does your family know you've been delayed?"

Palmer had a distinctly unhappy look on his thin face. "I called the wife, but I didn't say much. I didn't want to upset her."

"Just a few details for now, Mr Palmer, it shouldn't take more than a couple of minutes and then we'll take you home. We'll need a statement from you but we can leave that for now. We know you've had a bit of a shock, so I'll keep it short. Please tell us how you came upon the victim."

"I went out for my morning jog, as usual..."

"What time was that?"

"I usually leave the house about a quarter to seven. About fifteen minutes later, I left the pathway, to cut through the woods. That's my normal route."

Brody said, "Some distance from the path, probably why you were the first on the scene."

Palmer drew his hands onto his lap and locked his fingers together. His face wore a desolate look and he was struggling to describe what he had seen. "The – the body was just lying there, on its side. It was horrible – *horrible*."

Royce said, "We understand, sir. Take your time."

Palmer's head jerked up. "My first thought was to call the emergency services, so I did." He unlocked his fingers and spread his hands. "What else could I do? I couldn't help him, could I? Then the police car arrived."

"Were you waiting long?"

"Not long. Three or four minutes, maybe. I went to the lay-by to flag them down."

"And nobody else came along?"

"No. At least, I didn't see anyone."

Royce altered his position, turning to face forwards. "Thank you, Mr Palmer. Sergeant Brody will take you home now. Please give him your number and we'll contact you about the statement." He opened the door and then as an afterthought spun around and asked, "Just one more thing, sir. Sorry to have to ask, but were you physically sick?"

Palmer bristled. "What? No, I did feel nauseous, but I didn't throw up."

"Unfortunately, somebody did, close to the body." Royce stepped out of the car. "Take Mr Palmer home, Sergeant."

Brody started the engine and steered the car onto the road. Sergeant Bates left his patrol car and came over. "All done, sir?"

"For now. I just want to go back to the scene for a minute."

"I'm waiting here for the ambulance," Bates replied. "Taking their time, aren't they? Still, there's no hurry."

Royce began to walk back to the pathway. So Palmer had

felt 'nauseous', had he? Must be good to be well spoken, even when under pressure. *Probably been captain of his college debating team, or had a degree in English, or something.*

Later, after a harrowing visit to the murdered man's widow, Royce and Brody were returning to their base.

Brody said, "Poor woman. I don't want to see anything like that again."

"You will, lad, for sure, if you stay a copper," Royce replied quietly. "And you'll see plenty more that'll make you want to throw up again. Comes with the territory. You get used to it, in time. You have to learn to deal with it and move on."

"If you don't mind me saying, sir, the way you handled things at the house, you seem to know a lot about Muslims. I mean, about what they have to do and such, in situations like this."

"Twenty-five years since I joined the force. Weren't a lot of Muslims around then, or mosques. I've watched them grow and learned a bit along the way. They have a special feeling for the deceased – reverence, you might call it, for the body. It can cause problems when an autopsy's needed. With Muslims the next of kin always want to get on with the burial. Within twenty-four hours, if possible."

Brody's eyes widened. "Surely Doc Granger's not going to do a PM on a Sunday?"

"I don't think he'll do it today, but he won't hang around, he knows it's important for the family. You have to respect people's customs, Colin. You need to remember that."

They were approaching a roundabout and Brody slowed,

looking to his right. "That WPC did a good job."

"Sinclair? One of the best." Royce took out a photograph they had acquired from the widow and looked at it briefly. "That reminds me, time to give that MP a call."

CHAPTER THREE

In Somerford, Edmund Lafitte was dozing in the bed that he shared with Stella. He had woken briefly when she rose to take her shower and he was still half asleep when his mobile trilled on the bedside table.

He groaned, turned over and groped for it. He enjoyed his Sunday morning lie-ins and was not happy. He glanced at the bedside clock. Twenty past eight. Who the hell wanted him at this hour on a Sunday?

"Lafitte," he growled.

"Is that Mr Lafitte the MP?"

"Yes."

"I'm sorry to disturb you, sir. Chief Inspector Royce, Donfield CID."

Donfield? Edmund cleared his head. "Uh, what can I do for you, Inspector?"

"Sorry about this, but we need to ask you something."

"What?"

"Do you know a Mr Sayeed Iqbal? A Muslim gentleman."

"No, I don't think so, who is he?"

"A local businessman. He was unfortunately murdered; early hours this morning."

Yes, that would be unfortunate. How could it possibly concern me? "I've never heard of the man, Inspector. What's it got to do with me?"

"Your card was in his pocket. That's how we got your number."

My card? Khan! "I had a visitor in my constituency office yesterday and I gave him a card. Maybe he passed it on."

"Yes, that's possible, sir." He hesitated. "I was wondering, could Iqbal be the man who visited you?"

"Could be, I suppose. But he said his name was Khan."

"If it was the same man, I'll need to speak to you. Can I email you a photo?

"Yes, the email's on the card. What was he wearing?"

"Brown trousers and a blue anorak."

The same clothes! "Could be the same man, Inspector. What do you want to do? I'm in Somerford at the moment, but I'll be going back to London in the morning."

"Well this is a murder enquiry, sir, and we can't do an interview on the phone. Can you see me today? This afternoon? I've a few things to do but I can get to you about three o'clock."

"If you think it's really necessary. Around three is OK. I'll give you the address. Can you email the photo now? In case it's not the same man."

"I'll do that. And I'll call you again after you've had a chance to look at it."

"OK." Edmund gave him the address, adding, "Just one thing – how was he killed?"

There was a slight pause. "A messy business, sir. He was decapitated."

Edmund was sitting up in the bed, still holding the mobile and mulling over the implications when Stella emerged from the bathroom, rubbing her hair with a towel. She moved towards the dressing table but stopped when she saw his face.

"What's the matter? You look like you've seen a ghost or something."

He collected himself. "I had a call, some bad news."

She came over. "What is it?"

"It was the police. About a man who came to the office yesterday. He's been – he's had an accident."

"Nothing to do with you, surely?"

"No, but could be he's the guy who told me he's been threatened. They want to talk to me and I said it was OK to come today." He put the mobile back on the table.

"Today? Why do they want to see you?"

Edmund shrugged. "Because he came to see me?"

"Oh." Stella moved to the dressing table. "We're in today, anyway." She started drying her hair again. "When are they coming?"

"About three o'clock."

"Does he know you're not here weekdays? I don't want them coming round when you're not here."

"He knows. I told him I live in London."

She patted her hair and checked the mirror. "They'd better not be early. I'm doing a roast. I don't want them turning up while we're eating."

"Be a bloody miracle if they do, they're in Yorkshire." He swung his legs off the bed. "And they're not the Flying Squad."

She rolled her eyes and Edmund went to the bathroom for his shower.

CHAPTER FOUR

Kemal Abdullah was a big man, well over six feet tall, with broad shoulders and a strong, muscled body. A full black beard decorated his face, below a straight nose. Striding down Kitchener Road in the Yorkshire city of Donfield that morning after a hot shower and a change of clothes, he turned up the collar of his jacket, pulled his baseball cap further down over his eyes and quickened his pace. Rain, always fucking rain. He hated England; a cold, miserable place where he had never really settled. Life had been so much better in Baghdad, where he had been part of a loving, prosperous family in a large house that was in a peaceful district. Kemal always recalled it as being a place of sunshine and warmth. One day, he vowed, he would go back. That time was coming, soon.

His parents had fled Iraq fourteen years earlier, leaving behind everything they owned. They had lost their comfortable home and lifestyle, becoming penniless refugees who settled, eventually, in Donfield. Kemal clenched his teeth when he thought about those turbulent first days in England.

He would never forget the shock of suddenly being homeless, poor and cold. He would remember forever how his father, a respected university lecturer, could not find work in this alien county and it had broken him. They said he died as a result of a stroke, but Kemal knew better. His father had died of a broken heart, a victim of the British invasion of his country.

He pushed open the wooden gate of number fifty-five, strode up the path to the front door and rang the bell. He was here to see the man whom he believed would make a difference. The man who was a beacon of integrity showing the way forward, with God's help, through this materialistic cesspit of a country.

The door was opened by Imam Zulfikar Ali Mahmud, who welcomed him with the traditional greeting, in Arabic.

"*Assalamu Alaikum.*"

Kemal smiled. "*Wa-Alaikum-Salaam.*" He removed his sandals, left them by the door and followed the Imam down the hallway into his living room.

The cleric took a seat in an armchair, looking calm and composed. "Where did you park?"

"The supermarket car park. I wasn't followed."

"Good."

"Not good. It's too far to walk in the rain."

"Buy an umbrella," the cleric responded drily. He changed the subject. "Come, sit and tell me how it went."

"No problems." Kemal took the other armchair. "Only the card; it had some blood on it. I don't think we should have put it back."

"I have my reasons. The man is a Member of the British Parliament. I want him to learn he must stay out of our business. It was a good way to send him that message. Speak to our people in London. I want this man leaned on. Nothing physical, just make sure he knows we can make trouble for him any time."

"Won't the card be enough? It's a long way to go, just for that."

The Imam snapped, "You know my rules. No phone calls, no emails, no texts. Do it face-to-face." He waved a hand and his tone hardened. "The card may not be enough and maybe he won't be told about it, but I want to make sure he understands that we will not let him interfere."

Kemal nodded. "I'll go tomorrow."

"Good. Make sure they do it."

Kemal asked, "How's the boy?"

"He's resting. I told him to shower and go to bed."

"He was not looking good, so I dropped him outside the house."

The Imam's expression darkened. His eyes narrowed behind the round spectacle lenses. "I told you to leave him at the end of the road. Your car could have been seen here, an unnecessary risk. You should have done what I said." The waspish comment sounded like a reprimand.

"He was in shock and I didn't want to leave him on the main road. Anyway, there was nobody around. Rafiq agreed." He was referring to Rafiq Al-Ghani, a war-hardened veteran who assisted Kemal when required.

The cleric raised his head and thrust his chin out. "The boy is eighteen, old enough to be a *man* of eighteen. In the Caliphate they are twelve and thirteen when they start. At eighteen they are already veterans. It's time for him to see for himself what we can do."

Kemal said quietly, "Boys become men sooner in Syria. Here, he's been sheltered. It was the blood that upset him. After I used the sword he knelt down and was sick. He got blood on his hands."

The Imam showed no emotion. "Good. It's over this time, next time he will be stronger, *inshallah*."

"Next time? I thought he was with you for Islamic studies."

"If I thought that he needed only doctrine, I wouldn't have agreed to take him. Doctrine he could have learned in Pakistan. My brother put him in my care and I will teach him everything that he needs to know." The Imam lifted his chin. "Everything."

Kemal left shortly after. He walked back to his car slowly, deep in thought. The Imam's remark had him wondering if young Ibrahim had been sheltered too much before he came to England. Hard to say. The boy gave the impression of being shy, perhaps even a little introverted. Had it been a mistake to induct him so soon into the hard realities of jihad? Kemal respected the Imam's single-minded fervour but wondered if he was right to have taken the risk of involving the boy. *A worrying thought*.

CHAPTER FIVE

Just after three o'clock that afternoon in Stella's house, the doorbell chimed. Edmund was in the living room, slouched in an armchair, going through his notes on a matter that was to be debated in the House the following week. In the kitchen, Stella was arranging flowers that she had brought in from the garden.

"I'll go," she called out, wiping her hands on a towel. She made her way to the hall and opened the front door. The middle-aged man facing her was of average height, thick-set and stocky, wearing a slightly crumpled grey suit and holding a leather document case. His shirt collar was undone and he was not wearing a tie. He had bushy eyebrows under combed-over, thinning brown hair. Behind him stood a slimmer, taller, young man in a smart suit.

The older man spoke in a soft Yorkshire accent. "Chief Inspector Royce, madam, to see Mr Lafitte." He turned slightly. "And this is Sergeant Brody."

"Come in, please, Inspector." Stella turned to let them in and indicated down the hallway. "I'm Stella Tudor, Edmund's partner." She led them to the living room.

Edmund was standing by the armchair when they entered. The older man wore a serious expression.

"Inspector Royce," Stella said, taking a seat on the settee.

The man came forward. "DI Royce sir, and Sergeant Brody."

Edmund eased himself into his chair. "A nasty business, Inspector, I can hardly believe it. What can I do for you?"

"Not the usual sort of thing we have to deal with, I'll grant you." Royce took a seat. Brody sat down and flipped open a notebook.

Royce cleared his throat. "This man Iqbal, are you quite sure it is the same person who came to your office yesterday?"

"From the photo, it looks like him."

Royce unclipped the document case on his lap but did not open it. "We're trying to piece together his movements before he was killed. What time did you see him?"

"He was the last one before I closed the office at about a quarter to twelve. I was meeting Stella for lunch and I was five minutes late getting to the restaurant."

Stella interjected drily. "More like ten."

Edmund smiled. "Ten."

"So he left you about eleven forty-five?"

"Yes."

"Did he say where he was going?"

"No. Back to Donfield, I guess."

Brody was making notes. "Why did he come to see you, sir? You're a long way from Yorkshire."

"He said he and his family were being threatened by people working for the Islamic State. He seemed to think I had influence with them."

Royce nodded. "As we thought. You've been in the news with the Stanway hostage business."

"I told him the Foreign Office is dealing with the case and

I didn't think I could help him."

"But he had your card in his pocket."

"I felt sorry for him, that's all. I said I'd make some calls and told him to call back in a week. Khan – Iqbal – isn't a constituent, so really I shouldn't get involved. But he said a few things that were interesting. If they're true."

"Like what?"

"For one thing, that the police aren't doing anything about threats against Muslim businessmen in your city. Not true, surely?"

"No, it's not. We know there's a problem but sorting it's easier said than done."

Edmund was watching Royce's face closely. "He said there's a protection racket against Muslim businesses in your area. Run by people called the Brotherhood. Is that the problem?"

The policeman stiffened. "Nowt but rumours. How can we do our job when nobody's prepared to talk? There's no records of Iqbal coming in to any police station and no report of threats to him or his family."

"He said his cousin, a cab owner, couldn't pay the protection and was murdered. Drowned in a canal, he said, made to look like suicide. He didn't believe the man took his own life."

"Is that what he said? With respect, sir, I can tell you that on the evidence it looked like suicide. He left a note, and his business was going down. He was depressed, by all accounts."

"Iqbal said that the note wasn't his handwriting. Strange, don't you think?"

The policeman appeared to be losing his patience. "What

I think doesn't matter," he huffed. "Anyway, that's nowt to do with this investigation. Was there anything else?"

"He also said that the Brotherhood killed another man in a hit-and-run."

Royce reacted, gesturing impatiently. "There was a hit-and-run involving a Muslim but we couldn't trace the car or the driver. We had no reason to suspect the people called the Brotherhood, let alone prove it. And I don't see what that has to do with Iqbal's murder. That's what we're investigating and why we're here."

"So you do know about the Brotherhood?"

"Rumours, like I said. Can't do much with rumours. We need cooperation from the community and we're not getting it. That's the real problem."

"I understand. It must be difficult for you."

Royce had calmed down. "Not our fault if people won't talk to us."

Sergeant Brody spoke. "Did Iqbal say anything else?"

"He was really scared. When I suggested he talk to his Imam he went berserk. Said the Imam's the leader of the Brotherhood and that he's completely crazy; he wants to kill non-Muslims and everybody's frightened of him. So I told him to see his own MP. He said the MP and the Imam were in it together."

"Maybe he had reason to be afraid," Royce said. "And maybe not. But like I say, nobody's talking. It's like trying to get milk out of a stone."

Edmund asked, "If it's true – about the connection to IS, it could explain the unusual murder weapon, don't you think? How did it happen? I mean, Donfield's a city, how could something like that have been done in secret, even in the middle of the night? It's bizarre. If the Imam's responsible, he really is crazy."

Royce hesitated and glanced at Stella. She said, "It's all right, Edmund told me what happened. And I'm a solicitor, I'm not easily shocked."

The policeman nodded. "Cutting off a man's head cleanly; not easy, is that. Takes a sharp sword, maybe heavy, too. Not many of those around and it would have been difficult to hide, even before it was used, if you get my meaning."

"Where was the body found?"

It was Brody who answered. "In a wood in the suburbs, by a jogger."

Royce cut in. "His hands were tied behind his back and they'd been through his pockets. There was nothing on him except your card."

"Then how was he identified?"

"A car near the scene. We checked the plates and it was registered to Iqbal. And his wife phoned Bull Street nick just after three in the morning. She said he took a call on his mobile around midnight, then left the house and didn't come back. So we knew who he was before we went to the house. And before you ask, there was no sign of the mobile, either. Like I said, nothing except your card."

Edmund grimaced. "Tragic. The people who did this are worse than animals."

Royce's face hardened. "It has to be stopped, but it won't be easy. Just one more thing for now, sir. We have photos of the card." He turned to Brody. "Sergeant?"

Brody took out his mobile. "It was in an evidence bag, I took shots of the front and back." He came over to Edmund, holding the phone, displaying a photo. "This is the front. Can you confirm it's your card?"

Edmund looked carefully at the image. "Yes, it is."

Brody scrolled the screen. "This is the back."

Edmund peered at it. "Is that blood? Looks like a fingerprint."

Royce answered. "It's blood, a thumbprint. Not the victim's, obviously. Unfortunately it doesn't match any on record."

After a few more minutes' discussion, the policemen took their leave, saying that they would be in touch again.

Later, Edmund and Stella were in the kitchen, where she was making sandwiches for their supper. He was seated on a stool at the breakfast bar with a bottle of wine, staring into his half-empty glass.

"Mustard?" she asked, holding a butter knife.

Edmund looked up. "Thanks."

She tilted her head. "You were miles away. Grain or Dijon? It's ham."

"Uh, Dijon."

Stella opened the pot of mustard and began spreading the yellow condiment onto a slice of bread. "You OK?"

"Yeah, fine."

"You don't look fine. What's the problem?"

"Just thinking."

She assembled the sandwiches, put them on plates and brought them over, placing one in front of him.

"Ham with Dijon." She put the other plate down and climbed onto a stool. "What were you thinking about?"

"What sort of guy the killer is. He commits a brutal crime

and then calmly empties the victim's pockets. Unbelievable!"

"Takes all kinds, I suppose." She picked up the wine bottle and poured herself a glass. "People like that are insane, don't look for logic."

Edmund spread his hands. "But – think about it. He's just killed a man in an incredibly bizarre way, in the middle of the night, and there's blood everywhere. Then what does he do? He goes through the man's pockets, takes out everything including my card, and then puts the card back, *and nothing else*. Why?"

Stella had been munching. She swallowed and picked up her glass, waving it in an arc. "Who knows? It's irrational. You can't explain something like that. Only a madman would do such a thing. Stop worrying."

Edmund's brow furrowed. "No, there's a reason, there must be. He saw the card, so if he went to the trouble of putting it back, there was a reason. He would've known it would be found by the police. And it was blood-stained." A nasty thought occurred and he raised his head. "I think that Iqbal was murdered precisely because he visited me."

Stella's eyes rounded. "What?"

"The card. The killer knew that if he put it back the police would pay me a visit and show it to me. It was the only thing that he left on the body. Even the bloodstain makes sense."

"What do you mean?"

"I think it's some sort of warning, maybe a threat. They *meant* me to see it."

Stella's mouth fell open. "Good God!"

Edmund's brain went into overdrive. "The murder itself must have been a warning. They probably killed him because he came to see me, but why choose such a bizarre way?"

"Publicity, maybe?"

Edmund slapped his hand down onto the table. "Exactly. If Iqbal was right, the other murders were deliberately made to look like accidents. This was different. It was a clear warning to Muslim businessmen. This time it was out in the open, a brutal killing. As good as a public statement."

"Meaning?"

"They meant it as a threat to anyone who they think is a potential enemy. Putting the card back included me."

The blood drained from Stella's face.

Much later, Edmund was slouched in his chair, morosely nursing a glass of scotch. Stella was curled up on the settee opposite with her legs tucked under her. They had been watching the late evening news and the sensational murder in Donfield was the main item, dominating the broadcast. In a filmed statement, Chief Superintendent Flack of Donfield CID expressed sympathy for the victim's family and promised that no effort would be spared to bring the killer to justice. When the broadcast moved to another story, Edmund picked up the remote and turned the set off.

"No mention of my card."

"He kept his word, then, the policeman. He said there's no reason for that to come out."

Edmund drained his glass. "Let's hope it stays that way."

Stella uncurled her legs and sat up. "It's getting late. Come to bed, you'll feel better in the morning."

"That's for sure."

"Have you decided what you want to do?"

He raised his glass. "One more?"

"Not a good idea, you need to be up early. But I was talking about the threat."

Edmund eased himself up. "OK, no more whisky." He put the glass down. "As for the other business, I can't make up my mind. Putting the card back was deliberate, so there are only two options: I could ask for police protection, absolutely not what I want, or I could do nothing."

"That's not an option," she snorted. "You have to do something to protect yourself."

"There'd be no problem if the police find the killer. What did you think of them? Can't say I was impressed."

She shrugged. "I found that inspector difficult to read. Maybe he's smarter than he lets on?"

"My impression is that he's a typical plod."

"Pedantic, you mean? That's a bit unfair. How can they do their job if an entire community clams up?"

"You may have a point. But if my life depended on him, I wouldn't be happy. Maybe I should have a quiet word with someone in Security."

"Security?"

"Stephen Miller's department. Minister of State responsible for Security, to give him his full title. I've been dealing with one of his staff, Angela Fraser."

"On the Stanway case?"

"Yes. I could speak to her. Informally, because there's no actual proof that I'm at risk. Not good if they think I'm wasting their time."

"I see what you mean. Why don't you ask Amir what he thinks? Maybe he could help, though he's not your typical Muslim, is he?"

Edmund brightened. "Not a bad idea. He's not a Friday

prayers guy, but he's a Muslim. And he's smart."

"Well, that's a start. Two people you can speak to. Informally, as you put it."

Edmund stood up. "And as soon as possible, while watching my back twenty-four seven."

CHAPTER SIX

The following morning, Edmund took his reserved first class seat on the seven-forty express from Bristol to London, tablet propped up on the table in front of him. He checked his emails and found nothing urgent, so he closed it down. Stella was wrong; he felt no better now than he did the previous evening. He'd had a terrible night of disturbed sleep. Now he was worried, wondering if the issue would continue to be a problem. Was he really a target, or was he being paranoid?

He checked his watch. Angela Fraser would surely be up by now. The clever and ambitious woman, called 'the Freezer' by her staff, lived in south London, from where she usually arrived early at her desk in Westminster. He took out his mobile and called her. She answered promptly.

"Angela Fraser."

"Angela? Hi, Edmund Lafitte."

After the briefest of pauses, she replied, "Edmund?" Instantly, her tone sharpened and she snapped, "What's happened?"

"Relax, it's nothing to do with the Stanways."

"Oh?"

"Not directly, anyway, it's something else. I've got a problem and I need your advice, off the record. Can you spare me a few minutes sometime today?"

"Presumably it's urgent, or you wouldn't be calling me at this hour?" Her tone was waspish.

"It is. Sorry about the hour, but is there any chance we could meet?"

"What's it about? I'm tied up today but if it's important I'll make the time."

"I'm on the train, on my way in. It's a bit sensitive and I don't want..."

"OK, let me check."

"Thanks." He gazed out at the unending succession of suburban back yards with their patios and washing lines streaming past, impatiently tapping his fingers on the table. Moments later she was back.

"I'm in a meeting in Portcullis this afternoon, should be finished around four. I can clear a space around four-fifteen, will that do?"

"Super, thanks."

"How about the Atrium, or if it's sensitive, I can come to your office."

"Not the office, I share. The Atrium's better."

"Right, four-fifteen. Now maybe I can get some breakfast."

"Thanks, Angela, I'm..." She rang off.

Just after four o'clock that afternoon Edmund went down from his office to the Atrium on the ground floor of Portcullis House, the new extension to the Houses of Parliament. The complex had been built to create more space to accommodate the needs of Members of Parliament. He looked across to the area where tables were reserved solely for Members' use. There was no sign of Fraser but he had not expected her to be early. As usual, this light, airy central meeting place was busy, but less so in the Members-only area. He put his tablet on a table and drew up a chair. Then he switched on the device and opened his file on the Stanway case.

Ten minutes later, Edmund looked up to see Angela Fraser striding towards him, smartly dressed in a perfectly cut trouser suit. This was a woman who seemingly never missed an opportunity to show that she was politically and intellectually the equal of any man. She approached, flashing a brittle smile.

"Edmund, sorry I'm a few minutes late," she said, apparently without conviction. She took a seat and placed her tablet and a leather document case on the table.

He was mildly surprised to receive the apology. "No probs, I've not been here long."

In a brisk, business-like manner she came straight to the point. Elbows on the table, she tossed her head and leaned forward. "You said you've got a problem. What is it and how can I help?"

"Uh, I could be wrong, but I think that I may be the target of an IS cell."

"*What?* You, personally?"

"I'll explain. But first, is there anything new in the Stanway situation?"

Her eyes widened. "What makes you ask?"

"To be honest, when you took my call this morning you asked if anything had happened. My impression was that you thought it could be bad news."

She blinked and her face hardened. "Rubbish. Why should you think that?"

Edmund smiled crookedly. "That's a yes, then. I expect you'll tell me when you want to." She said nothing, responding only with a stony stare, so he went on. "When you hear what I'm about to tell you, that could be now."

He went on to relate what had happened to him over the weekend and she listened without commenting. He concluded by saying, "That's it. It's driving me mad and I'm losing sleep. What do you think? Should I be worried?"

Without a word, she unzipped her document case and removed a notepad and a silver ballpoint. "You asked for this to be off the record." The pen clicked as she depressed its cap. "For what it's worth, and considering it concerns the Donfield murder, I think you may be right to worry and we need to look into this. But you'll have to agree that it can't be off the record." She paused, holding the pen poised above the pad.

Edmund nodded. "OK, I'll go with that."

"You can start by giving me the names again. The murdered man, the police officers and the other victims."

He told her what he remembered and added, "I can speak to Royce again to see if there's anything else."

She shook her head. "No, not a good idea. We'll deal with it and I'll get back to you."

"And in the meantime?"

She put the notepad and pen away and zipped up the case with a flourish. "Watch your back."

"Is that it? *Watch my back?* Can't you at least tell me what's going on with Stanway?"

For a few moments she seemed to be thinking about it. Then she said, "Right now the country's on high alert. We have reason to believe that one line being monitored may concern Peter Stanway."

"In what way?"

"I'm not at liberty to say. You know how intelligence is gathered. Call it straws in the wind."

"Not at liberty?" Edmund was aghast. He could feel the blood rising in his cheeks. "That's just not good enough. My life may be on the line here."

Angela Fraser busied herself collecting her case and tablet, apparently in readiness to leave. She paused and asked, "Where will you be for the rest of this week?"

"Here – in the city, at my flat in Bayswater. I'll be there until Friday next week."

"And after that?"

"In my constituency for the weekend." He grimaced. "If I'm still around, of course. Why?"

Fraser's lips formed a thin smile. "My guess is that on the balance of probability, you'll still be around. But since you're so concerned, I was about to ask if you would like personal protection."

"What?" He frowned. "No, of course not. That's ridiculous."

She stood up. "As you wish. But I'll have to put on record the fact that you've declined my offer. It won't be an email; I'll send you a letter by courier." She flashed the faux smile again and stood up. "Let me know if anything develops."

Edmund was speechless. The Freezer was covering her backside.

Edmund preferred to use the London Underground from Westminster to his local station, Bayswater, when returning from the House of Commons to his flat. When the weather was bad he took a cab. But this day was different. Although it was dry and mild, he used a taxi. Avoiding the crush of people on the Underground, he reasoned, was nothing to do with a possible threat to his life. *No need to take unnecessary risks; just being prudent.*

In his kitchen preparing supper, he opened the fridge and removed a bottle of beer and a ready meal of curry. He put the beer bottle on the worktop and turned to place the meal into the microwave.

He was mulling over the matter that had preyed on his mind all day. "Being prudent? Don't kid yourself," he muttered, "you're scared shitless." Heroics were for brave people who were also stupid, not for the likes of Edmund Lafitte. Life was too good. He felt a little better for the admission, but the gut feeling of sickening apprehension persisted. He was setting the timer on the oven when his mobile trilled. He had left it on the coffee table in the living room. "Shit," he muttered.

Stella. He tapped the display. "Hi, sweetie."

"You should've called me. What's happening?" There was anxiety in her rebuke.

"Oh, sorry, just getting supper. I was going to call you later."

"OK, so now we know what your priorities are. Don't you know I've been out of my mind with worry? Did you talk to that Security woman?"

"Yeah. They'll look into it and get back to me. Worry not."

"What do you mean, look into it? If they think it needs looking into, it must be serious."

"Maybe, maybe not. They keep tabs on what's happening in their undercover world. Routine surveillance stuff, on-going. I'm guessing they'll check to see if there's anything that connects me to the murder."

He could hear only the regular rhythm of her breathing. Then she snapped, "I don't buy that, it's not good enough. You're on your own, which is bad. Can you get a friend to put you up? Or go to a hotel?"

"I can't think of any friend who'd put up with me. My pals are all married or in relationships and I don't have any close female friends. Mind you, if you insisted, maybe I could...?"

"Knock it off, Edmund, that's not funny. This isn't something you can make jokes about." She sighed audibly. "God, sometimes you're impossible."

"OK, if you insist, I'll do something."

"I insist. What will you do?"

"Oh, I don't know. A hotel, or maybe Popplewells," he said, referring to his London club.

"Yes, good idea, that would be best."

"A hotel would be cheaper."

"The club would be safer and you can afford it. They know you there."

He gave in. "All right, the club it is."

"Promise?" She sounded relieved.

"I promise. But only until I'm back in Somerford. Or before, if the spooks say there's no problem."

He ended the call when Stella said she was satisfied.

Next morning, but for the stubble shortly to be removed, the face that Edmund Lafitte had begun lathering with soap looked better in the mirror than it had the previous night. More relaxed. The bags under his eyes were empty now. He leaned closer to the mirror, touching a sideburn. Was there a tad more grey in his hair? *No, of course not.*

He had slept soundly, untroubled by the issue that had been haunting him for days. The worry worm was still there, but now pushed to the back of his mind. The murder was still the lead story in the media and the Donfield police had been under immense pressure, but there was nothing in the news to connect him to the story. The blood-stained card was being kept under wraps, no need to worry. It had been scary, but with no developments in the past three days there seemed no reason to think that it had been a real threat. But he had promised Stella that he would stay at the club, so that's what he would do. He decided to pack what he needed and return later to collect his bags and take a taxi to Mayfair, where Popplewells club had been a fixture since Victorian times. Satisfied, he finished shaving and stepped into the shower.

Edmund's ground-floor apartment was in an elegant Victorian terrace where most of the buildings had been converted into flats. From Bayswater the journey on the Underground to Westminster was short, though invariably as crammed as a rugby scrum, but without the camaraderie and banter. On one memorable occasion he had been jammed up against a couple who exuded both garlic breath and body odour. Unforgettable.

On the two previous days he had chosen the safe option of using cabs to get to and from his office but he decided to revert to using public transport. The Underground was quick, cheap and convenient. Probably just as safe, too. Nothing untoward had happened to back up the suspicion that he could be under threat. With a spring in his step he emerged from the front door of the building and stood for a few moments at the top of the short flight of stone steps to look around.

Cars parked on both sides of the road, narrowing it to a single lane in the middle. A few people about on foot, hurrying on their way. In fact, a normal weekday morning, nothing to worry about. Then he chided himself, muttering, "Get real, relax." He went down the steps and made his way to the corner of the road, heading towards the station.

Less than ten minutes later, Edmund was standing on the pavement of Queensway, opposite the entrance to the station. He waited for a break in the traffic so that he could use the pedestrian crossing. A dozen or so others waited with him. To his right, two dark-skinned men were speaking a language he did not recognize. One turned to look directly at him for a few seconds, before all surged forward onto the crossing. Edmund paused to allow the pair to enter the station before him. He wondered briefly why he felt the need to do that. Was it instinctive caution or just illogical, unnecessary fear?

Edmund passed through the ticket barrier. Did the look that had been levelled at him have any significance, or was he imagining it? Feeling distinctly uncomfortable, he made his way onto the crowded platform to await the next train. He looked around. The two men were standing a short distance away, apparently deep in conversation. They raised their heads briefly and both looked directly at him. It was an unsettling moment. Edmund looked away quickly.

The familiar sudden strong draught of warm air from the tunnel to his left heralded the approach of the train, followed by its clattering progress alongside the platform. The noise abated, reducing to squealing complaints of the wheels as the train slowed and finally pulled up, throbbing rhythmically. Edmund found himself positioned between two doors; he could use either. He glanced across at the two men who were standing behind a knot of people waiting to board through the door to his right. Edmund joined the group to his left. As a few passengers eased themselves out of the packed mass inside to disembark, Edmund held back, glancing across at the two men. They had not moved and did not appear to be part of the group waiting to board. He stepped forward to clamber on quickly and seconds later the sliding doors hissed to close behind him. *Made it!* He breathed a sigh of relief and turned to ease himself into a more comfortable position, before stooping to place his briefcase between his feet. As he straightened, he glanced down the packed carriage. The two men were staring at him from their position just inside their door. *Shit!* Edmund Lafitte felt sick. He was suddenly, horribly, afraid.

Time to stay calm and steady his nerves. He made a conscious effort to concentrate. But was it really a problem? He still wasn't entirely certain but he needed to work something out, just in case. Just in case what? He was suddenly aware that his armpits were damp with sweat. Damn.

The carriage lurched and he swayed in harmony with the standing passengers, as if engaged in a sort of weird choreographed dance. In another minute or so they would be approaching the next station, Notting Hill Gate. After that there were six more stops before they reached Westminster. He needed to think this through. Come on, he urged himself, *think*.

Edmund turned his head slightly so that in his peripheral vision he could look past the strap-hanging passengers at the two men. He did not want to make direct eye contact again. They were in the same position near the door ahead but now the taller man had moved so that he was looking at Edmund, while still conversing with his colleague. The train began to decelerate, gently at first, then more strongly, to the accompaniment of squeals of protest from the wheels as the brakes began to bite. Usually when passengers disembarked at stations along the way, Edmund moved further into the carriage to be more comfortable. This time he stayed where he was and flattened himself against the bulkhead to let people squeeze past him and through the door. When the train started up again, he changed his stance so that he could check on the two men. They were still there.

By the time they arrived at the next station, Edmund had worked out a plan. He reasoned that if the men intended to leave the train, it would probably be at Victoria, a hub for transport services, including the link to Gatwick airport. Victoria was two stops before his destination, Westminster. If they disembarked at Victoria, all was well and he could stop worrying. But if they stayed on and alighted at Westminster, he would stay on board to give them the slip. He could get a taxi from the next station back to the House of Commons. *A good plan*. He relaxed a bit and waited.

The two men did not get off at Victoria. Edmund gritted his teeth. They did not leave at the next station either, St James's Park. When the train started up again it was on its way to Westminster. Would they get off? As it slowed to enter the station, Edmund tensed and his heart was hammering. He could feel a trickle of cold sweat down his back. He bent to pick up his briefcase and turned to face the doors, as if making ready to disembark. Through the corner of his eye he watched the two men. They appeared to be preparing to leave the train. *Bad news*. The train rolled to a stop, the doors sighed open and Edmund stepped out onto the platform. He stood still while others disembarked, then when those waiting on the platform clambered aboard, he stepped inside quickly just before the doors hissed shut again.

As the train gathered speed on its way out of the station, Edmund caught a fleeting glimpse of the two men. They were still on the platform. He smiled to himself. He could not be absolutely certain that he had been in danger but if it really was some sort of psychological contest, he had won that round.

CHAPTER SEVEN

In Donfield, a bearded man wearing wire-framed, round-lensed spectacles, a knitted white skull cap and a serene expression, sat quietly in the waiting room of his doctor's surgery. Imam Zulfikar Ali Mahmud was a man who had long since developed the ability to sit absolutely still, allowing his mind to dwell on matters more important than anything in his immediate surroundings. Distractions like that annoying little boy sitting opposite, staring and pointing, whispering loudly into his mother's ear.

It was no effort to ignore the child, doubtless destined to become just another typical English teenager. Selfish, undisciplined, rude and ignorant, of no value to society. Just like the ill-bred, beer-sodden animals who had mocked him on a bus only a few months ago. Not one of the dozen or so other British citizens present had intervened as the louts sneered, telling him to go back to his own country. He had remained sitting quietly in dignified silence, looking straight ahead, not responding. No point. Soon, very soon, there would be no more country to go back to. No national borders, just one country, world-wide. One state, one nation: Islam, the Caliphate. Allah had so decreed, it was Kismet.

A buzzer sounded briefly to draw attention to the electronic notice-board on the wall. It scrolled a new message: *MR MAHMUD TO DR SHAH'S ROOM PLEASE.*

Zulfikar stood up, briefly fixing his gaze upon the child and its mother, with just the trace of a thin smile on his face. He made his way through swing doors into the corridor where the doctor's room was located. The door was ajar and he entered and closed it gently.

A minute earlier, in his consulting room, Doctor Aziz Shah had been trying to stay calm. He pressed the button to signal that he was ready to receive the next patient. But was he?

He sat with his elbows on the desk, seething. Aziz was dedicated to his career in medicine. Being a family doctor in general practice was all he had ever wanted. He reflected bitterly that he did not deserve to be in the wretched position in which he found himself. The man who was about to enter his room was not even sick; not physically, anyway. Mentally? Another matter altogether. Unquestionably deranged, bordering on psychotic.

His stomach knotted as he tried to condition his mind. He must stay calm. The bastard was on his way in, Aziz had no choice, he had to get on with it.

The door swung open and Zulfikar Mahmud entered. The doctor said nothing, merely indicating towards the chair across the desk.

Mahmud came forward. He smiled, greeting the doctor in the traditional manner. *"Asalaam Aleikum*, I trust you are well," he said, in Arabic.

Aziz did not respond. He glared at his visitor, saying nothing.

Mahmud took the chair. "Is something the matter?" he asked, again speaking in Arabic.

Doctor Khan folded his arms on the desk and replied

coldly, in English. "For a start," he said, "you know perfectly well that in my consulting room I insist on speaking English."

The man shrugged. "Your room, your rules, though you would have learned Arabic as a child."

"Only to study the holy book. Arabic is not my mother tongue and we are not in the mosque now."

"No. And in your case, not at all, recently. We can speak in Urdu, if you prefer."

The doctor stared at the cleric. "English, only."

The Imam leaned closer. "Tell me, why are you in such a bad mood?"

"*What?* You ask me that? You of all people?" he sputtered, barely able to contain his anger. "Do you take me for a fool? I will ask *you* a question. Do you know where I was yesterday?"

The cleric did not answer. He merely blinked briefly and shrugged.

The doctor took his hands off the desk and sat up. "No? Let me tell you. I was called to the mortuary to identify a body. A man murdered in such an obscene way that the police called me to identify him. They did not want his wife or his family to see him until the pathologist has finished his work. That man was one of my patients." He was breathing heavily. "But of course you know who I mean."

With his face devoid of expression, the Imam replied, "I don't know what you're talking about. You know why I'm here and I don't need to talk about anything else."

Aziz stared at the man. Unbelievable! It was like talking to a robot; an inanimate, unfeeling monster. Without another word, he drew forward the briefcase that was on the end of his desk, flipped the lid open and removed from one of its pockets a padded brown envelope. He handed it to the cleric.

"Yours. It was delivered to me by one of my patients."

Mahmud took the envelope. "I know. We will keep using this system. We need our funds and this way is best, for now."

The doctor slammed down the lid of his briefcase. "I don't need lessons in morality from *you*," he spat. "And what others think is of no concern to me."

The Imam stood and moved to the door. "It should be. You are a prominent member of the community. People look up to you, the medical professional. You with your big house and your fancy car. As a Muslim, you should be doing much more to support our people. More than just being a post box."

"I am a doctor. I do my best to support all my patients. And for your information, I do not measure the strength of my faith by how often I visit the mosque."

"But maybe others do?"

The cleric opened the door. He curled his lip to say, "Give my regards to your English wife. I hope that she and your children will continue to enjoy good health." The implied threat was made in Arabic. Then he left, closing the door behind him.

The doctor leaned back and muttered, "I don't need reminding, you bastard. I haven't worked all these years to be lectured to by the likes of *you*, you ignorant, arrogant, hate-peddling piece of shit."

He reflected with simmering anger that only his need to protect his family had prevented him going to the police months ago.

Across the city, Inspector Charles Royce stood before his superior, Chief Superintendent George Flack. Royce knew the man was not happy. Flack, a large man with bushy eyebrows and fleshy jowls, leaned across his desk with his arms crossed. The surface was untidy, littered with papers and files. It looked like some had not been touched for weeks. Flack frowned, his eyebrows protruding above a steely glare, seemingly determined to make his point. He jabbed the air with a stubby finger.

"Not good enough, Charlie. Not fucking good enough. The press bastards are crawling all over us and the Chief Constable's on my back."

"It's not all bad news, sir. There's the thumbprint. No match yet but chances are the killer doesn't know we've got it. And there's the DNA from the vomit. It's not the victim's and it won't be the killer's, so we have something else to go with."

Flack frowned. "How do you know it's not the killer's?"

"People throw up when they're shocked. Unlikely to be the bloke who used the murder weapon. The killer would have done it before, I reckon. At least once."

Clearly, Flack had not thought it through. "Well, anyway," he said, "I want the Chief off my back, get on with it."

Royce stood his ground. "No bugger's giving us anything, sir. Not a sniff."

"What about your snouts?"

"We've only got one informant who's a Muslim, and he's clammed up, like the rest. I reckon he's been warned off. They're a pretty close bunch and we've no one else on the inside."

"Have you spoken to that Asian constable at Bull Street? Kumar, is it? Maybe he can suggest somebody you can lean on."

"No, sir. He's the last person any of them would talk to."

"Because he's a copper?"

Suppressing a smile, Royce said, "No, because he's a Hindu, not a Muslim."

Flack frowned. "Oh." He eased his bulk upright. His suit didn't fit at all well. The jacket hung around the barrel-shaped torso like a tent. No doubt about it, the man was not happy and at that moment, neither was Royce. This was not going well.

Flack glared at his subordinate. "Three days now and we got nothing. Fuck-all, Charlie. What's your job title again? Inspector? *Detective* Inspector?" Royce did not answer. Flack growled, "Then fucking *detect*. If you got nothing to go on, find something. Make it happen. I learned that when I was a young DC." Royce groaned inwardly. Here we go again, another 'when I was' lecture. *Shit!*

The Chief Superintendent took his time and gestured, waving an arm in the air. "Go shake a few trees, see what falls out. Rattle some cages, you'd be surprised what a bit of pressure in the right place can do."

Like I never thought of that. But he knew when best to stay quiet. Aloud he said, "Yes, sir."

"A man gets topped on our patch and we got *nothing?* What do we know about the victim? Enemies, grudges?"

Royce inclined his head. "A good citizen, by all accounts. Family man, small business, wife and two kids." He shrugged. "Considering how he was killed, it's not likely a neighbour with a parking problem, is it? Or a family fight, none of the usual reasons for murder." The irony seemed to have passed over his superior's head. *Of course* it was no ordinary sodding murder. The man was decapitated with medieval savagery, almost certainly to serve as an example to others in the Muslim community.

Flack's impatience surfaced. "Well, what are you going to do about it?"

There were times when Royce wondered how the man had made it to the rank of Chief. He stayed calm. "It's the Brotherhood mob and that trouble-making preacher. Nobody else fits the bill, but we need someone to cough. I'll have another go at the informant. Maybe I didn't push him hard enough first time."

Flack nodded. "Do that. And go back to the family. Maybe one of them is more angry than scared. Enough to open up."

"Will do, sir." Royce turned to leave, rolling his eyes.

CHAPTER EIGHT

It had taken Edmund Lafitte thirty minutes longer than usual to get to the office that he shared with Jonathan Dace, another MP, in Portcullis House. They also shared the services of a secretary, Diane. When he entered, she was at her work station.

"Morning, Edmund." She smiled. "Overslept?"

"Hello, Diane. Something like that. Is Jonathan coming in?" Edmund slipped his jacket off and hung it on the back of his chair.

"Not today." She looked at her notepad. "There's a message. Harry Mason called."

"Really? Haven't heard from him in ages. Did he leave his number?" Edmund's cousin Harry was a director of a company that made films for television.

"No, but he said he'd call back later."

That suited Edmund. He had been wondering if he should speak to Angela Fraser about the men who had been watching him that morning. Or were they? At the time he felt sure that he was being stalked, but now it had begun to seem a bit improbable. He really was in two minds about it, but maybe best to be on the safe side. He decided not to call her office, mobile to mobile would be better. Across the room Diane, wearing headphones, was working at her keyboard. He called Fraser and she answered.

"Angela Fraser."

"It's Ed Lafitte. Can you spare a minute?"

"A minute? Yes, but I'm due in a meeting. What is it?"

Suddenly, Edmund felt foolish. How could he describe his unease? "I, er, had some company on my way in this morning."

"What?"

He marshalled his thoughts. "Normally I walk from my flat to Bayswater tube station and take the Circle Line to Westminster. This morning was different." He lowered his voice. "I think I was being watched."

"You think?" She sounded annoyed. "You *think*? Like you don't know?"

"I can't be certain, but..."

"If you don't know, what do you expect me to do? You've been offered protection, are you now saying that you want me to arrange that?"

"My problem is that I'm not sure."

"Then why are you calling me?"

"I'm trying to tell you that something happened today that was – unusual. I'm not comfortable with it and I need to know more about what's going on. How else can I decide if I need what you're offering? What's happened to change the Stanway situation?"

There was a brief pause before she answered. "There's some evidence that his situation could be about to escalate. I can't say any more."

Well, that's not much help.

He replied, "I really don't want to be stalked by heavies." He noticed that Diane had glanced across sharply and then looked away. He decided that he was getting nowhere. "Looks like I'm wasting my time, then."

"It's worse than that," Fraser snapped. "You're wasting mine. Call me again when you have something to say."

She rang off.

CHAPTER NINE

In an unmarked police car parked discreetly in a side street in Donfield, Detective Inspector Royce and his sergeant had a good view of the betting shop. It was diagonally across the main road, about a hundred metres away. Royce refilled the cup of his vacuum flask.

"That's the last of my coffee."

Brody slid back his seat and stretched out his legs. "That's better. I was getting cramp." He looked across at the betting shop. "Doesn't look like your man's coming today, does it, sir?"

Royce slurped a mouthful of lukewarm coffee. "Give it time, he'll come. He works shifts at the hospital and today's his payday. Knocks off at two, so he'll be here. The betting shop's his first port of call after he gets his wages."

Brody glanced at the clock on the dashboard. "It's nearly twenty past. Are you sure he's coming? If we know where he lives, we can just go there."

"No, we can't. He's my only contact on the inside and I don't want to lose him. When you spend a lot of time and effort working on a grass, it's important that nobody knows he talks to us. If we keep him off the radar, we'll get more out of him."

"Wouldn't it be easier to phone him? Everybody's got a mobile."

Royce turned to give his subordinate a derisory look. "Aye, and nearly everybody knows how to hack 'em. He never wants me to phone him and I promised I wouldn't."

"Why doesn't he just change it? New mobile, new server even."

"Better this way. He knows it can be hacked, so as long as he's careful he's in control. His calls and texts are routine. Friends and family, nowt suspicious."

"Doesn't that make it harder for you? To get hold of him, I mean."

"Rule number one: he never gets in touch with me. When I need him I go to one of his hangouts."

"Like this betting shop? I thought Muslims aren't allowed to gamble."

"Folk do things they shouldn't." Royce smiled. "Do you want to talk about your expenses?"

Brody bristled. "There's nothing..."

"Only joking, lad." Royce lifted his chin, indicating. "There he is now. My man Anwar."

Brody looked across at the informant, a slim young individual in a shabby blue anorak, who was approaching the entrance to the bookmaker's premises. "OK," he said, "let's go."

The Inspector held up a hand. "No, you stay. I don't want him spooked. I'll go on my own." He opened his door and stepped out. "I'll give him a couple of minutes to do his business first."

There was another reason why Royce wanted to see Anwar alone. Something best kept to himself for now. He took his time. No hurry, the man would be a few minutes placing his bets and perhaps collecting some winnings, if he'd been lucky. Royce strolled across the main road to a travel agent's, two doors from the betting shop, where he looked at the window display. It was partly obscured by cards on which deals and offers were written in marker pen. Royce smiled to himself. *Travel agents who can't even spell Fuerteventura!*

There was little traffic through the doors of the betting shop. Two people had entered and one had left, before the door swung open again. Royce's informant Anwar emerged. He paused briefly and glanced at Royce without showing any sign of recognition. Then he turned and walked away. The policeman glanced around casually before starting to follow a short distance behind. A minute later he quickened his pace until he was alongside the man. Without breaking step and keeping his gaze fixed ahead, Royce spoke quietly. "Afternoon, Anwar. Who won, you or the bookies?"

The man dipped his head slightly. "Mostly them, Mr Royce."

"I need a word, I'll not keep you long."

Anwar turned his head a fraction towards the policeman. "I told you all I know on Monday."

"You told me nothing new."

"I don't know anything about the killing, Mr Royce."

For a few moments Royce did not respond. Then he said, "Remember Victoria Avenue? Five years ago?"

Anwar slowed. "I remember. What about it?"

"You were what – fifteen?"

"Sixteen."

"And hanging out with a bad lot. Brought into the nick with three of your mates, accused of assault. Actually, kicking the shit out of a guy lying on the pavement."

"I didn't do it. I was just there. You know that, Mr Royce."

"Only because I took the trouble to talk to your parents. Good people. My boss said you were just another Paki layabout. He told me not to bother."

"I didn't know that."

"I took a chance on you. Remember what I said before I left your house?"

"You said I could show I wasn't a troublemaker. I was grateful, also my parents."

"You didn't let me down, you went back to school. Six GCSE passes, was it?"

"Seven." He snorted. "But not good enough to get me a job. I know guys smarter than me with university degrees and it's the same for them."

"It's tough, I know."

"No jobs here for the likes of me, not good ones, anyway. I'm the wrong colour, wrong background, wrong religion."

"You doing OK at the hospital?"

Anwar shrugged. "It's a job. Lousy pay and no prospects, what do you think?"

Royce answered quietly. "I think you deserve better. You work at the mosque as well?"

"Clerical stuff for the management committee, letters and such." He smiled thinly. "No money in it. I was volunteered, if you see what I mean. Being broke all the time's no fun. It started me gambling."

They were approaching a marked pedestrian crossing. Royce indicated. "Let's cross, I have to get back to my car." A vehicle stopped to let them across and they turned to head back in the direction from which they had come, walking more slowly.

"This murder," Royce said. "A bad business." Anwar said nothing, so he went on. "It's not good for your people, you know."

Anwar lowered his head. "Not my fault," he mumbled.

"You can do something about it. We know it's probably the Brotherhood. Come on, give me a name. Nobody will ever know."

"I can't, Mr Royce."

"You must know who's responsible."

Anwar shook his head. "No, I don't."

"All right, tell me this. Who do you *think* did it?"

Anwar stopped and stared at Royce. "These people are animals, they make me sick. They're not true Muslims. Do you know what they'd do to me, or my family if they found out I talk to you?"

"All the more reason. I give you my word, lad, I will never reveal anything you say."

They walked on a few paces before Anwar replied, in a voice no louder than a whisper. "You're right, they must be stopped." His face looked grim. "I'll tell you this – the Imam is the leader of The Brotherhood, I know that for certain."

"The hate preacher? So he would have given the order to have the man killed?"

The informer was breathing heavily. He stopped walking, stared into the policeman's eyes and nodded slowly. "Most probably."

Royce was elated. Now was the moment to push his luck. "Give me a name. Who do you think actually did it?"

Again the young man paused, clearly deeply troubled. He shook his head.

"No, I can't do that. I've said too much. I have to go now."

They were close to the side road where the police car was parked. Royce turned and put a reassuring hand on Anwar's arm. "I have something for you." He reached inside his jacket and drew out a mobile phone. "Take this. It's a pay-as-you-go, registered to me in a false name and never been used. Pre-loaded."

Anwar's eyes rounded. "A police mobile? No, I can't..."

Royce thrust the phone at him. "Take it. It's nothing to do with the police. You can throw it away if you want. But I'd like you to keep it. Put it somewhere safe. In case you want to get in touch if anyone threatens you, or if you have anything to tell me. Just send a short text. It'll go to another clean phone that I keep at home, not my normal one."

Anwar hesitated and then took it. He nodded, saying nothing.

Royce said, "Thank you. I'd be a lot happier knowing that you can contact me if you need to. And I meant what I said about us meeting today. No one will know we've talked."

CHAPTER TEN

At lunchtime two days later, Edmund Lafitte stepped out of a taxi on Goodge Street in the West End of London. It dropped him off at The Mask, a fashionable restaurant that was a favourite with journalists and people in the broadcasting media. His cousin Harry Mason had invited him to lunch, saying that he wanted to introduce him to Naomi Porter, one of his film producers.

Edmund checked his watch. Twelve forty-five; he was on time. He made his way past the bar in the reception lounge to the dining room. The place was busy, with nearly every table occupied and waiters bustling about their tasks. The head waiter led him between sets of garrulous diners to a table at the rear of the room. Two people were seated there; a heavyset, balding man with a round, open face, and a blonde, smartly-dressed woman.

The man stood up. "Edmund, you old dog," he said. "How are you?"

"I'm good, Harry. You're looking well, too."

Harry Mason beamed. "Really? I've lost a bit of weight; glad you noticed." He sat down, indicating towards the woman, who stayed seated. "Meet Naomi Porter, the best producer in the business."

Edmund caught his breath. Her startlingly blue eyes looked up with an intensity that momentarily unnerved him.

"Er – hello," he stammered.

Naomi smiled. "I've been looking forward to meeting you, Edmund."

Harry Mason said, "She's been at me for a couple of weeks to set up this meeting. Driving me mad ever since I mentioned that I knew you."

"Oh?"

Harry cupped his hand to his mouth and in a theatrically loud whisper said, "She's obsessed with the Islamic State."

Naomi smiled. "Not exactly. But to be honest, what started as a three-month project has run on a bit."

They paused when a waitress came to the table. She took their orders and Harry asked her to bring them a bottle of the red house wine. She left and Naomi spoke to Edmund again.

"He makes it sound like I bullied him into it. But I just want to get on with the job and getting hard facts about IS hasn't been easy."

"It's the Foreign Office that's negotiating to get Stanway back. I've not had direct contact with IS but if I can help, I will." He smiled. "But politicians rarely turn down a free lunch."

Harry said, "That's a fact."

Edmund asked Naomi, "Didn't you do the *Inside* series? *Inside Serbia*, *Inside Estonia* and some others?"

"Yes, we did six."

"I'm afraid I only saw a couple. Did you use the same format for all?"

"Uh-huh. We tried to get a feel for what life's like for ordinary people. We focused on families from different backgrounds, one from what we call 'middle class' here and another from lower down, typically tradesmen. We didn't want to compare the very richest and the poorest. Viewers relate better to the middle ground."

Harry interjected. "We followed the two sets of families. My favourite was the job in Saudi. You'd be amazed what she had to do to get that one in the can."

"Not easy, I'm guessing," Edmund murmured.

"She was a journalist before she joined us," Harry declared.

Naomi shrugged lightly. "In some countries being a woman doesn't help. But on the Saudi one I got away with quite a lot more than I should have."

"Is that where you became interested in Islamic State?"

"It started me thinking. Saudi's a Muslim country. Well run, on the whole. So how's it possible for a bunch of thugs in Syria to draw lines on maps and say they're a nation? And in the name of Islam? That's what I want to find out."

Edmund tilted his head. "Come on. I can't believe they'd let you in to do vox pops on camera."

It was Harry who replied. "No, of course we can't do that and there's no way I'd let any of our people even try."

Naomi added, "We've spent weeks trying to find out what life's like inside IS. It's not easy. We know a bit about how they raise money and how they get recruits. But not much about how their people actually live. What's family life like? Are people free to move around? What sort of social life do they have? What about leisure activities? As for actually going there, Harry's right. It's not possible at present. Their borders aren't fixed. They change all the time, war zones in effect. I wouldn't want to get caught on the wrong side."

"Exactly what happened to Peter Stanway," Edmund observed. "I'm curious, how can you do an *Inside*-type program without going into the territory?"

"A good question," Naomi replied. "And the answer is that we can't. We'll have to use a different format, but it'll still be interesting. It's a challenge."

"I'm sure you're up for it." Edmund had been wondering if he should say anything about his strange predicament. If he really was being stalked by British jihadists, it would certainly be an IS-related issue. The murder had been reported at length on television and in the press, but so far there had been no mention of his involvement. The police had not made public the finding of his business card and for that he was grateful. But what could he say about his strong suspicion that he was being watched? Nothing, really, since he himself was not certain that was so. He decided that it would be best to keep it to himself for the time being. He turned to Harry. "Can I ask a favour?"

"Sure, what is it?"

"I'm not really comfortable talking about this here." He made an apologetic gesture. "Wrong time, wrong place."

"What do you want to do?"

Edmund looked at Naomi. "I'd prefer to meet you again somewhere else, to do this properly. How about one day next week?"

Her eyes widened. "Of course, no problem. I think you're right, this really isn't the best place."

"You can come to Westminster, if you like."

Harry's mouth twisted into a grin. "Best chat-up line I've heard in years."

Naomi picked her handbag up off the floor. To Edmund

she said, "Don't take any notice of him. Actually, I've never been to the House of Commons, I'd love to come." She opened her bag and removed a card, which she handed to Edmund. "My number's on this."

It said she was a producer at Tolgate Films. "I'll give you mine," he replied. "Any day except Wednesday. I don't like to miss Prime Minister's Questions."

"Sounds fascinating."

Edmund looked away, breaking eye contact. The experience had unsettled him. He had never before seen a pair of eyes that were so strikingly beautiful.

CHAPTER ELEVEN

In Donfield, Royce and Brody were on their way in an unmarked car through a district known as Middle Meadows, one of the less salubrious inner suburbs. They were behind a bus on the main road.

Royce stared out of the side window, taking in views of the parades of shops, most of which had been established to serve the needs of Asian and other ethnic minorities. Grocery stores that had expanded displays of exotic produce on tables extending out onto the pavements. Halal butchers, specialist garment, sweetmeat and spice emporia, all attesting to the constantly changing nature of the inner suburbs of the cities of modern Britain. Branching off the main thoroughfare were terraces of tired old buildings on roads made narrower by vehicles parked on both sides. Middle Meadows? How many years had it been since this place was any kind of meadow? His musings were interrupted by a question from his subordinate.

"Are you sure he'll be home, sir?"

"Mid-afternoon, I'm guessing he will."

The bus slowed and pulled up at the kerb, allowing Brody to pull out and move forward. "Mid-afternoon?"

"He's the Imam. He leads daily prayers at the mosque." Brody's eyebrows arched so Royce said, "If you'd done a bit of homework, lad, you'd know they pray five times a day. Between sessions he should be home. Like mid-afternoon."

"Only thing I know about him is his reputation for stirring things up."

"Aye, there's that. But he's still the Imam. You were probably lucky to catch him on Monday. What time of day was it?"

Brody was looking ahead. "Just after eleven."

"A short interview, then. They have mid-day prayers at the mosque."

"Ten minutes at most. Waste of time, I got nothing out of him."

"I know."

"Said he'd never heard of the Brotherhood and didn't know anything about the Islamic State." Brody snorted. "Bullshit. Did he really think I'd swallow that crap? The bugger was lying through his teeth and he knew I didn't believe him. He just stared at me." Brody's jaw tightened. "He was taking the piss."

Royce smiled. "Winding you up. But somewhere round here there's a man whose print is the one on the card, and it's odds-on the Imam knows who it is. I'll do the questions, it'll help that I've not met him." He glanced at Brody. The sergeant's knuckles were white as he gripped the wheel. Royce continued. "We can't have you losing your cool now, can we?" Changing the subject, "How much further?"

Brody lifted his chin, indicating forwards. "Not far. Kitchener Road, first left after the lights."

Number fifty-five on Kitchener Road was a terraced house. Brody eased the car forward between the dual lines of parked vehicles, slowing as they approached a speed hump. Royce scanned the house carefully as they passed. It was scruffy, with black paint peeling off the wooden window frames. The curtains were drawn.

"Doesn't look like we can park near," he said.

"I'll find a space further on. The walk will do us good," Brody replied. "I know how much you like exercise, sir."

"Yeah, very funny. At my age, a recipe for a coronary."

Fifty metres further Brody found a space. They made their way back along the pavement towards the house, stepping aside to allow a woman in Punjabi dress to pass. She was pushing a baby in a buggy, with a boy of about four toddling behind. He swivelled his head, his round, inquisitive eyes locked on the policemen as he passed.

The front door of number fifty-five appeared to have had a coat of black paint recently, unlike the frames around the bay window. Royce pressed the doorbell and stepped back.

Behind him, Brody stood with his hands in his jacket pockets, looking over the fence at the adjacent property. "We've got an audience," he muttered. "Couple of young guys next door."

Royce looked downwards, then turned casually and raised his head. "Never seen them before. You?"

"No. Maybe they're just nosy."

"Around here we stick out like monks in a brothel, I reckon."

The door was opened but only partially, by a short, dark-skinned youth. His round, fleshy face wore a frown and the beginnings of a beard.

"Yes?"

Royce answered politely.

"Good afternoon. Donfield Police. Is Mr Mahmud in?"

The detective was unprepared for the youth's reaction. The boy's head jerked upwards and he blinked rapidly. "Wait," he said, shutting the door in their faces.

"Did you see that?"

Brody turned. He had been watching the two men next door. "What?"

Royce rolled his eyes. "Never mind." He was thinking about the youth's reaction, wondering whether he himself had betrayed his surprise and dropped his guard. Years of policing had equipped him with the ability to use a deadpan mask whenever he chose, but this had been an unplanned moment. Did that boy have something to hide?

Two minutes later, the policemen were still waiting and Brody's impatience surfaced. He fumed. "They're sodding about, taking the piss again." He took a step forward. "I'll lean on the bell."

Royce put out a restraining hand. "No, we'll wait. If he's trying to wind us up, it's working. With you, anyway. Stay calm, act normal, and let me do the talking."

Brody scowled, shoved his hands into his pockets and turned his back. At that moment the door was opened again by the young man.

He avoided eye contact. "Mr Mahmud says have you got identity?"

Brody spun around and seemed about to react so Royce shot him a disapproving look. He showed the youth his warrant card, saying, "Mr Mahmud has already met my colleague. Please tell him that we need to speak with him." He smiled thinly. "Either here or, if it's more convenient, at the police station."

This time they did not have to wait. Within moments Zulfikar Ali Mahmud appeared behind the young man. Royce thought that he must have been lurking out of sight in the background.

Royce looked up and asked, "Are you Mr Mahmud, sir?"

"Yes. What can I do for you?"

"Can you spare us a few minutes, please?"

Using a language that the policemen did not understand, Mahmud spoke to the young man, who left, retreating down the hallway. The cleric lifted his chin and addressed Royce. "What's this about?"

"We need to clear up a few things, sir."

"What sort of things?"

Royce nodded towards the two young men next door. They had moved forward, closer to the fence. "Maybe better if we came in?"

Mahmud opened the door fully and moved aside. "All right." As the policemen entered he added, "Those are my neighbour's boys. It's not their fault they have no jobs." He shut the door firmly.

Mahmud's feet were bare and there were sandals in the corner by the door. Royce asked, "Do you want us to take off our shoes?"

The man glanced down at the policemen's feet and shook his head. "Not necessary."

In the narrow hallway they stood aside to let Mahmud pass. The wooden floor was partly covered by a faded, threadbare strip of carpet and the walls were decorated with floral-patterned wallpaper that clearly had been there a long time. This was not what Royce had expected in the home of a senior cleric in a relatively prosperous community. The odour of spicy cuisine pervaded. A not unpleasant, if slightly stale, smell.

Mahmud opened the first door off the hallway. "In here."

The room was dark but clean and sparsely furnished with a settee and two armchairs that did not match. In the centre was a circular rug upon which was a round wooden coffee table. The policemen stayed by the door while Mahmud went to the bay window and pulled the curtains aside, letting in daylight.

"That's better," he said. "Sit, please."

Royce could not decide if the Imam's manner was genuinely polite. No matter, he was here to do a job.

The Imam sat back. "How can I help you?" he asked, glancing at his watch.

Royce thought the gesture contrived. "We won't keep you long."

"I have to go to the mosque but I can spare a few minutes."

Royce said, "As you know, we're investigating the murder in Milford Park on Sunday morning." He waited but there was no answer. The Imam stared, unblinking. Would a provocative statement get a meaningful response? Royce was studying the man's face closely as he said, "There's some new evidence that we need to check out."

There was a momentary flicker of interest. "New evidence?"

The detective waited a few seconds. "Is there something you may wish to tell us now, sir? Anything at all?"

The stony stare returned. "No. I told your sergeant I don't know anything about it. That has not changed."

Royce held his gaze, waiting to see if he could squeeze

anything out of this man. After a few moments the Imam spoke. "I am a law-abiding citizen. If I can help you, I will. What's your new evidence?"

"Gathering evidence is on-going. We get new information a bit at a time." The detective avoided giving a direct answer, not that he had much to say, he thought. He was fishing, but did the cleric realise that? He continued. "Just now we're looking into something promising, but we can't be certain at this stage."

Again there was silence. Finally, the cleric asked in an apparently casual manner, "Do you have a question for me, Inspector?"

At last. The mask had slipped, the man had blinked first. A small edge, but satisfying. Royce had intended to use the existence of the thumbprint, his only piece of real evidence, to shake something out. But now he felt sure that his informant was right and that the Imam was probably directly responsible for the crime. He decided to save his evidence and use it to better effect later. The Imam himself would not have been present at the murder, but there could be no doubt that the MP's card was deliberately put back on his instructions. Unlikely, then, that he would know about the thumbprint. Maybe this was not the best time to reveal its existence.

The detective was looking directly into the cleric's eyes. "Do you know a Mister Edmund Lafitte?"

Not a flicker of interest. "No."

"He's an MP, a Member of Parliament."

The Imam's mouth twisted. "I know what MP means, Inspector. But I know nothing of the man."

Royce held his gaze for a few moments. Then he said,

"Perhaps the new evidence is not relevant to you, sir." He smiled and stood up. "But we do appreciate your cooperation and thank you for your time."

There was a look of astonishment on Brody's face. But the Imam looked distinctly smug. The policemen departed.

As the front door was shut behind them, Royce murmured, "Right-hand side, across the road. There's a 'To Let' sign in the window. About six houses down."

Brody looked up. "I see it."

"I want a surveillance unit there, soon as possible. Keep it low-key and set it up after dark. Tell me when it's done."

They went through the gate at the end of the path. "He'll be watching us from behind his curtains," Royce said. "You don't need to look."

"Cunning bastard. We've drawn a blank again, sir.

"Yes, he is and no, Sergeant, we haven't. He's now a worried man. And that boy is hiding something."

Royce increased his pace. He was looking straight ahead, when Brody asked, "Any target, sir? The surveillance, I mean."

"Eh?" The inspector had been deep in thought. "Identification," he snapped. "I want to know who comes and goes, and how many times. We need to find the man who used the weapon. He'll be strong, probably big."

Brody pressed the remote to unlock their car. Royce pulled open the passenger door. "Round the clock, Sergeant. Twenty-four seven." He settled into his seat.

CHAPTER TWELVE

In London the following morning, Edmund was at his desk in Portcullis House, going through a file. He was making notes on a pad when he put his ballpoint pen down, groaned aloud and wiped his face with his hands.

"This is bloody impossible," he complained. Diane was at her computer. She looked up briefly.

Across the room Jonathan Dace, the MP with whom Edmund shared the office, was gathering papers and putting them into his briefcase. "Problem?"

"Yup. A planning application and I'm in trouble."

Dace, a stocky man who had been a Member of Parliament for many years, shut his briefcase. "Planning? Nothing to do with you, surely?"

"Depends. A supermarket's looking for permission to build a new store and some local big-wigs are against it. They want me to take up the cudgels."

"So?"

"Actually I'm in favour. It'll be near a housing estate."

"No problem. Go with whatever trawls in the most voters." Dace was clearly in a hurry to get away. "Can't stop, committee meeting." He scooped up his mobile and shoved it into his pocket. "Or you can sit on the fence. You're a politician."

Edmund muttered, "Thanks a bunch." His mobile rang. It

was a number he did not recognize.

"Edmund Lafitte."

"Edmund? It's Naomi." It was a few moments before he made the connection.

"Oh, hi."

"You OK to talk?"

"No problem." *What could she want?*

"Only I wouldn't want to interrupt anything."

"Just doing some paperwork. It's OK, really."

"About your invitation to the House of Commons. I was wondering, any chance we can do it tomorrow?"

What? We've only just met. "Tomorrow? Saturday's not the best day."

"Oh."

"Too many rubber-necking tourists. Weekdays are better."

"Can we meet somewhere else then?"

Somewhere else? Was she really in a hurry to interview him or – was there something else going on? "Well, I suppose…"

"Oh, I forgot. You're probably in your constituency at weekends. Silly me."

"Actually I'm here this weekend and tomorrow's fine. What do you suggest?"

"Harry said you have a flat in Bayswater. How about lunch somewhere near you?"

"I'm not using the flat just now, I'm at my club. Popplewells, do you know it?"

"Popplewells? Isn't it one of those stuffy old Victorian places?"

"It's quiet and comfortable, perfect for a meeting. Long

as you don't mind stuffy old Victorians. And they do a superb lunch, the chef is a genius."

She chuckled, a delicious sound. "OK, it's a deal. Where is it and what time do you want me to come?"

"Mayfair, Brook Street. Five minutes' walk from Bond Street station. If you come around twelve, we can talk before lunch."

"Sounds good."

"Just ask for me in reception."

"See you tomorrow, then."

She rang off and Edmund put his mobile down, feeling elated and slightly bemused. Had he just made a date?

That evening, after an early dinner, Edmund retired to his room at the club to catch up on news about the murder. He was watching the TV when his mobile rang. It was Stella.

"Hi, sweetie. I was going to call you. Everything OK?"

"I was expecting you to call this morning. Are you still being followed?"

"Not since Tuesday. I've been a good boy, only using cabs."

"Good." She sounded relieved. "Have you got anything planned for tomorrow?"

"I've got a lunch appointment."

"Can you get out of it? I'd like you to come out. I called Amir and he's happy to come over. Tomorrow or Sunday, but I think the sooner the better."

"Why?"

"Why? Because I'm worried, that's why. You need to talk to him."

This is getting a tad ridiculous. "But it's a two-hour drive for him. A bit over the top, isn't it? Anyway if you're really worried, I can call him from here."

"Not the same as being face-to-face. Can you get out of the lunch thing?"

Edmund was not happy to cancel the meeting with Naomi. "Not really," he said. "What about next weekend?"

"He can't make it. His cousin's visiting from Canada."

"Ah. Yes, he told me. Tell you what, if you're really worried, I can get a train back tomorrow evening, so Sunday would be OK."

She seemed pleased with that. A nuisance, but worth it if it kept her happy.

CHAPTER THIRTEEN

Late the following morning, Naomi Porter, carrying her tablet and handbag, made her way from the Underground station towards Brook Street, thinking about Edmund Lafitte. Harry Mason had described him as being highly intelligent and a bit of a political maverick, not afraid to speak his mind. Also, Edmund was unmarried but in a stable relationship. Good, she thought, suits me perfectly.

Naomi had known since her teenage years that men found her attractive. Dealing with it had been a pleasant game but after a disastrous marriage that left her a divorcée at twenty-one, all that changed. Her bitterness passed as she learned how to use to her advantage the good looks that fate had bestowed on her. When she met a man whom she found attractive, she played him like a hooked fish. Yes, she thought, Edmund Lafitte will do. He was just the type she preferred. She thought of it as 'sampling' a man she liked without the baggage of risking a full commitment. She could back out any time, as she had done several times recently.

Naomi went up the wide steps to the glass double doors of the building that housed the venerable club. It had been named after its founder over a century before. Only the modest polished brass plate upon the wall revealed that this was Popplewells, one of London's oldest, most exclusive gentlemen's clubs.

The reception desk was in a wide hallway. The young woman behind it was flicking through a fashion magazine as Naomi went over.

"Can I help you?" she asked.

"I'm Naomi Porter, here to see Mr Lafitte."

"He's expecting you, madam," she said, indicating. "In the Green Room, second on the left down the corridor."

Corridor? It was as wide as a road, expensively carpeted, with walls displaying ornately framed portraits in oils. Images of men who looked to be persons of substance, prosperous and comfortable. Naomi paused at the entrance to the room and looked around. A place steeped in an atmosphere of quiet, unobtrusive wealth. Exactly what she might have expected, with faint, musty odours of furniture polish and old money.

High-backed armchairs upholstered in dark red leather were grouped around low wooden tables. Only two were in use, one with three men around it and another in the far corner, where Edmund Lafitte was sitting alone.

All heads turned immediately. As she made her way forward, conversation at the table of three ceased. She was the centre of attention and the men were staring at her. She looked ahead but in her peripheral vision saw that their faces swivelled to follow her as she passed. Edmund stood up. "Welcome to the lair of stuffy old Victorians."

Naomi put her handbag and tablet on the table and unbuttoned her coat. She smiled and slid it off. "Pretty much what I was expecting. No cigar smoke, though."

"Not in here, but we've got a room where members can indulge their habit." He indicated. "Take a pew."

She took a pad and a ballpoint pen from her handbag.

"This is impressive, but there's nothing green in here. Why is it called the Green Room?"

"No idea, never thought to ask. But better for a quiet meeting than a restaurant. Would you like a drink?"

"Can I leave it until lunch? I'm looking forward to seeing what your genius chef has to offer."

"You won't be disappointed."

"Let's make a start, then." She picked up the pad and pen. "How long do we have?"

"The table's booked for twelve forty-five, but we can continue after lunch. Until about four o'clock, anyway. I'm going back to Somerford this evening."

"We should be done before then. I thought you were going to be here for the weekend?"

"Change of plan."

"Is it serious? We can do this another day, if you like."

"No, it's OK. Something's come up that I have to deal with."

"Long as you're sure." She frowned. "Can't be easy, having to divide your time between two places."

"I manage."

"That reminds me; something I was wondering about." She crossed her legs and rested the notepad on her knee, taking her time. She was amused to notice that Edmund's eyes had been busy. "I mean, you've got a flat of your own and this place must be expensive. Even for someone of independent means."

Would mentioning that upset him?

Edmund's lips curled into a half smile. "My family's loaded, but I've always made my own way. My father told me that I'd have to fend for myself."

Naomi persisted. "But you joined the family firm, didn't you?"

"My first job and I was a dogsbody. Didn't enjoy it much and I wasn't too keen on staying." He smiled. "The chairman's son and all that. Actually, it was my father who suggested politics. He said it's the last resort for people who can't do anything else."

"Well, you should know."

"He had a dry sense of humour. He passed away two years ago, I still miss him. But when he suggested politics I thought, why not? I got involved in local council politics."

"Which led to you becoming an MP?"

"Yup." His brow furrowed. "But what's this got to do with IS?"

"Just background. I like to do my homework."

"Clearly."

She raised her pen and pointed. "You haven't answered my question."

His eyebrows arched. "What question?"

"Why stay here if you have your own place?" For some reason the question seemed to unsettle him. He looked away briefly and shrugged.

"Why not?"

"Just curious."

"It's really not too expensive. And it's quiet."

"Uh-huh." She flipped open her pad. "Well, let's get on. How did you get involved with the Islamic State?"

"I'm not. As I told you, the Foreign Office is doing the negotiating."

She made a note. "Do you go to their meetings with the IS people?"

"Only the first one."

She looked up. "Only the one?"

"They don't tell me much." He smiled. "Goes to show how much they value my presence."

"Who represented the other side?"

"A diplomat from the Middle East, a lawyer. After that the FO pretty much told me to butt out. They promised to keep me in the loop."

"Have they?"

Edmund hesitated. "Not really."

"Uh-huh." Naomi's journalistic experience kicked in. Edmund was prevaricating. No matter, she'd dig deeper some other time. Right now she needed him to relax and open up. This was a man she definitely intended to get to know better. She smiled, sat back and said, "Tell me what happened at that first meeting, the one that you went to."

The following morning Edmund was in Stella's living room, watching television. When the Sunday politics show ended he made his way to the kitchen. Stella was at the worktop, chopping vegetables.

"What's for lunch?" he asked.

She looked up and a strand of hair fell across her forehead. Using the back of her hand she brushed it aside. "I'm doing a beef casserole."

"Sounds good." He nodded at the steel saucepan. "You going to fill that? It'll be too much."

"No it won't. Not for three of us, but if there's anything left I'll freeze it. Lunch will be a little later than usual. I don't think Amir will be here before two at the earliest. If you want something now, I can make you a sandwich."

"No, it's OK, I'll wait. I still think I could've called him, much easier. It's a long way for him to come just for a chat."

Stella scraped a pile of chopped vegetables into the saucepan. "It is, but I want you to talk to him face-to-face. We can't risk leaving it another two weeks."

Edmund perched on a stool. "I can't help wondering if you're taking all this a tad too seriously."

"Am I?" Stella's face hardened. "Get real, Ed. The murder's been in the news every day and the police are getting nowhere. If you're being threatened, you need all the help you can get." She went to the sink and began washing her hands.

"What did you tell him?"

She answered over her shoulder. "I just said it was important and that he should hear it from you."

"All right. If he's happy to come, I suppose it's OK."

Later, Stella was in the kitchen pouring coffee into three mugs. Amir Hakim had arrived and the men were in the living room. She overfilled one, spilling the liquid. "Damn," she muttered, pausing to mop it up.

It had been her suggestion that Edmund should seek advice from Amir and she was pleased he had come. Edmund had been edgy and morose but his mood improved after Hakim arrived. Telling his friend about his fears seemed to have relaxed him.

She put the mugs on a tray and took them into the living room. Hakim was speaking in his high falsetto that always sounded odd, coming from a man of his stocky build. He was leaning back, legs stretched out, fingers steepled on his chest.

"I can't believe it. It's been a week now and there's not

been a word about you." He unlocked his fingers and gestured. "The murder's been in the news every day, practically twenty-four seven. With media vultures pressuring the cops, your card's not been mentioned. Not once. That's amazing, but it can't last." He inclined his head. "What are you going to do?"

"About what?"

Hakim's eyebrows arched. "Come on, Ed. Sooner or later some Muslim guy or bent cop is going to bank a fat cheque for leaking the info. Any minute now somebody's going to stick a mike in your face, wanting to know how your card got into the victim's pocket. With blood on it, too. I'm amazed it hasn't happened already."

Edmund muttered, "Oh shit."

Stella said, "We never thought about that."

Hakim drew his legs in and sat up. He leaned forward, took a sip of coffee and asked Edmund, "Have you been in your club all the time? I mean, do you go back to your apartment?"

"I'm staying at the club but I've been to the flat a couple of times, by taxi. And I've been using cabs to get to the House."

"Do you still think you're being followed? Noticed anything suspicious?"

"Nothing certain that I can put my finger on."

Stella cut in. "But you told me you're looking over your shoulder all the time."

Edmund shrugged. "OK, that's true. I can't shake off the feeling I'm being watched." Hakim said, "I'm sorry but I don't know if I can help, much as I'd like to."

Edmund wiped his face with his hands. "I just needed – well, another opinion. Specially yours."

"Because I'm a Muslim?"

"Partly. Do you know anything about this Brotherhood?"

"I've heard of them, but I don't know any personally. I've met one or two high profile Muslims from Donfield, maybe I can nose around a bit."

Edmund was cradling his mug in both hands, staring into it. He raised his head. "The Donfield police say they know about the Brotherhood but can't get anyone to open up."

Stella commented, "Are you surprised? You weren't too impressed when they came here."

Hakim asked, "When was that?"

Edmund replied, "On the day of the murder, two CID officers."

"Have they been back?"

"No, not even a phone call."

"Strange. They're being crucified in the media. You'd think that your card being left by the killer would at least make them wonder if you've been threatened. Why don't you tell them you think you're being followed?"

Edmund seemed reluctant to answer. He grimaced, saying, "I tried to tell Angela Fraser but..."

"The Security woman dealing with the Stanway case?"

"Yes. She said suspicions weren't enough. But she did offer me police protection."

"And?"

Edmund looked away, shrugging lightly. "I turned it down."

"Why?"

Stella interjected. "He thinks it would screw up his life."

Edmund said, "I told her I thought I was being followed, but wasn't sure. She said to get back to her when I was. In fact, she was quite rude."

Hakim nodded. "I can see her point. But she's nothing to do with the Donfield police. They're the ones dealing with the case."

"Yes, but when I mentioned the card she told me not to contact the police. She said that her lot would deal with them."

Stella said, "But that was before you were followed."

Edmund looked down into his mug again. Stella thought he was stalling. Hakim was looking at him, apparently waiting for an answer.

Edmund drained his mug. "OK," he said, "I'll think about it."

Stella rounded on him. "For heaven's sake, Ed, get real. If there's the slightest chance your life's threatened, you have to do something. OK, you don't want police protection, but you should at least *tell* them. Not just the Donfield lot, you need to tell the Met police, too. You're an MP, you should have some clout." She waved a hand. "It's their job."

Hakim said, "She's right, Ed. You need to tell them. Sounds like someone's trying to rattle you. You can't ignore that."

Edmund conceded. "All right, I'll speak to Fraser tomorrow. At the risk of getting my head bitten off."

Hakim replied, "Good. You go to London by train?"

"I take a local to Bristol and catch the seven-forty to Paddington. My Monday routine most weeks."

"From Paddington you take the Underground to Westminster?"

"I used to, but not anymore."

"Since you were followed?"

He nodded. "Now I use taxis to get to the House."

"And to your club?"

"Yes."

"I was going to suggest that you vary your routine, but it sounds like you're doing that."

"As much as I can, avoiding public transport. But there are times when I'm..." He seemed to be trying to find the right words, "out in the open. I still have to take the train to and from London." He grimaced. "There's a limit to how much I can keep my head down."

A short while later Hakim left, saying he would make enquiries with people he knew in Donfield. He was not optimistic about finding out anything that could help.

CHAPTER FOURTEEN

On the Monday morning, Edmund followed his routine, taking the local train from Somerford to Bristol Temple Meads station. He boarded the express to London, made his way to his reserved seat and placed his tablet and document case on the table.

Some of the faces were people he had seen before. But familiar though they were, they never seemed to acknowledge one another's presence, save for an occasional nod. Any sort of conversation, he mused wryly, seemed out of the question. They were, after all, English.

Edmund opened his tablet to look at the Saturday edition of *The Globe* online. On an inside page he found the article that Beth Stanway had seen. In a report on the Red Cross in Syria, there was a two-line reference to Peter Stanway and two other hostages. It was believed that they were to be moved to a more secure location. *Is that all?* Unlikely then, that Angela Fraser would have anything to tell him. He didn't really want to speak to her anyway. As for Stella's insistence that he should tell Metropolitan police about being followed, on reflection he felt that there was no hurry.

"It's Mr Thorneycroft, returning your call," Diane announced. "I'll put him through." The editor of *The Globe* had been unavailable when Edmund had tried to call him earlier. He picked up.

"Edmund Lafitte."

"Hello, Edmund, you wanted a word?" The man's manner was brusque.

"Thanks for getting back, Sam."

"This place is manic on Mondays. But the Stanway business is always a priority; Peter's one of ours. What news?"

"Actually, I was hoping you could tell me. I saw the piece in the Saturday edition about the hostages being moved but I've heard nothing from the FO. Is there any more to it?"

"Oh? I thought you were calling to tell me something new." He sounded disappointed. "Not much to it, really. We had a tip from a stringer in the Red Cross. The hard info is that Peter and a couple of others have been moved. Nothing else we can print. Reading between the lines, we think that the place where they were held was getting too much attention from Syrian army shelling. But that's just a guess, really. Could be other reasons." In a sharper tone he asked, "You sure you don't have anything for me?"

"Sorry, Sam, I don't. But if I do I'll get back to you."

"OK, you do that." The comment had come across as sceptical.

Edmund replaced the receiver thoughtfully. He could not help feeling that there was something else going on, but as long as the Foreign Office chose to keep him in the dark, there was nothing he could do.

Shortly after, Edmund's mobile rang. It was Naomi.

"Hi."

"Hello, Ed, good weekend? I missed you."

"Can't complain. What's up?"

"Um, when we had lunch in your club, I said you were right about your chef? He really is a genius."

"Uh-huh."

"As good as any celebrity chef you've met?"

"Yup." Edmund wondered where this was leading.

"Do you know Doogie Cameron? I mean, personally." She was referring to a notoriously abrasive Scottish chef who hosted television cooking programmes.

"Ah. I've met him a couple of times. Don't actually know him, though."

"I've always wanted to meet him. How about dinner at his Chelsea place?" She added, hastily, "My treat."

"What? Impossible, they're booked up weeks ahead."

"But you're an MP. And you're well known, a celebrity."

Edmund chuckled. "Nah. You've got to be a VIP to jump the queue, and I'm not."

"Do you always sell yourself short? Worth giving them a call? Any evening this week or next would do."

Edmund thought he could at least try. "All right, I'll call them, but don't count on it. A weekday may be possible, no chance of a table at weekends. Not for months."

"It'd be great if you can get us in. I'd love to meet him."

"OK, I'll give it a shot and get back to you."

Later, and to his surprise, he was able to make the booking. He sent her a text. He had achieved what many would have believed close to impossible, They had a table at Doogie's for dinner the very next day.

"Miss Porter's here, sir," the night manager at Popplewells announced. Edmund was in the Green Room, reading *The*

Times. He folded the paper and put it aside. "Thanks, Roger." He followed the man out. Naomi's taxi was at the kerb and Edmund climbed in.

She was wearing a navy blue trouser suit and a wide smile. Edmund's first impression was that she looked like something out of a fashion magazine.

"Hi." He pulled on his seatbelt. "You're looking gorgeous."

She tilted her head. "Thank you." The cab moved forward and she added, "I've told the driver it's Doogie's."

Edmund replied, "Table's booked for seven-thirty, good timing."

Traffic was light and they arrived at the restaurant in a side street in Chelsea just over ten minutes later, pulling up beside its distinctive striped awning. Two men stood talking on the pavement, one casually dressed with a camera slung around his neck, the other, larger, man wearing a dinner jacket. He came over to open the door while Edmund paid the driver.

The man greeted him as he stepped out. "Good evening, Mr Lafitte."

"How you doing, Jake?"

"I'm good, sir."

The other man took a step forward, his camera raised. Then with a disappointed look, he lowered it again. Edmund smiled to himself as the couple followed the large man into the restaurant.

The air in Chelsea on that late spring evening was crisp and cool. Edmund and Naomi had left the restaurant and made their leisurely way down Cheyne Walk to the Embankment, strolling by the riverside. At the scene were groups of young people chatting animatedly, couples with eyes only for each other, and the ubiquitous tourists, carrying bags bearing the logos of fashionable London shops.

Edmund breathed in deeply, savouring the ambience. He felt pleasantly content and completely relaxed. "So, did it live up to your expectations?"

Naomi slid her arm through his. "Marvellous, though I didn't get to meet the man himself."

"You disappointed?"

"A bit. I'm a fan."

"We did meet Sarah." He was referring to Doogie Cameron's protégé Sarah Stewart, who ran the kitchen in his absence. She had come out to meet the diners.

Naomi said, "She seems a bit young for the job but she's good, the meal was fantastic."

"She was a bit miffed when you asked where Doogie was."

"I didn't mean to be tactless."

They were approaching a bench. Edmund said, "You weren't. Let's sit." They settled and he added, "Maybe she's ticked off playing second fiddle. But when I said you're a fan, she was OK."

For a few moments they were silent, gazing across at the activity around the boats moored at Cadogan pier. Naomi asked, "How did you manage to get the table? You said it was impossible."

"I'm an A-list celebrity," he replied, deadpan.

"What?"

"Kidding." He grinned. "They had a 'no show'. Seems they get calls every day asking if there's a cancellation.

Even then, it depends on who you are. I was lucky, they'd heard of me."

"That doorman knew you. Welcomed you by name."

"Jake. His name's Jake and it's his job to know who's expected. But don't call him a doorman. He's a 'greeter' and he's there to welcome guests."

"He looks like he can handle himself. I wouldn't want to be around when someone upsets him. That guy with him was one of the paparazzi, hanging around to get shots of celebs."

"Uh-huh."

"He didn't try to get one of you."

"Like I say, I'm not A-list. If there's a D-list, I'm on it." Edmund was sitting with his legs extended, completely at ease. He had a sudden urge to yawn and tried to suppress it by putting his hand over his mouth. "Sorry," he apologised.

Naomi smiled. "Am I boring you?"

"A leading question." He made a dismissive gesture. "You're never boring. It's me, I'm whacked. Or it could be the wine." He took out his mobile. "Time to get you home; I'll call a cab."

Comfortably ensconced in the back of a taxi, they were heading for Pinner, the suburb where Naomi lived. Edmund insisted that they take her home first.

Naomi protested. "This is going to take you miles out of your way and really it's no problem. Why don't you drop me off here? I can use the Underground. My place is close to the station."

"I won't hear of it." Changing the subject he said, "I've been through Pinner, but don't know it. Do you have a house or a flat?"

"A house. It's a quiet, middle-class area. Commuter land." She rolled her eyes.

"You don't like it?"

"It's OK, a bit boring. But I love my house. Spoils of war."

"What?"

"Best thing I ever got out of Andrew. Divorce settlement; I agreed to give up my maintenance claim in exchange for the house. My reward for marrying him and putting up with his lying and womanising. He can afford it, he's a high flyer in a bank."

"Sounds like you came out all right."

"In the end, but it was a bad time. I was eighteen when we married and he was twenty-five, climbing the greasy pole. It lasted only two years. I loved him but he never loved me the same way. All he wanted was to show off. Flash cars, the gold Rolex, that sort of thing. And the house, a detached villa. I finally realised that I was just another trophy." She smiled. "But now the house is all mine. So yes, I'm happy."

Forty minutes later, the taxi pulled up at a T-junction. The vehicle was fitted with an intercom to allow the driver and the passengers in the back to communicate. A red indicator on the device lit up. The driver's voice came through in a metallic tone. "We'll be at Grove Crescent shortly, Miss. What's the number?"

"Twelve. It's on the left."

"Twelve, OK." The indicator light went out as the cab moved forward.

Naomi put a hand on Edmund's arm. "It's been a fabulous

evening, Ed. I've had a great time."

"You know what? Me too."

She hesitated. "It doesn't have to end just yet. Why don't you come in?"

"I'd love to, but it's late and I've got an early start tomorrow." Her face fell, so he explained. "There's a meeting I have to attend in the morning."

"Why not stay over?"

Overnight? He wasn't expecting that. The prospect hadn't even occurred to him and he struggled, stammering, "I – er..."

"If you go to your club tonight it will be another hour before you get to bed. Much easier if you come in, have a nightcap and crash out. In the morning you can make an early start and go your club or straight to your office."

The intercom light came on and the device crackled. The driver said, "Just turning into Grove Crescent now, miss. Where do you want me to pull up?"

Naomi leaned forward. "The sixth house on the left." She pointed. "Just behind that beech tree, you can pull up there."

"OK."

The half-minute or so had been just enough time for Edmund to sort himself out. He took Naomi's hand and spoke calmly. "Maybe next time. Right now I'd be lousy company."

She shrugged lightly, pulling her hand free. "OK." Without warning she reached up, cupped his face between her palms, drew his head down and kissed him, slowly and passionately, full on the mouth.

CHAPTER FIFTEEN

What was that all about, Edmund wondered? After their lingering kiss, Naomi had stepped out, waved briefly through the window and strode up the drive without a backward glance.

The cab eased away and the intercom light came on. "Popplewells, was it, sir?"

"That's right. How long will it take?"

"This time of night, about forty minutes, I reckon."

Edmund peered out at the darkened street. It had started to rain and there wasn't much to see. He returned to his deliberations. Naomi had been flirting with him ever since they met. He felt flattered because she was a beautiful woman. But also smart and calculating, a woman who was prepared to do whatever it took to get what she wanted. Did she really want him? More likely all she wanted was a casual fling. OK, so what's wrong with that? *What possible harm could it do?*

His thoughts turned to Stella, with whom he had not spoken that day. He checked his watch; it was after eleven, too late to call. Stella, lovely Stella who had come into his life when he won the seat in Somerford. She was a widow and at that time a voluntary worker for the local Conservative party, advising on legal matters. They became friends and not long after started a relationship that had endured. He reflected that he was fortunate to have such a loving, close companion. He would never do anything to hurt her. Unthinkable. But could a casual fling with the gorgeous Naomi count as cheating? Lost in thought, Edmund was only vaguely aware that the driver was talking to someone. He could not hear what was being said and assumed the man was communicating with his base. The indicator light came on again.

"My controller's just called, guv. Traffic's jammed on the A40 and there's a tailback."

"Will we be held up?"

"Nah, we can go round it. I'll divert through Harrow and Ealing, no problem."

"What caused it?"

The cabbie took a hand off the wheel and made a dismissive gesture. "Could be anything. Accident, most likely." He slowed the vehicle and used the indicator, making a turn. "There's a football match tonight, England against some East European country at Wembley. Should be over by now. Anyway, most of the traffic will be heading the other way, out of the city."

Edmund was not familiar with the route that the taxi was taking, but he wasn't concerned. The cabbie seemed to know what he was doing and traffic was not heavy. Twenty minutes later, the situation changed. They were moving more slowly, down the Harrow Road with its signs indicating Wembley and the stadium ahead. They slowed at a large roundabout, with Wembley signposted to the left and Ealing straight ahead. With its diesel engine throbbing impatiently, the taxi filtered into the stream of traffic slowly encircling the roundabout. A minute later, the reason for their crawling pace was revealed. The exit they had been heading for was closed off. Edmund peered forward through the rain-spattered windscreen, his view blurred by the wiper blades swishing over the glass. A police car with its blue roof light flashing was blocking the road. Standing in front of the vehicle was a uniformed policeman, rain-drenched and looking distinctly unhappy, impatiently waving vehicles back around the roundabout.

The cabbie said, "Bad news, another diversion."

Edmund leaned forward. "What now?"

The man took his hands off the wheel and shrugged. "Who knows? I'll check with the office, see if they know what's going on." He turned the intercom off and flicked a switch on the radio console, while guiding the vehicle around to join the stream heading off towards Wembley. A minute later he turned the intercom on again.

"Not good, guv. Some sort of incident on Wembley High Road. Barriers and diversions all over the place. I reckon we're stuffed, if you'll pardon my French."

"Bugger! That I don't need. Did they say what it is?"

"Right now they don't know. No choice, I'll just have to follow the diverts."

The traffic was crawling again, nose to tail. Edmund resigned himself to the situation, sat back and checked his watch. Ten to midnight. He was tired, no telling when he would get to bed this night. Half a mile further there was another police barrier. This time the way ahead was coned off and two uniformed policemen were diverting vehicles into a side road.

"Oh shit!" The cabbie's muttered expletive betrayed his frustration. The man had left the intercom on. Traffic stopped and the taxi was now waiting to join the queue of stationary vehicles that had been directed off to the side. Edmund looked ahead through the rain and darkness. Beyond the cones three police cars were parked in the middle of the road and further behind there appeared to be considerable activity. He could not make out exactly what was going on, but there were several emergency vehicles involved. The rain and darkness made it difficult to tell, but there appeared to be two fire tenders and at least three ambulances attending, all with amber and blue lights flashing. People wearing fluorescent vests were moving between and around the vehicles. No doubt about it, whatever had happened was serious.

Edmund raised his voice. "What's that up ahead?"

The driver had also been watching the scene through the windscreen. "They've coned off the High Street, it don't look good."

Edmund was now alert, his fatigue forgotten. He took out his mobile to access Twitter. Within moments he knew what the problem was. Somebody had set off a bomb!

Horrified, Edmund exclaimed, "Driver, I want to get out. Right now!"

"What? We're stuck in traffic. What..."

"Pull over to the side. I need to speak to those policemen."

"I don't think that would be a good idea, guv."

Edmund snatched the door handle but it would not move. He had forgotten that the passenger compartments of London cabs in use were routinely locked by the driver. "Listen," he hissed, "I'm an MP. A bomb's been set off on Wembley High Street. I want to find out what the hell's going on. Pull over to the side and let me out, *now*." His outburst had been delivered with a degree of urgency and enough authority to get the response he wanted.

"Right." The driver swung the wheel immediately and propelled the cab to the side of the road. He must have released the door lock because the handle now worked. Edmund swung the door open and scrambled out, to be assaulted instantly by the cold, driving rain.

One of the policemen reacted immediately, shouting, "Oi! You can't stop here." He strode forward holding a torch, its beam directed at Edmund's face. "Get back in your cab," he bellowed.

Edmund blinked and put up a hand to shield his eyes. "I'm an MP, Edmund Lafitte. I want to help."

"You can help by getting back in your taxi. I want it moved. There's emergency vehicles coming through and you're in the way."

The policeman was now only a few feet away. He was quite young and appeared to be severely stressed. Edmund said, "A bomb incident is it, Officer? I'm sure there must be something I can do."

The man's brow creased and he snapped, "Look, mate, I don't care who the fuck you are. If you're not a doctor or a paramedic, just bugger off." He waved his arm to emphasise the point.

"Surely there must be something..."

The policeman came right up and thrust his head forward. His helmet dripped water and his clothes were soaked. His eyes bulged and with his face contorted, he snarled, "You deaf or something? Yes, it's a fucking bomb. Set off in a crowd and I've been stood here watching body parts being bagged." Shaking with fury, he raised his voice. "An MP, are you? If you're serious about helping, *do something to stop this madness*. Now sod off. If you don't go right now, I'll do you for obstruction." He waved his arm again and shouted, "Bugger off." Then he turned and strode back to his companion.

Edmund was staggered. The constable's unexpectedly savage, near-hysterical outburst stunned him. The words *do something* kept ringing in his ears. With rain lashing his face he was suddenly aware that he was getting soaked. He walked back to the cab and stepped in. Cars were now moving forward slowly and the cabbie, waiting to ease the taxi into the line, looked up and spoke. "My office has been on, guv. They said it's a bomb and I've been told to get out of the area as quick as I can."

Edmund did not reply. He was wiping his face with a handkerchief. A van paused to allow the taxi to pull into the line of traffic and the cabbie moved the taxi forward. He looked up into the mirror at Edmund. "I've put my radio on. It's the London News. They said there's been an explosion on Wembley High Street, outside a pub." He indicated with a thumb. "Just down the road there."

Edmund looked across at the road block. "That policeman was in a bad way. Traumatised, poor bugger."

The queue of traffic was moving again. In the background Edmund heard the radio station's terse announcements, but could not quite make out what was being said.

"Can you turn your radio up?"

The man reached over and adjusted the volume. "I'm not really supposed to use it when I'm carrying, but I reckon it's OK, this being an emergency."

"Leave it on, please."

Edmund's mind was locked onto the senseless horror of the incident that had taken place only yards from where they were. It was going to be a long night.

Much later, in his room at Popplewells, Edmund was sitting on the bed, having gone through the motions of readying himself for the night. He never used pyjamas, preferring instead to sleep in boxer shorts. He took off his watch, glanced at it and placed it carefully on the bedside table. Ten minutes past two in the morning. It had been a long, tiring day, yet despite his fatigue he could not unwind.

He had arrived at the club twenty minutes earlier and was let in by Roger, the night manager; an ex-marine who had seen service in Bosnia. He had not batted an eyelid, as if a member returning at that hour was the norm. After a brief exchange of views about the atrocity, Edmund had dragged his weary body to his room, turned the television on to the news channel and left it on as he went through his routine of preparing for bed.

It was believed that a lone suicide bomber had targeted a crowd outside a pub on Wembley High Street. So far ten were known to be dead, with many more injured. Most were football fans who had been at the match. The people known as Daesh or Islamic State were quick to claim responsibility. *What is the world coming to?*

Edmund sighed, drew his hands down his face, pulled back the covers and eased himself into bed. Sleep. That's what he needed. Deep, flat-out, dead-to-the-world slumber. But, no matter how hard he tried, he was unable to relax. Sleep stubbornly eluded him as his mind buzzed in overdrive, constantly churning over all that had happened that day. Uppermost were his concerns about safety, for himself and for those closest to him. What kind of people deliberately set out to kill innocent civilians? Had they been playing cat and mouse with him? An odd but apt phrase. Cats often toy with mice before killing them. And he was a target, wasn't he? An unbearable, painful thought occurred. Stella or Naomi could be injured or worse if they were with him when IS struck. *God, what a mess.*

After what seemed like an age and no nearer sleep, he threw off the covers, switched on his bedside light and sat up. He had been sweating and had a throbbing headache. He checked the time. Twenty-five past four. Wearily, he padded to the bathroom and had a long drink of water. Then he turned the television on for an update. The coverage was much the same, except that it was now known that twelve people were dead and at least fifteen others injured. He turned the set off in disgust and returned to his bed.

This time he did achieve a degree of rest, but only intermittently. Small doses of shallow, fitful sleep with occasional bouts of near-consciousness. And throughout, constant, continuous mental activity. Over and over again, the interweaving threads of his subconscious meanderings were interspersed with the image of the face of that young, frightened and angry policeman. *If you're serious, do something to stop this madness!*

In the twilight state somewhere between sleep and full consciousness, very slowly his anxiety and fears gave way to feelings of mounting anger, rising to an overwhelming fury at Islamic State and all that it stood for. So strong was the feeling that it caused him to wake suddenly. He sat up, paused briefly to clear his head and then went over to the wooden chest of drawers, on top of which he kept his briefcase. He needed a notebook to jot down his thoughts and set out a framework for the speech that he was now determined to make in the House of Commons. Prime Minister's Questions would give him the perfect opportunity to launch an attack on Islamic State. His burning anger was enough to brush aside any lingering fears for his own safety.

He, Edmund Lafitte, an elected Member of Parliament, would set in motion something that would lead to the final and permanent destruction of that evil establishment. His jaw tightened. To hell with them.

CHAPTER SIXTEEN

In his office adjacent to the incident room at Donfield Police headquarters, Chief Inspector Charles Royce sat with his elbows propped on his desk and his hands cradling his face. He was morose. Ten days since the murder of Sayeed Iqbal and they had made little progress. He stared unblinking at the large whiteboard that covered most of the wall opposite, his brain churning, seeking inspiration.

In the centre was a picture of the Imam, his beady eyes staring through the round, wire-framed spectacles. Around the periphery were photographs of individuals who could be suspects in the murder investigation. Or maybe not. Images of people who had visited Imam Mahmud's modest house since the surveillance unit had been set up. The instructions to the team specified that a special note should be made to mark any person who looked capable of wielding a sword. The problem was that there were at least ten individuals who qualified. Why so many? And because most had visited the house several times, when added together the number of visits by all of these people totalled a highly improbable forty-two. In just ten days? Something was not right.

The door hinges squealed to announce an entrance. Sergeant Colin Brody came in, using his backside to keep the door open as he eased himself in. He was holding two polystyrene cups, one in each hand.

"That machine's playing up again," he complained. "No sugar."

Without taking his eyes off the board, Royce grunted. "Tell maintenance." He nodded towards the door. "While you're at it, tell them to oil the hinges on that bloody door. How many times do I have to ask?"

Brody put one of the cups on the desk in front of his superior, placed the other on the opposite side and pulled up a chair.

Royce pointed at the board. "You know what? Something's not right with this. It doesn't add up, unless Mahmud's running a club for weight-lifters."

"What do you mean, sir?"

"We set up the surveillance ten days since. Why have that many heavies called on him?"

Brody took a sip from his cup. He shrugged. "Can't say. Who knows?"

Royce drew forward a brown folder that was on the desk. "Let's take a look at the log." He flipped open the folder, checked through the papers and pulled out the record sheets. Then he skimmed through the first few pages, frowning as he ran a finger down the list of entries.

Brody put his cup down. "What you looking for?"

Royce ignored the question, concentrating on the entries on the page. "Hah," he exclaimed. "Look at this. First four days, all the same. Then from day five, there's a stream of heavy blokes calling in. Why?"

Brody seemed to be considering this for a few moments. Then his face lit up. It was as if a light bulb had been switched on in his head. "He's rumbled the surveillance."

"Yeah, that's what I think too, Colin."

"The crafty sod!"

Royce said, "I've got a nice little job for you. I want you to go through the file and make a spreadsheet of all the men logged as heavies. Then note how many times each came to the house and on what days. Also if they came alone or with others."

"Will do. Have we got names for them all?"

"Yes, so far. The team's done a good job. But get the logs for yesterday and today and if there's no names for any new ones, make sure you get them. I want it all bang up to date."

Brody's expression displayed a distinct lack of enthusiasm. "Yes, sir," he said in a downbeat tone.

Royce snapped, "Basic policing. You're a detective, when it's painstaking, that's what you get. Pain." He closed the folder and handed it to his sergeant. "The info's already there, all you need is to set it out so it can be analysed. It's not rocket science, get on with it. Drop everything else, if they know they're being watched we might as well shut down the team. Get moving, Sergeant, I want it as quick as possible."

Across the city Imam Zulfikar Ali Mahmud was in his living room with Kemal Abdullah, who had just arrived. "Take a seat. Five or ten minutes is enough. Do you want some coffee?"

The big man shook his head. "No, I have to get back. They don't like me taking time off and I don't want to push my luck." Abdullah worked as a fork-lift driver in a parcel distribution centre a few minutes' drive away.

"What did you tell them?"

"I said my mother fell over and hurt her foot and I'm doing her shopping until she can walk again. But they're not happy."

"You've done well. The police are stupid, now also confused. Idiots, do they think we don't know about their circus across the road?" He chuckled. "They will be busy checking out every brother who's been here." His face broke into a wide grin. "And they will find out nothing."

Inspector Royce had just finished taking a call from the Deputy Chief Constable, berating him for the lack of progress on the murder investigation. He slammed the handset down. Why the hell didn't they leave him alone to get on with his job? Why didn't the DCC settle for the daily updates he got from Flack? Not that his superior was a bad boss, he just wasn't the brightest copper on the Force. And his way of dealing with pressure from above was to pass it on. The constant attention from the press and broadcasting media was just being shovelled down the line. This case was like a clam with its jaws welded shut. He needed a break, and soon. His musings were interrupted by a double knock on the door. He looked up and saw through the glass panel his sergeant's face, wearing a smug expression.

Royce waved him in. "What have you got?"

Brody put the file on the desk and placed a printed spreadsheet on top. "Look at this, sir." He pointed. "In the first four days nothing much, except for one guy who called twice. He came back again after the fifth day like the others, except he's the *only* one who'd come before." Brody went over to the whiteboard and put an index finger on the photo of a man with a dark, bushy beard. "This man," he said, firmly. "Kemal Abdullah."

Royce sat up. If the Imam discovered the surveillance on the fourth day, that man had been calling on the cleric *before* he muddied the waters by calling in the others. Interesting. He said, "What do we know about him?"

Brody returned to the desk and opened the file. At the top were two pages stapled together. He removed them and held them up. "This is what I have so far. I'm sure there's more, but I'm guessing you'd want this now."

"Let me see."

Brody handed it to him.

CHAPTER SEVENTEEN

Next day in his room at the club, Edmund watched the news on television. Eight o'clock in the morning was probably not a good time to try to get hold of the Prime Minister, but Edmund needed to speak to her. He phoned the ex-directory number for Downing Street and identified himself. He was told by the switchboard operator that the Prime Minister was not taking calls.

In that case, he thought, I'll talk to her PA. "Can you put me through to Michelle Jackson, then?"

The operator said, "Mrs Jackson has four callers on hold. Do you want to wait, or can you call back? Or I can take a message, if you prefer."

Unbelievable! Maybe he could cut through the crap. "Look, I'm sorry, but this is extremely urgent. I have to speak to the PM about today's PMQs. Can you..."

"I'm sorry Mr Lafitte, but today's session of Prime Minister's Questions has been cancelled. There'll be an emergency debate instead."

"What?"

"It's because of the bomb incident, as a mark of respect to the victims." Edmund did not reply, so she added, "What do you want to do?"

"I'd like to leave a message. Please ask her to call me; it's urgent. Tell her I was near the bomb scene."

"Ah. Yes, Mr Lafitte, I'll make sure she's told."
Edmund thanked her and rang off.

Barely ten minutes later, Edmund was on his way down to breakfast when his mobile rang. It was a call from a shielded number. Probably Michelle Jackson. He answered immediately.

"Edmund Lafitte."

"I got your message, Edmund." She spoke briskly. "You were there when it happened?"

"No, just after. I was stopped at a road block close to the scene by a police constable. He refused to let me get closer. Any chance of a word with the PM?"

"Impossible, right now. You said it's urgent. Can I help?"

"I saw the chaos and the effect it had on the policeman. I want to speak in the debate."

She paused for a moment and then said, "I'll put you through. She's on a call and there's another one waiting. Can you hold?"

After a brief delay, he was put through. His conversation with the Prime Minister lasted no more than a few minutes but Edmund was satisfied. He would get his platform. He was determined to use it as effectively as possible, even if that meant raising his voice to shouting level when necessary, to overcome the volume of baying and near-constant banter that was the norm when the chamber was full.

At precisely eleven-fifteen, Edmund was in his seat in the House of Commons. The benches were all occupied, as expected. As usual on occasions when the chamber was full, Members who could not be accommodated on the benches stood in the aisle at the side of the chamber.

The Speaker of the House commenced proceedings and after the usual formalities the debate began. At that point, in time-honoured fashion, the Prime Minister rose to her feet to make a short announcement before the first member to speak was called. The chamber fell silent as she invited the House to join with her in offering sympathies to those who were injured in the bombing atrocity of the previous evening and condolences to those citizens who had been bereaved. She promised a full investigation and assured the House that steps would be taken to maximise security against the recurrence of such incidents in the future.

The Member who was to speak first, rose to his feet. Edmund and several others also stood up and immediately sat down again, thus indicating to the Speaker in the manner proscribed by convention their desire to be called. Also as expected, the Speaker first called upon the Leader of the Opposition. A quiet, taciturn man, he rose and made a short statement, echoing the sentiments expressed by the Prime Minister about the victims of the bombing. He then went on to criticize the Government's failure to make adequate provisions for the funding of policing in the community. To the noisy banter and baying by unruly Members on the Government side, he concluded his statement and went back to his seat on the Opposition front bench. The speaker then called the Member who was to be the first to speak.

The MP rose to his feet. He drew attention to the security implications caused by proposed reductions in the armed forces. The Prime Minister answered, assuring the House that no measures taken would compromise the security of the country. When she resumed her seat on the front bench,

Edmund and the others stood up. Edmund looked directly at the Speaker, who nodded towards him and declared in a loud voice, "Mr Edmund Lafitte."

The others sat again while Edmund remained on his feet. He was holding a notepad but did not speak until the hubbub in the background had died down. Then, raising his voice he said, "Thank you, Mr Speaker."

Edmund glanced at his notepad before continuing. "Mr Speaker, I join with the Prime Minister and the Leader of the Opposition in offering my sincere condolences to those who have been bereaved, and express my deepest sympathy with those injured, as a result of the appalling atrocity committed in Wembley last night. That senseless act of savage, unspeakable brutality, carried out against innocent civilians, has affected me profoundly."

He paused for a few moments and then continued, speaking clearly, his voice slightly raised. "Mr Speaker, I am tired and angry. Tired because I have had little rest during the past fourteen hours, and angry because I happened to be very near the scene of the atrocity shortly after it was perpetrated." Instantly, the chamber fell silent. Edmund was aware that he now had the full attention of all.

He looked around, taking his time. "I was close enough to visit the actual site of the incident to assist in any way I could, but I was prevented from so doing by the presence of a police road block across the High Street," he paused briefly, "and a constable doing his duty. That young man would not let me pass. When I told him that I was a Member of this House and wished to help, his reply was that unless I was a paramedic or a doctor, I should leave immediately. His manner, to put it mildly, was short. I persisted, and he answered forcefully, telling me that he had been obliged to stand and watch body parts being bagged." There were gasps around the chamber. Nobody spoke.

Edmund held up his notepad and said, "May I tell you exactly what that young officer, exhausted, clearly deeply stressed and certainly traumatised, said?" He looked at the pad. "Mr Speaker, the man said that if I was an MP and serious about helping, I should – and I quote – *do something to stop this madness*." A few seconds of total silence followed. Then Edmund said, "That, Mr Speaker, is what I meant when I said that the incident had affected me profoundly. Today I am a changed man."

There followed another brief silence, broken when a Member on the back benches behind Edmund shouted, "Question?" To the background sounds of general hubbub, Edmund nodded and addressed the Speaker.

"Mr Speaker, I thank the honourable gentleman for his prompt. My question to the Prime Minister is this: Will the right honourable lady now consider, as a matter of urgency, greater involvement of our armed forces in the fight against the evil of Daesh, as it is known?" The noise in the background increased and shouts of approval were expressed, as Edmund went on. "The time has come for us to join with other nations in this endeavour by putting troops on the ground." The baying and shouting of Members on both sides rose in volume.

Edmund raised his voice. "Mr Speaker, it is clear that aerial bombardment is of little value. You cannot..." He was interrupted by the cacophony of noise in the chamber, but he continued. "You cannot destroy a nest of poisonous ants by throwing stones at them. They have to be eradicated by appropriate action *on the ground*. It is time for all democratic, sovereign nations to unite in a single endeavour: the total and complete destruction, by an alliance of troops and armament on the ground, of this evil entity that dares to call itself the Islamic State."

Breathing hard, Edmund sat down and the chamber fell silent. Moments later, he was patted on the back by some nearest him, while others rose to their feet. The House of Commons has a strictly observed convention that speeches are not applauded. It has been breached only twice in recent history. But after the briefest, stunned silence, Members began clapping, slowly at first, then with increasing intensity with whoops and shouts of approval, a combined cacophony that rose in volume, drowning out the Speaker's efforts to restore order.

On the Government front bench a Minister remarked, "A brave man." Beside him a colleague observed drily, "But courting trouble, I fear."

Late that afternoon, Edmund was in the anteroom to the Cabinet Office in Downing Street, having been summoned to a meeting with the Prime Minister.

"Wait here." The Cabinet Secretary used an imperious tone, indicating a row of padded, ornate straight-backed chairs. He was a dapper man, dedicated to his job but not generally liked. His preference for built-up shoes was one of the worst-kept secrets in Westminster. He started to move towards the door of the Cabinet Office, but stopped and turned. "Do you have a mobile phone with you?"

Edmund nodded. "Yes."

"Turn it off, please. The PM has a house rule – no mobiles

here or in the Cabinet Office." He went to the door, knocked and entered.

Edmund had been given no reason for the summons, but was not too concerned. He did not expect any problems and did not mind being kept waiting, but wished that he could use the time to better effect, like making phone calls or sending texts. Ten minutes later, the Cabinet Secretary returned and ushered him in.

The Prime Minister was seated at the far end of the long oak table that was used for Cabinet meetings. Head down, she was making notes on an A4 lined pad, using an old-fashioned fountain pen. Beside her sat the white-haired Home Secretary James Houghton, with a brown file open on the table. His bespectacled, lined face was grave. Walking behind the Cabinet Secretary, Edmund became aware of the near total silence in the room. Their footfalls were soundless on the thick Axminster carpet.

Houghton glanced up at Edmund and his mouth turned down. The PM, without looking up from her writing, addressed the Cabinet Secretary. "Thank you, Patrick," she drawled, dismissing him. He muttered "Prime Minister," before leaving. Edmund was left standing behind a chair, he had not been asked to sit. He felt like a schoolboy who had been summoned into the headmaster's presence to be reprimanded for a misdemeanour. Still without looking up, the PM used the pen to point, saying, "Do sit down."

Edmund drew the chair out, murmuring, "Thank you, Prime Minister." He had begun to worry. *What was coming next?*

Finally, the lady re-capped her pen, placed it carefully on the table and looked directly at Edmund. She frowned and snapped, "Don't believe in half measures, do you?"

Sharply taken aback, Edmund answered with a querulous, "Prime Minister?"

She waited a few seconds before answering in a level but firm tone. "When we spoke this morning I don't recall you saying anything about making war on the ground in Syria."

Edmund had a sudden hollow feeling in his chest. "I didn't think…" he stammered.

She interrupted forcefully. "No, you certainly did not. We have procedures that we follow when making foreign policy decisions, especially when it comes to deciding when and where to use our armed forces. And there's the small matter of seeking a UN resolution first."

Houghton leaned forward. "This is a serious business. I simply cannot understand why you didn't run it past me. Or mention it to the Prime Minister when you had the opportunity."

Edmund felt his blood rising and realized that his face was reddening. "There wasn't time. The bombing incident occurred only last night and…"

"Time?" The lady had interrupted again. "You were talking to me and you made an emotional appeal to be allowed to speak against the evil of Islamic State. That I agreed to, given the bad experience you had." Her nostrils flared and her tone was now cold and measured. "What I did not do, *Mister* Lafitte, was to give you carte blanche to demand that we lead our allies into another war on the ground. How much time would you have needed to tell me that was your intention? A minute would have sufficed."

Edmund knew that he was now blushing with embarrassment. He had no answer. After a few seconds

Houghton sat back and said, "There's another issue to be considered and it needs to be addressed as a matter of urgency." He lifted his chin to scrutinise his papers through the bottom halves of his bifocal lenses. "Safety. You are foolish enough to risk your own life, but you don't seem to have given a thought for anyone who may be nearby when you are attacked." He leaned forward again. "And I do mean 'when' and not 'if'. You know nothing about the Islamic State or its methods. You are now a walking target and everyone around you is at risk."

Edmund was stung into responding. "I'm not a fool. And as for the risk to my life, I have good reason to believe that I was already a target before last night's incident."

The Prime Minister said, "We know. We also know about your involvement in the Donfield murder. That's precisely why I felt you could be trusted to speak on the IS issue. It never occurred to me that you would say anything that would actually make your personal situation worse. Why would it?"

Edmund did not reply. Then Houghton said, "We understand that you have declined personal protection. It is no longer up to you to decide. You have put us in an impossible position. We will now have to provide you with protection around the clock and that isn't cheap, to say the least. If we don't, we'll be blamed for not protecting you. If we do, as we now must, the Opposition will have a field day attacking us for what it is going to cost the taxpayer." He grimaced. "Thanks a bunch."

The Prime Minister had the last word. "Or you can pick up the tab yourself," she said drily.

In Somerford, Stella Tudor arrived home after her day's work, steering her car onto the drive. The journey from her office in the town took around fifteen minutes and she was glad to be home. It had been a trying day. As she drew up in front of her garage, her mobile rang. She picked it up. Amir Hakim. Unusual, he rarely called her.

"Hello, Amir."

"Stella? Where are you?"

"In my car, just got home. I'm about to go in."

"Has Ed called you?"

"No, but I'll be phoning him this evening. Is there a problem?"

"Did you speak to him last night?" He sounded anxious.

"As it happens, I didn't. What's the problem?"

"He made a speech in the House and..."

This did not sound good. "And what?"

"It was a bit strong. Dynamite, in fact."

"What, *Edmund?* That's not like him. What was it about?"

"Turn on your TV. He's on the news, lead story."

Stella grabbed her handbag off the passenger seat and scrambled out of the car. Holding the mobile to her ear she slammed the car door shut. "What's going on? Tell me."

"He's attacked the Islamic State."

She was heading for the front door and stopped. "*What?*"

"You need to see the footage, it's on right now. The news channel."

"I'm on my way."

"Call me back when you've seen it."

She ended the call but in her haste to open the front door she fumbled and dropped the keyring. "Damn," she muttered, stooping to pick it up.

Once inside, she put her handbag on the hall table and threw the keyring down beside it, before hurrying to the living room. She grabbed the TV remote, switched it on and jabbed the number for the news channel. At that moment her landline phone rang. Edmund! She muted the television, rushed over to the phone extension that was in a corner of the room and picked up the handset.

"Edmund?" she blurted.

A brief pause. "Er, no, Stella. It's Freddie. Freddie Pollard, *Somerford Times*."

It took a few moments for her to adjust her thoughts. She knew Pollard, but was caught off-guard. "Oh, hello, Freddie. What can I do for you?"

"I was wondering if you know where Edmund is."

Stella was anxious to get back to the television. "I'm not sure where he is right now, but he'll be here on Saturday week. He comes to his constituency office most Saturdays, as you probably know."

"I'm looking for a quote. I've tried his place in London but no luck."

"He's staying at his club in Mayfair at the moment, have you tried there?"

"Which one is it?"

"Popplewells, in Mayfair," Stella replied, instantly biting her lip, regretting what she had said.

"OK, thanks. And by the way, we think he's amazing, a brave man."

Stella did not comment. She ended the call and immediately pressed the speed dial button for Edmund's mobile, whilst turning the television sound on again.

Fifteen minutes later, after several frustratingly failed attempts to phone Edmund, she returned Hakim's call. He picked up at once.

"Yes, Stella."

"I can't get hold of him, Amir. His bloody phone's off, it's so annoying. He must know I'm worried."

"I can't get him either, but it's not surprising, considering what he said. Did you see it on the news?"

"Yes, I did. Bloody stupid. What's he playing at? I've never seen him do anything so – so *rash*. Has he taken leave of his senses?"

"I have to say it's not like him, but it looks like he meant it. Ed's no fool, Stella, he probably had his reasons. I'm sure he'll call you as soon as he can."

Stella had calmed down. "OK, I'll wait, but there's no excuse for him not calling, or texting." She rang off and went into her kitchen to see what she could muster for a supper snack. She was not hungry.

In the taxi on his way from Downing Street to Popplewells, Edmund sat back wearily and closed his eyes. What an extraordinary day! His mobile had been switched off, but now he could relax and give Stella a call.

Her response was an immediate reproof. "It's about time," she snapped. "Where the hell have you been?"

"Stella? What's the matter? I'm in a taxi on my way to the club."

"What's the matter? Why haven't you called? I've been trying to get you but your phone's been off."

"Oh, sorry. I was asked – well actually, ordered – to turn it off. I've been with the Prime Minister and the Home Secretary."

"What the *hell* are you playing at?" She had raised her voice. Edmund was astonished. Casually dropping the names of two of the most powerful people in the country seemed to have made no difference. She was clearly very angry. "Have you gone mad?"

This was something he was not ready for. Still smarting from the verbal lashing he had suffered at the hands of his political masters, he had been expecting support from his partner. Or at least a bit of sympathy. He decided to back off and give her time to cool down. Once she had heard about his encounter with the policeman, she would come round.

"Let me call you again from my room," he said. "Something happened that you should know about. Give me fifteen minutes."

Ten minutes later, when the cab pulled up in front of the entrance to Popplewells, it was immediately besieged by a mob of yelling, pushing cameramen and reporters.

Edmund shut his eyes and groaned. "Oh, shit!"

Getting through the mêlée had not been easy, but Edmund held his nerve and said nothing at all to the press. He entered his room, put his tablet down and took out his mobile. First things first, he stripped off his jacket, loosened his tie and kicked off his shoes. Relief. Then he sat on the bed and called Stella. She answered immediately.

"You're late," she snapped.

"Hello, sweetie. Sorry about that. I had to fight through a mob of media vultures outside the club, worse than a rugby scrum. Quick off the mark, aren't they? How did they know I'm staying here?"

It was a few moments before she answered. "Uh, I can't

say. You know what they're like."

"I expect there's another lot outside my apartment, too. Maybe one of my neighbours there said something."

"Yes, I expect so."

She seemed calmer. Edmund said, "Something I have to tell you. Last night, when that bomb went off in Wembley, I was at the scene."

"What? You were there?"

"Actually, close by. I was in the traffic jam it caused. I tried to get to the scene but was stopped by a policeman. I think he was traumatised. When I told him that I was an MP, he went berserk, telling me that if I wanted to help, I should do something."

"That's why you made that speech?"

"Yeah. Stayed up all night writing it. Just didn't realise how much shit would hit the fan. I'll have to keep my head down for a bit, until it's all died down."

"Are you going to get police protection?" She sounded anxious.

"They told me I've no choice."

"Why not?"

"It's political. They're worried that if they don't, they'll be hammered by the Opposition. Especially if..." He did not finish the sentence.

"I can understand that. Will you be coming over on Saturday?"

"Let's see how it goes. I may have to ask Amir to cover for me."

"Maybe that would be best." The words were spoken in a tight, nervous manner.

Thinking that concern for her own safety was the reason,

Edmund wanted to set her mind at rest. "For what it's worth, the PM said that she'd get the security people to come up with a plan. I'll be meeting them on Friday. Far as I'm concerned, anything that puts you at risk is a non-starter. You must know that."

"Call me after you've seen them." She paused and added, "Be careful, Ed. I love you." She rang off.

Edmund put the mobile down slowly.

He was at last beginning to appreciate the true enormity of the predicament that he had created.

CHAPTER EIGHTEEN

Seven o'clock in the evening and traffic was light in Donfield. Unusual, in this part of the inner city at this time of day. In the passenger seat of Brody's car, Royce was checking through the documents on Kemal Abdullah. The file was open on his knees.

"Not much here," he complained.

Brody was looking ahead. "It's enough to be going on with, sir."

"Has he been abroad? When, where? Nothing here to say."

"Sir?"

"Has he been back to Iraq, where he was born? Raised in this country, but is he a British citizen?"

"Didn't think to check, sir."

Royce snapped, "If he's our man, he would've, wouldn't he? Where'd he learn to chop off a man's head? Not something you learn in evening class, is that."

"Sorry, sir. I'll get on to it." He added, "Anything else you're looking for?"

Royce closed the file. "Motive. If it was him, why?"

Brody shrugged. "Following orders? That Imam's the organ grinder, calling the shots."

"What I'm saying is, this file's about a man who seems normal. What happens to turn an ordinary bloke into a robot committing brutal murder like it's some sort of ritual? Normal folk don't do that. He'd have to be insane."

Brody used the indicator to signal a turn. "Maybe he is."

"That's not how this file reads. Young guy, practising Muslim, living with his mother, a widow." He had a thought. "What happened to the father?"

"Died about ten years ago."

"How?"

"Don't know. But it couldn't have been anything to do with him becoming a murderer, could it?"

"I'll ask him, maybe it did." He added, "How much further?"

Brody glanced at the satnav. "About five minutes. Do we know if he's home?"

"He finishes work at six. I'm guessing it's his dinner time now." He put the file on the floor.

Brody said, "I can't see him giving us anything, sir."

Royce was gazing out of the side window. Drab streets, drab people. He turned to face his sergeant. "No chance of a voluntary confession. Sometimes all you have to do is ask a good question to get the truth. But don't mention the MP's card. I want to keep that back in case he's not the man we want."

Brody seemed surprised. "But he must be, surely? I reckon we've enough to pull him in."

"Not enough to charge him. When we question him I'll know one way or another, if it is or isn't him. A few minutes and the right questions is all it takes."

The house was at the end of a terrace of Victorian dwellings, built to house labourers and their families in the late nineteenth century. Later, they were occupied by successive waves of immigrants, because they were always the cheapest dwellings available.

Brody drove slowly, steering carefully between cars parked on both sides, while Royce checked the house numbers.

"That's thirty-two," he said, pointing with a finger and counting forward. "Up there on the left, it's the last one, forty-two." It was the end house of the terrace. There was a short concrete driveway, its surface cracked and oil-stained, upon which was parked an old white Ford Escort van.

"No room on the street," Brody said. "I'll park up behind the van." He glanced at his superior. "I'm guessing we won't be here long, sir."

"Make a note of that van's number, Colin. Run a check on it."

Royce rang the doorbell and they heard the chimes sound somewhere inside the house. The door was opened slightly, to reveal a face that was several inches above his own. The face of Kemal Abdullah, full-bearded and impassive.

Royce raised his head. "Good evening, sir. Are you Mr Abdullah? Mr Kemal Abdullah?"

"Yes." The man's feet were bare.

Royce took out his warrant card and held it up. "Donfield Police. Chief Inspector Royce and Sergeant Brody." He waited, but there was no response. The man just stood there, stone-faced. From somewhere inside the house a female voice called out, in a language that the policemen did not know. They recognized the first word. It was 'Kemal', spoken in a querulous tone.

Abdullah replied over his shoulder, apparently in the

same language. Then to Royce he said, "My mother. She wants to know who you are. I told her the Social."

Royce nodded. "Sorry to bother you, sir. We're wondering if you can spare a few minutes."

Abdullah glanced at Brody, then looked back at Royce. "Why?"

It was Brody who answered. "We're carrying out an investigation and we're hoping you can help us. Can we come in?"

The man stood there like a colossus, showing no signs of moving, let alone asking them in. Royce was fleetingly reminded of the time when he played rugby as a young man and always felt intimidated when facing someone of this stature and stubborn demeanour.

Abdullah did not answer. Instead, he moved his head to peer past Brody at the car parked on the drive. "Your car?"

"Yes, it's ours," Royce replied. "No space on the road." He lifted his chin slightly. "Could we come in, please?"

The big man replied slowly, "Do you have to?"

"No, but we would like to ask you a few questions. Either here or, if you like, at the police station."

Abdullah stared down at Royce, his face betraying no emotion at all. He was still holding the door ajar. Finally he nodded. "Ask, but I don't want you in the house. My mother is not well."

"As you wish," Royce replied. Brody took out his notebook and Abdullah's eyes flicked across. Royce continued. "Can you tell us where you were on the night of Saturday the sixth, around midnight?"

"Here. I am always at home on Saturdays." The reply had been immediate and delivered without a flicker of emotion.

Brody made a note on his pad.

"Are you sure about that, sir?" Royce asked.

"Yes."

Royce nodded slightly. "Do you know a Mr Sayeed Iqbal?"

"No."

"He owned a food take-away business." The detective used the past tense deliberately.

"I don't know him." Again, no reaction.

So far, the man had shown no emotion at all. Royce thought he should try a softer approach. "Thank you, sir," he said, moving back a step. "Just one more question." He inclined his head and with a half-smile, asked, "Have you heard of Edmund Lafitte?"

"No."

"He's an MP, a Member of Parliament." Was there just a trace of alarm on that inscrutable mask?

Abdullah blinked briefly. "I don't know any MPs."

Royce smiled. "Well, we'll be on our way, then. Thank you for your time." He turned as if to leave, but stopped, nodded towards the van on the drive and said, "Is that your van, Mr Abdullah?"

"Yes. It's insured, everything legal."

"I'm sure it is, sir. Would you mind if we had a quick look inside?"

The question seemed to catch the man off-guard. "Why? Just now is not convenient."

"It'll not take a minute. No reason us taking a quick look would be a problem?"

Abdullah frowned. "Wait, I'll get the keys." He closed the door and retreated.

Brody muttered, "Are you going to ask about his father?"
"No need, just now."

A minute later, Abdullah returned and stepped out. He was now wearing sandals. "It's only got tools in." He went over to the back of the vehicle with the policemen in tow. Abdullah opened the rear doors fully, stood aside and said, "Look, only tools."

Royce stepped forward and looked in, carefully scanning the load area. It seemed reasonably tidy. There was a small trolley jack, a steel folding toolbox, some power tools and a roll of what appeared to be a strip of carpet. Apparently no sign of anything suspicious.

Royce nodded. "Thank you, sir. We'll be in touch if we need to ask for your help again." The big man's face remained impassive.

In the car Brody paused to make a note of the van's number before reversing out onto the road. Then he said, "He didn't give us anything, sir. We should've taken him in and rattled his cage."

Royce had been deep in thought. He answered quietly. "Not so, lad. We learned quite a bit. He's guilty, all right. I'd lay odds he's the one swung the axe. Or sword, or whatever."

"Can't we get forensics to go through that van?"

"Not without the right paperwork. Can't get that without a good reason."

"What about the surveillance log? "

"Circumstantial. We need something better. But now I know he's our man. Maybe not much, but it's a start."

CHAPTER NINETEEN

Edmund was in the shower with his eyes shut, trying to clear his mind. Slowly, he began to relax, letting the warm flowing water slough off his mental cares as it cleansed his body. Had he really done something incredibly stupid? Maybe he was wrong and the others were right? That morning he had been filled with a single-minded, burning determination to do whatever was necessary to start a crusade that would lead to the total and final eradication of the Islamic State. Now it seemed that he had written his own death warrant. What was it that Houghton called him? A walking target. *Shit, what the hell happened?*

In a sober mood later, he was about to go down to the club's dining room. Time to check his mobile. Two text messages that did not need replies and six missed calls, only two of which he felt inclined to answer. Amir and Naomi. He scrolled down to her number and tapped the screen.

"Well, *hello*," she chirruped. "I've been trying to get you but after your star performance you seem to have stepped off the planet."

"Hi, Naomi. Sounds like a good idea. I'm holed up at the club to get away from the media."

"You OK? You sound downbeat." She seemed anxious.

Edmund had not meant to flag up his mood. He replied in a more cheerful tone. "I'm fine. I'm going to be in a protection programme, as they call it. For a while, anyway. Can't say I'm too happy about it."

"At least you'll be safe."

"Police heavies." He snorted. "No choice, that's the problem. I'll have about as much freedom as an inmate at Belmarsh." He was referring to the notorious high-security prison in London.

"Not good. But you did the right thing and I'm proud of you."

"It's going to change my life, for the next few months at least."

"When do you put on the ball and chain?"

"I'll get the details on Friday. So I'm guessing it'll start on Monday."

"Right. So the bad guys take weekends off?"

For an instant Edmund was tempted to be flippant, but thought better of it. Not the moment for a wisecrack. He said, "I'll be OK, don't worry. And it'll all end, one day. Even bad guys have to give up, sooner or later."

Edmund placed his order for dinner and sat with his tablet propped up on the table. He knew that in certain parts of this august establishment, the use of new-fangled devices was frowned on. The dining room was one such place.

He recalled being told about the days when a member wishing to make a telephone call would summon a waiter to bring over a heavy Bakelite handset and place it on the table. The man would then gather up the cloth-covered cord and plug its end into the nearest phone point. He smiled to himself.

He'd had some disapproving looks but thought it unlikely

that anyone would take him to task. Not today, surely? He just wanted to be left alone. On the *Evening News* website he was watching a video of his speech when his mobile rang. It was Naomi.

"What are you doing this Saturday?" she asked. "Are you going to Somerford?"

"This weekend? I'm supposed to stay here and look at the walls. What did you have in mind?"

"Doogie Cameron's going to be at his place in Chelsea. Fancy another dinner there?"

He snorted. "What, spit-roasted MP on a bed of nails?"

She chuckled. "No, listen. I'm serious, what do you think?" She sounded keen and upbeat.

"I think it would be nothing short of a miracle. Weekends there are booked up for months."

"I've booked us a table."

"What? How did you..."

"I called them and said that I was your secretary." She paused. "Yes, I know. I lied, but you know what? They said no problem. No more D-list, Mr Lafitte – after today you're right up there with the celebs. So why not?"

Why not indeed? He had been ordered to stay at the club until Monday. But she'd gone to a lot of trouble and she sounded excited and pleased with herself. He just could not bring himself to disappoint her. Unlikely, too, that it would be much of a risk. Not enough time for anyone to have planned anything bad. And anyway, his masters need never know.

"OK," he said, "Let's do it."

CHAPTER TWENTY

Ibrahim had never before seen his uncle lose his temper. An hour earlier, the Imam had received a telephone call and then immediately turned on the television. He jabbed the controller to switch to the news channel. The main item seemed to be footage of a rowdy scene from the British Parliament.

The boy watched in horror as the Imam's reaction quickly turned from astonishment to anger and then total fury. This man, always in control of his emotions, had begun ranting. His eyes bulged and his face contorted with rage as he shouted and shook his fist at the television. It was an alarming and frightening experience.

Ibrahim closed the book he was reading and quietly left the room, retreating to the relative sanctuary of his bedroom. But he could still hear his uncle's rants clearly. He sat on his bed, put his hands over his ears and rocked slowly back and forth. He felt miserable and utterly alone. How desperately he wanted to be back in Pakistan with his parents and younger brother. There was peace in that home, where the atmosphere was always loving. Here it was different, so cold. His uncle demanded respect and total obedience and his aunt was completely subservient. Impossible to have any sort of meaningful relationship with either. He was deeply afraid of his uncle, who imposed his authority with an iron will. Ibrahim closed his eyes and in his mind willed himself back home in Pakistan, where life was warm and killing was something that was done by others, on television. Make-believe, not real.

He tried never to think about that night and the sickening scene that he had witnessed, but the memory haunted him. Of one thing he was sure: never again would he allow himself to be involved in such an event. He would rather die, by his own hand, if necessary.

Shortly after, his aunt called up the stairs to summon him to dinner. Ibrahim was apprehensive, wondering whether his uncle's mood had improved. And if not, how would he vent his anger? He crept down the stairs to the kitchen and without a word took his place at the table. His aunt was already seated and they waited for the Imam. He came in, took his place and said the prayer of thanks before they commenced the meal. Not another word was uttered. They ate in total silence.

Ibrahim knew that his uncle did not like to be disturbed when he was having a meal. Just as well that they had nearly finished when the doorbell rang.

The Imam indicated by jerking his head towards the door. "Ibrahim?"

The young man pushed his chair back and left the room. He returned a minute later. "Kemal is here, Uncle."

"Go to your room," the Imam ordered. "Your aunt will clear the table." He went into the hall, leaving the door ajar, and they heard him speak to Kemal Abdullah. Without greeting the man, he said, sharply, "In here," directing Abdullah into the living room. Ibrahim's aunt, head bowed, was already collecting and stacking plates. The boy went upstairs to his bedroom.

For several minutes the youth could hear only the muted sounds of verbal exchanges between the Imam and Kemal Abdullah, not clearly enough to discern what was being said. It did not matter because he was not interested. The situation changed when the Imam suddenly raised his voice, shouting at Abdullah, who responded by raising his own voice. Their meeting had become a shouting match.

Once again Ibrahim covered his ears. He was not listening but there could be no mistaking the anger in the room below. As before, he began to rock backwards and forwards. If only he could block out these people, this house, this damned country. "God help me, God help me," he prayed.

Kemal Abdullah slammed the door behind him when he left the house a few minutes later. Without a backward glance he strode down the road, still fuming. He had not seen the television news. How was he supposed to know that the MP had made a speech that day? Anyway, what did it matter if he wasn't punished immediately? Surely a few days would make no difference? How could the Imam, a man he admired and respected, fail to understand that sometimes there were limits?

He had ordered Kemal to go to London immediately to see the Kilburn group, telling him that it was imperative that the MP be eliminated. They were to be told that was an order, delivered in person by Kemal directly on behalf of the Imam himself, God's messenger. It had to be obeyed, at once. Kemal protested that if he took another day off he would almost certainly lose his job. Without his income, what would become of his mother? Why could the visit not be deferred until the weekend? He had pleaded in vain. The Imam was adamant. The job had to be done, if he, Kemal, were to avoid incurring the wrath of the Almighty.

The big man's jaw set and he was breathing heavily. Without realising it, his pace had quickened. He knew what he must do. He would pass on the order by telephone, just this once. Surely it could not be God's will that he lose his job, causing unnecessary suffering to his mother? God be praised.

Next morning, Inspector Royce went to see his boss. He wanted to access the records of phone calls made by Kemal Abdullah and Zulfikar Ali Mahmud. He knew that in order to meet the strict terms of the Regulation of Investigating Powers Act, he needed enough proof to justify the applications. Permission could only be granted at the very highest level and that was the problem.

He had no solid evidence to support either application and even if he did it could take days to get a warrant of authorisation from the Secretary of State's department. But he believed he could make a case for short-circuiting the usual procedure, on the grounds that this was now an emergency.

The Chief Superintendent tapped a pencil on his desk. "Run it past me again."

"I need RIPAs for both, sir. Abdullah because he's the man who committed the crime and Mahmud because he's the ringmaster."

"And what I need, Charlie, is grounds." Flack put his pencil aside. "What makes you think that Abdullah is our man?"

"No proper alibi for the time of the murder. Plus I've

questioned him in his home and I'm certain it's him."

Flack grimaced. "Hunches and gut feelings. Not good enough. What about Mahmud?"

"He's the key to the whole thing. If we can get his phone records we'll crack this case wide open."

"Same problem, Charlie. No proof that he's involved in the murder, so no grounds for the application. We've been watching him for what, five years? Stirring up trouble with his sermons. But never a sniff of anything like proof of criminal activity. You'd be wasting everyone's time."

Royce took a moment before replying. "True, until yesterday. Now it's different. Lafitte's stuck his neck out, good and proper. Made himself a target, publicly. We've kept his card and the thumbprint under wraps so far, but now's the time to use them. They give us a reason to pull Abdullah in for a fingerprint check. He told me he didn't know Lafitte, but he was lying. I'm certain he's seen the card, but it's odds-on he doesn't know about the print."

Flack's eyebrows arched. "Your point is?"

"We apply on the grounds we have an emergency and we have to act fast to prevent an act of terrorism. Lafitte made his speech yesterday. Today he's a target."

A look of surprise appeared on Flack's face. He seemed to have grasped the implication. "Possible terrorist threat, emergency. Yes, that's all we need to get the go-ahead from the Chief. And no need to go higher." He looked at his watch. "Leave it with me, I'll speak to him."

"We have to move quickly, sir. Could be big trouble if we don't and there's an incident." Royce pushed his notes across. "You'll need the details."

Back in his own office, Royce was wondering how much longer he could justify the expense of the surveillance operation. It was busted, anyway. He opened the file to look at the team's report on the previous day's activity. Abdullah's late visit was on the record. His arrival was logged at eight thirty-five in the evening and his departure twelve minutes later. In the limited space of the comments column the duty constable had written, "Looks very angry."

Angry? Nothing like that had been recorded before. The officer was Constable Ricky Masters, one of the three males posing as students renting the premises. Royce decided that he would call him to get a better description of Abdullah's behaviour. But why, this once, would Abdullah be angry? Angry enough to show it. What was different about this particular visit to the Imam's house? A few minutes' deliberation suggested the most likely answer. Lafitte's speech. *Bloody hell!* The MP was not just a possible target. It was worse than that, the man was probably in mortal danger.

But it was only a deduction, no more than suspicion. Should he tell Flack? He was still considering the matter when the phone on his desk rang. It was an internal call, from the man himself.

"The Chief's not happy, Charlie. My impression is he doesn't like being put on the spot. He wanted me to send both applications straight to the Secretary of State."

"That would take days. Lafitte could be dead by then."

"I told him. But Lafitte's a high profile target now, so the Chief agreed the go-ahead for Abdullah. I told him that when we take his prints we've nailed him and nobody's going to worry about how we got the RIPA. We'll have confirmation of the permission tomorrow."

"What about the Imam?"

"No chance. He said that messing with a Muslim religious person was the last thing he'd agree to. You'd need cast-iron proof the man's involved in the murder if you want a RIPA for him."

So, some progress at last.

CHAPTER TWENTY-ONE

"Can't for the life of me think why they call them 'gentlemen' of the press, sir." Roger, the night manager at Popplewells, snorted. "Bunch of hooligans, if you ask me. That gang outside the front are a bleedin' nuisance. The members are complaining."

Edmund was following the beefy ex-marine down a corridor leading to the back of the building. "Sorry, Roger. Wish I could do something about it."

"It's a bleedin' disgrace. You've not been outside for two days and they're still here."

Talking to reporters was the last thing Edmund wanted to do. Especially that evening. He simply had to stay out of sight. "Persistent buggers, aren't they? If they're still there when I get back I'll have to give them something just to get rid of them."

"I can think of a few things that would do the job," Roger replied.

They turned a corner past the kitchen and scullery to the end of the building where there was a fire escape door, kept shut by a quick-release bar. The night manager put a hand on the bar. "Let me check the alley." He pushed it down and opened the door, peering around it into the alleyway beyond.

"All clear, sir."

Edmund thanked him and went out. He headed towards the end, carefully picking his way past garbage bins, to the side street at the end of the block. He had spoken to Naomi a few minutes earlier and knew that she would be waiting there in her taxi. He would have to be careful, and quick.

Naomi had been looking forward to seeing Edmund again. Since his rant in the House of Commons he was big news and she was excited at the delicious prospect of having him all to herself for the whole evening.

But something was not right. Before opening the door, Edmund had glanced up and down the street quickly and then scrambled into the cab. Not like him to be rattled. She leaned forward, expecting a peck on the cheek, but he appeared not to have noticed. He had his head down and seemed preoccupied with his seatbelt, settling into the seat beside her.

"Phew, that's better," he said.

The intercom light came on and the driver's voice crackled through. "Doogie's, Miss?"

She looked up. "Yes, please." She turned to Edmund. "You OK? You seem a bit upset."

"Upset? Not really. Why would I be upset?"

"All this ducking and diving to avoid reporters."

He was looking straight ahead. "It's a nuisance, that's all."

"How did your meeting go yesterday?"

"OK. The security thing starts Monday."

"What's the plan?"

"I'll have a couple of heavy cops with me all the time." He snorted. "Hardly a plan."

He did not seem comfortable talking about it, so she waited a moment and then changed the subject.

When the taxi turned off the main road ten minutes later, the restaurant's striped awning came into view, with the formidable figure of Jake the dinner-jacketed doorman standing under it. This time there were two photographers with him, the one who had been there before and another, younger man. Both had expensive-looking cameras slung around their necks.

The cab pulled up at the kerb and the doorman came forward to open the door on the near side, where Edmund was sitting. Naomi picked up her handbag and placed it in her lap, while Edmund paid the driver. The photographers were on the pavement, holding their cameras at the ready. So different from the last time. Was it only four days ago? Celebrity, the price of transient fame.

She was looking past the cabbie through the windscreen, her attention drawn to a motorcycle that had made a slow U-turn across the road and pulled up in front of the cab. It was a large, powerful-looking machine, carrying two men. The helmeted passenger casually stepped off while its engine was still ticking over, burbling rhythmically. The driver appeared unhurried, straddling the machine in his black leathers and wearing a space-age helmet.

The doorman opened the taxi's door and Edmund stepped out and stood up. The greeter said, "Evening, Mr Lafitte. Nice to see you again."

Behind him the photographers had begun taking pictures, the rapid staccato clicks of their camera shutters snapping urgently.

Naomi leaned forward, ready to step out, when she was startled by the sudden, explosive roar of the motorcycle being revved up. The noise had caught the attention of all present and the men on the pavement were looking across at the machine. The helmeted man who had been the passenger strode forward and without warning flung himself at Edmund, knocking him to the ground. At once the motorcycle accelerated, weaved around the taxi and took off at speed.

So shocked was Naomi that later she was able to recall the entire incident in precise detail, as though she had seen it in slow motion. The assailant had spread himself over Edmund, pinning him down. Jake immediately lunged forward, hauled the man off and threw him to the ground. In a single, quick movement he fell on him, grabbed his right arm and raised it, shouting, "Get back, all of you, *get back NOW!*"

Trapped under the considerable bulk of the doorman, the assailant seemed to be clutching something in his hand. He was struggling to get his arm free; shouting, raving and apparently cursing in a strange language. The two photographers instantly turned their attention to the drama unfolding before them. They snapped away rapidly, crouching and moving around to make the most of what must have been for them a heaven-sent bonus.

The attacker was proving difficult to restrain, despite Jake's best efforts to subdue him. The doorman's florid face contorted as he bellowed angrily over his shoulder at the photographers, "For fuck's sake stop farting around and call the police. *He's wearing a bomb.*"

The man was still fighting to get free. The fingers of his

right hand were closed around something and he was staring at it, shaking his fist and screaming maniacally. Jake raised himself briefly and quickly adjusted his position, using a knee to hold the assailant down. He leaned forward and grasped the man's upraised arm firmly with one hand. Using his other hand, he forced the forearm backwards against the elbow joint, causing it to fracture instantly. There was a loud crack as the wretched man screamed in agony. His fist opened, releasing the object that he had been holding as his arm folded limply. The doorman sat back on his haunches, his face puce as he breathed heavily. "You won't be using that for a while, pal," he muttered.

Later Edmund told Naomi that she had been screaming, but although every other detail of the incident was burned into her memory, she could not remember that at all.

The evening had gone horribly wrong in every sense, Edmund reflected, sitting in the back of a speeding unmarked Metropolitan Police car. And it could end in misery in his room, with a plate of cold sandwiches and a tasteless beverage made by pouring hot water over brown powder labelled as coffee. Unless he could coax the chef at the club to rustle up something. He checked his watch. Well past last orders time. He sighed. Maybe there'd be some leftovers.

He was tired and hungry. "You might have let us have our dinner," he complained.

The man sitting beside him in the rear was looking straight ahead. "Just following orders."

Conversation seemed impossible. They had been in the car only a few minutes, yet Edmund's innocuous comments were met with truculence bordering on rudeness. The man seemed charmless and about as garrulous as a house brick. His companion, sitting with the driver in front, had said nothing at all.

Edmund was starting to feel aggrieved. He said, "Look, if it was just me, I wouldn't mind, but my friend booked it as a special treat and you sent her home on her own. Hungry, too. Surely we could have stayed long enough to eat something?"

The policeman turned, his face and demeanour betraying barely controlled anger as the words tumbled out. "You really don't get it, do you? So you're hungry, big deal. Whose fault is that? Listen: my son-in-law's with the bomb squad in the army. Not the lot who came to disarm that arsehole, thank God. Has it even occurred to you that while you're moaning about missing your fucking dinner, some poor sod had to risk his life getting the vest off that creep? He took a *hell* of a risk; it could have gone off anytime. What about him?" He hissed, "We haven't ruined your evening, pal, you did that all by yourself." He was almost snarling when he added, "And for your information, I was dragged out of a family party to nursemaid you. It's my daughter's birthday..."

He stopped abruptly, interrupted by the muted ringing of his mobile. Still glaring at Edmund, he reached into his jacket to snatch it out and glance at the display. He turned away. "Sir?" He cupped his hand over the phone. Moments later he nodded, saying, "Yes, sir." Then he handed the phone to Edmund. "It's for you."

"What?" Edmund was still reeling inwardly from the verbal assault. He took the mobile. "Lafitte."

An unfamiliar voice barked, "Richard Bennett here, SO15."

Edmund recognized the abbreviation used by the Counter Terrorism Command section of the Metropolitan Police. "Mr Bennett, I'm..."

"It's *Commander* Bennett. You're being taken to your club. Now listen to me. You are to stay there until you are contacted again by us. Do not, repeat, *do not* under any circumstances, leave the building. Do you understand?"

Edmund's immediate reaction was one of astonishment. It was a long time since anyone had spoken to him like that. Who do these people think they are? With his hackles rising, he replied, "You don't have to..."

"Yes, I *do*. I'm telling you, Mr Lafitte, that I'm obliged to warn you in the strongest possible terms and with the backing of the highest authority, that you must do exactly what we tell you. You ignored the instruction to stay indoors. It is only by a stroke of luck, undeserved in my view, that you are still alive. Have you any idea just how much trouble you've caused? You risked the lives of emergency response personnel and members of the public and wasted police resources, all of which would have been avoided if you had done as you were told. Are you getting all this?"

Edmund's stomach churned. It was all he could do to mumble, "Yes."

"Good. Right now you are a danger to all around you, and we will not allow this to continue. Sergeant Monroe and Constable Thorne will be with you at all times, so get used to the idea. Now, do you have your mobile with you?"

Edmund was breathing heavily. Was this really

happening? He answered tersely, "Yes."

"Good. Give it to Monroe, right now."

"What? Why..?"

"Good God, man, do I have to spell it out for you? Your table was booked three days ago. How did the bombers know exactly where you would be and when? Did you tell anybody that you were going to the restaurant tonight?"

That feeling of stunned horror was there again. Edmund knew he was well out of his depth. "Not that I remember."

"There are other possible sources for the leak, but your phone is top of the list. Give it to Monroe, now."

"But I need to make some calls. And there'll be people trying to contact me."

"You won't be using that mobile again. Use the room phone at your club, but keep the calls short, and as few as possible. We'll get you a new phone with a new number and you'll have it tomorrow. Now give your mobile to Monroe and then put him on again."

Without another word, Edmund did as he was told.

During the next few minutes there was total silence in the car and Edmund had plenty to think about. Uppermost was the need to communicate with those closest to him. He desperately wanted to call them because he knew that news of the attempt on his life would be breaking in all the media. His thoughts were interrupted when Sergeant Monroe's mobile rang. The policeman took his phone out, checked the display and responded.

"Yes, sir." Moments later he spoke again. "I'll tell him." Another brief pause before he said, "Understood. I'll tell Thorne. Thank you, sir."

Monroe tapped the phone and put it back into his jacket. To Edmund he said, "You're being moved to a safe house tomorrow."

"I thought they wanted me to stay at my club."

Monroe shrugged. "Orders."

This was something Edmund was not expecting. "Where am I going?"

"No idea. You'll find out tomorrow." He leaned forward to speak to his constable. "We're booked into his club. Our overnight bags will be picked up and brought to us."

Thorne said, "Shit. I wanted to watch the football."

"Yeah, me too." Monroe had a sour look on his face. "Corridor duty, you do the first shift."

Thorne snorted. "Great."

The car turned the corner into the street where the club was located. Edmund groaned. There was a sizeable mob of media people waiting on the pavement, cameras and microphones at the ready.

Monroe grunted. "As we expected." He leaned forward to say to the men in the front, "We'll muscle him through." He turned to Edmund. "No interviews, no statement. Say nothing at all. Clear?"

Edmund nodded. He had no intention of saying anything, anyway.

Flanked by the SO15 men, Edmund ran the gauntlet of the media scrum and scrambled through the door. It was immediately shut firmly behind him by the night porter. When he finally made it to his room, the first thing he did was to turn on the TV. He watched, fascinated, as the incident was reported. There was no video footage, but several still photos had been used to play out the sequence of events, the last of which was a picture of the terrorist secured to the railings outside the restaurant. An interview with Doogie Cameron followed. The chef praised his staff and said that the MP had been extremely lucky. The item concluded with a statement issued by the anti-terrorism unit at Scotland Yard, naming the assailant and urging anyone with information about the man or the powerful motorcycle to come forward.

Edmund muted the sound, relieved that there was no mention of Naomi. He picked up the room phone, annoyed with himself for not retrieving from his mobile the numbers that he needed. Why were they called 'smart' phones? *Ridiculous, not smart at all.* He would have to use the online phone directory. The only number that he knew from memory was the landline at Stella's. He dialled it and she picked up.

"Stella Tudor."

"Hi, sweetie. I'm sorry..."

She blurted, "Ed? Thank God. Are you OK? I've been out of my mind. Where are you?"

"At the club, I'm fine. I've got a bump on my head but that's all."

"I've been trying to call you but your phone's off." There was a note of anxiety in her rebuke.

"They took it from me, the security people. That's why I couldn't call you before."

"What? They took it? Who? Why?"

"Scotland Yard. They think it's been hacked. Probably how the bombers knew where I'd be."

"You sure you're safe at the club?" She was speaking more rapidly. "What are they doing to protect you?"

"I've got two policemen for company." Hardly company, he was thinking, but he said, "Don't worry, nothing can happen to me here."

"I've had calls from people wanting to know where you are."

"I'll be here until tomorrow, at least. They're taking me to a safer place."

"Where?"

"Don't know. They'll tell me tomorrow." He could hear her breathing heavily.

"When will you get your phone back?"

"They're giving me a new one. I'll call you as soon as I can."

"I'm guessing you won't be here next weekend? At least you'll be safe." She was starting to sound calmer. "What the hell got into you? You're in it up to your neck. How are you going to get out of this?"

"Oh, I'll manage. You know me."

"What were you doing at that restaurant, anyway? Not your sort of place."

"Er, I was invited to dinner by a film producer." Not a lie.

"A film producer? What for?"

Edmund had his answer ready. "Nothing special. They're looking for background on the Islamic State and thought I could help."

"God, what a mess. When will it end?"

"It'll blow over sooner or later." He had to reassure her, but he also needed to make a few more calls. "Look, I have to make a couple more calls. I'll get back to you as soon as

I can. Meantime, you take care and for heaven's sake, stop worrying. Pour yourself a glass of wine and put your feet up."

After a moment's hesitation she said, "I will. And Ed..."

"What?"

"When are you going to stop patronising me?"

For the first time in hours, Edmund smiled. She was OK.

There was only one Mrs Naomi Porter living in Pinner. Edmund found her number in the online directory. He dialled it and at first there was no response. He had just started to worry, when she picked up.

"Naomi Porter," she said, briskly.

"Naomi? It's Ed. You OK?"

"Edmund? Sorry, I was in the bathroom. Where are you? I've been trying to get you all evening but you're not answering."

"Long story short, the police took away my mobile. I'm at my club with a couple of heavies for company."

"I can guess why they took your phone. The heavies are no surprise, either."

It was her journalistic experience kicking in. At least she was calm. "Are you OK?" he asked again. "Last I heard they'd shoved you in a taxi without saying goodbye."

"Or giving me the fare, or a chance to speak to you properly. To say nothing about the dinner we'd booked. But since you ask, I'm fine."

She really was calm. He relaxed. "Have you seen it on the news?"

"It's in every bulletin, TV and radio. You'll be spread all over the dailies in the morning."

"That I don't need. And I don't much care for being on the A-list. The sooner I'm a nobody again, the better."

"Don't worry about it. You're hot news at the moment but I'm guessing they'll hide you away out of sight somewhere until you cool down."

He was impressed. "Spot on."

"So where? Have they told you?"

"No, not yet. They probably think I'd blab to some journalist or TV producer."

She chuckled. "Perish the thought. Although, come to think of it, an interview with you right now would be worth a fortune."

He was smiling when he replied. "As you say, perish the thought. I know I'm being moved tomorrow, but not where."

"Will I be able to contact you?"

"They're giving me a new mobile. I'll call you."

"Unless you're headed somewhere too remote for a good signal. Quite likely, I should think."

"Ah." He hadn't thought of that. "I'll find a way round it." He changed the subject. "What about you? If it gets out you were with me, you'll have to keep your head down, too."

"At the moment I'm not worried, I'm not in any of the photos. If it comes out, so what? I'll deal with it. Anyway, it was a business meeting."

"Er, yes, of course."

"Wait a minute. Did you think it was something else?" She giggled. "Whatever gave you that idea, Mr Lafitte?"

He didn't mind her teasing him. "Course not. I meant it could be taken the wrong way."

"Whatever."

She was clearly enjoying herself. But after all that had happened, he wasn't concerned. "I'll have to go. I have some calls to make. I'll call you again as soon as I can."

"OK, make sure you do."

Edmund put the phone down slowly. A huge difference between Naomi's reaction and Stella's. *Food for thought?*

Edmund was checking the other numbers to call, when the room phone rang. He picked it up.

"Yes?"

"Roger in reception, sir. Chef says he can knock you up an omelette with a bit of salad on the side. That OK?"

"Sounds good. I'll be down in ten minutes."

"No need, sir. It'll be brought to your room."

"Really?" That seemed to be taking protection too far. "OK, no problem. I know the police have a job to do, but that's a bit over the top."

"It wasn't them. One or two of the members thought you'd be safer in your room."

"What?" He should have realised. It was a message to remind him that this dignified establishment did not like publicity, especially of the wrong kind. "OK, fine, Roger." As an afterthought he added, "Can you make sure there's a bottle of claret on the tray?"

He put the phone down. Maybe his membership of Popplewells was about to be terminated.

Edmund rose early the following morning, after a night of fitful sleep. Random thoughts and half-thoughts about the many ways in which his life would be changed had denied him proper rest. His first act on rising was to turn on the television news.

It was showing an interview with a journalist who was a specialist in terrorist-related matters. The man was speculating about how total personal security could affect the normal life and activity of a Member of Parliament. The piece appeared to be part of the lead story, repeating the account of the attempt on his life. Little had been added to what he had seen before, except for the fact that as yet no new statement had been released by Scotland Yard.

There was one new item; video footage taken from CCTV cameras outside the restaurant had captured the whole incident from the arrival of the taxi until the securing of the assassin to the railings outside. It had been edited down, but at the start it showed a fleeting but clear image of Naomi Porter.

A hot shower helped clear Edmund's head and crystallise his thoughts. If Stella happened to see the new footage it was unlikely that she would even notice Naomi, let alone draw any conclusions. He decided that he would call her after breakfast. That reminded him, would he be taking that in his room?

He called reception and Roger confirmed that his meal would indeed be brought to his room. "All you have to do is to call reception. I'm off my shift at eight o'clock so Derek will be here. Just tell him what you want."

"Thanks, Roger."

"You've had some calls but the police said not to put them through. I made a list. There were nine, all from TV and press people, except one."

That figured. He was relieved that he did not have to deal with them. "Who was that?"

"Mrs Tudor, she's called twice."

Edmund knew he had to respond. "She's a friend, nothing to do with the press. You can bin the list."

"No problem."

Edmund dialled Stella's number. She answered and her words were rapped out, seemingly impatiently.

"Stella Tudor."

"It's Ed. Are you OK?"

"Yes, fine. Sorry I snapped. This phone's been ringing off the hook and I've had enough. Are you still at the club? I've been trying to get you but they wouldn't put me through."

"I know, the police wouldn't let them. They don't want me talking to anyone."

"You're all over the TV and the papers. Who's the blonde?"

Bugger, she noticed. But he was ready for the question. "What blonde?"

"The one in your taxi."

"Oh, her. She's the film producer, works for Harry Mason's company. Harry's my cousin. You've met him, haven't you? Short, balding..."

"Yes, I've met him. What did she want?"

"She was the producer for the *Inside* series of TV films. They're doing an *Inside Syria* and they're researching ISIS."

"Oh."

"Couldn't turn down a free dinner at Doogies, could I?" He changed the subject. "They're taking me to a safe place today. And I'll be getting a new phone. Can you give me your mobile number? It's in the old one and I can't remember it."

She told him and he wrote it down. He said, "I've got to go now but I'll call you again as soon as I can. Why don't you put the house phone on answer?"

"I'll do that."

The room phone rang again while Edmund was reading *The Times* online. He picked up the handset.

"Derek in reception, Mr Lafitte. There's a call from the police, can I put them through?"

"OK."

There was a click. "Mr Lafitte? Richard Bennett."

"Good morning, Commander."

"Morning. We're moving you on. Can you be ready to leave in thirty minutes? It's a long drive."

"Where am I going?"

"Inspector Platt will tell you when you're on your way. Thirty minutes. Make sure you're ready."

"Will he have...?" The policeman rang off. Edmund wanted to ask about his new mobile. Thirty minutes, he had to start packing.

CHAPTER TWENTY-TWO

When Inspector Royce arrived in the CID office twenty minutes late for his eight o'clock shift that morning, Brody was already at his desk. The sergeant greeted him with a cheery, "Good morning, sir."

Royce grunted. "Is it? Third Sunday in a row. Not had a day off in three weeks, not even Sundays." He took his jacket off and hung it on the back of his chair. "Anything in?"

"Only the email you've been waiting for from the Yard. Phone records for the bomber's mobile. It should cheer you up." On his desk were a few sheets of paper stapled together. He handed them to Royce. "Calls in, calls out, in date order, going back four weeks, but you don't need to look further than the third page, I marked it."

Royce quickly scanned the first and second pages. Then he flipped to the next one and there, near the bottom, was one number marked in highlighter. He smiled broadly. "Well, now. That's the one, is it?"

Brody grinned. "Kemal Abdullah. The bomber took a call from him on Wednesday the twenty-fourth, at nine forty-seven that night. The day Lafitte made his speech. Not only that, but none of the other numbers match any other suspect's mobile."

Royce leaned back. "At last, a break. Maybe even a result."

"We've got him, sir!"

His sergeant's enthusiasm was almost contagious, but Royce was cautious. "It's a break. A good one, I'll grant you, but it doesn't actually prove anything. Have you been through the lot? Does Abdullah's number appear anywhere else?"

"No, only on that day and I went through it twice. We can pick him up now. How's he going to explain that call?"

The Inspector tilted his head back and rubbed his chin. "Hmm. We need to play this right, Colin. I can't afford to waste it." He brought his hand down on the desk. "Now, how about some coffee? I need to think."

Five minutes later the sergeant returned, entering backside first, as usual. The door hinges squealed. Brody was holding two polystyrene mugs and he placed one in front of his superior. "No sugar. It's still not working."

"Thanks." Royce brought the cup nearer. "I think maybe you're right, Colin, we should bring him in. I'll speak to the Super first to see if he agrees."

"Why shouldn't he? We've got the murderer, sir. Biggest case in the nick's history. We've got reason to pull him in and fingerprinting will nail him, for sure. We can take his DNA, too."

"Right." Royce reached for the phone and tapped a key. He waited, impatiently drumming his fingers on the desk. A minute later he said, "His mobile's off." He snorted. "Or as he'd likely say, the battery's flat. Funny how that happens on Sundays. I'll try his home." He held the handset to his ear for another thirty seconds and then said, "Royce here, sir. There's been a development in the murder case and I need to speak with you. Call me, please." He placed it back in its cradle. "Answer phone. He's out. Damn!" He started drumming his fingers on the desk again. He needed to make a decision at once.

"We can't risk the guy taking off while we're faffing around. It's too big a case and if we lose him it'll all go pear-shaped." Royce glanced up at the wall clock. "I'll call the Chief. God knows where he'll be right now."

Royce had to look up the Chief Constable's mobile number. He dialled and heard it ring several times while he hung on. Finally, there was a response.

"Yes?" the Chief barked.

"Royce here, sir, sorry to trouble you."

"Charlie? What is it?"

Royce realised he must have called at a bad time. He explained the situation as quickly and calmly as he could. Should he pick up Abdullah or not?

The Chief Constable answered, his tone short. "It's your decision, or George Flack's. If you can't get hold of him, it'll have to wait. Right now I've got to go, I'm on the tenth and there are people backed up." He rang off abruptly.

What? Had he heard right? The team had worked flat-out for three weeks, under relentless pressure. Not a day had passed without the bizarre murder and the apparent lack of progress by the police being featured prominently in the news. *They've been kicking the shit out of us, for God's sake.* Well, until today, when the attempt on the life of that MP was the main item.

Royce put the phone down. "It'll have to keep for now," he said. He stood up and took his jacket off the chair. "The Chief's playing sodding golf, Colin. And I'm going home. Call me if anything develops."

CHAPTER TWENTY-THREE

Edmund did not need all thirty minutes to pack his case. As he had no idea where he was going, or for how long, he would need to get back to his apartment to pick up a few things. More clothes and his overcoat, for a start. Wherever they were taking him, surely a quick stop at his flat would be OK? The room phone rang.

"The police are here, sir. Do you want me to send them up?"

"Thanks, Derek. No need, I'll come down."

"I'll tell them."

Edmund went down the wide Victorian staircase into the thickly-carpeted corridor on the ground floor. He was carrying his suitcase and tablet, his grey raincoat over his arm. At the end of the corridor a man and a woman were talking with Derek at the reception desk. The man was tall, well over six feet, with square shoulders and a thick neck. His back was straight and his bearing upright. He was holding a trilby hat in one hand. Who wore hats these days? Edmund was mildly amused. A Scotland Yard officer, that's who. In his dark grey suit and shiny black shoes he looked more like a businessman than a copper. Beside him the woman, a slight figure in a neat trouser suit, looked tiny, although as he approached, Edmund saw that she was actually of average height.

He went over to the man. "Inspector Platt?"

It was the woman who answered. "I'm Platt," she said. "And this is Sergeant Cosgrove."

Edmund turned. "Ah. My apologies, Inspector." She had a half smile on her thin face. Her companion said nothing, his expression deadpan.

She nodded towards the door. "No problem. My car's outside. Shall we go?"

The car was a large black saloon. The sergeant strode forward and opened the boot. Its dimensions were cavernous and there was luggage in it. "Put your stuff in here, sir," he said. Inspector Platt was already in the front passenger seat. Edmund settled in the back and the tall policeman followed.

Edmund asked, "Can we drop by my apartment? It's not far and there are things that I'll need."

The inspector turned and fixed her grey eyes on him. "Make a list. We'll have it picked up."

Edmund wanted to ask where they were headed, but thought better of it. He did not enjoy being treated like a criminal, transported under guard to an unknown place. He felt trapped, without even the means to communicate. And this taciturn bunch seemed unwilling to engage in simple conversation. That reminded him. *They owe me a phone.*

He leaned forward to address the woman. "I was told that I'd be given a mobile phone. Can I have it, please?"

She replied without turning. Staring ahead through the windscreen, she said, "When we get to our destination."

"How long will that take?"

She glanced at the driver. "About five hours, Briggs?"

The man nodded. "Yes, ma'am, allowing for the stopover."

Edmund asked, "Where are we going?"

"Mid Wales," she replied, tartly.

So, the middle of Wales. Remote, but not inaccessible. Lots of potential for a safe house there. He had at least drawn that much information out of them. And once there, he would be able to use the mobile to get back to the land of the living. He sat back and said, "Talkative lot, aren't you?" They ignored his comment, but he felt better for having made it.

That evening, Edmund looked across the long dining table and said, "Irene, this is absolutely delicious. Superb, all of it, the meat and the vegetables. Seriously good."

His hostess Irene Morgan smiled shyly. "Welsh lamb, nothing better." She nodded towards her husband. "And they're new potatoes, fresh out of the ground, home grown by Mal. You can't go wrong with the best ingredients."

Edmund said, "You know what we had for lunch? Burgers, from a drive-through on the motorway. I wasn't even allowed out of the car."

The table was an eight-seater, solid oak. Placed in the centre of the room, it dominated the country kitchen. Seated with Edmund were his hosts the Morgans, Inspector Mary Platt, Sergeant Alan Cosgrove, and the driver, Briggs.

Cosgrove raised his empty plate. "Marvellous. Is there any more?"

Irene answered, "On the cooker. There may be some potatoes left, too."

Cosgrove scraped his chair back and took his plate over to the cooker.

"Alan needs to keep his strength up," Inspector Platt said, rolling her eyes. "He says."

Edmund looked across. "You're all so relaxed. Not at all like you were in the car."

"Are we?"

"Using first names, for a start. It's like you're off duty."

Cosgrove was hunched over the saucepan on the cooker, helping himself. "We're never off duty. Except when we're home." He came back to the table, carrying his replenished plate. "Even then we can be called out anytime."

Platt waved her fork in the air. "While we're with you we're on duty. But we try to relax when we can. Like now, thanks to Mal and Irene."

Mal Morgan declared, "It's easy here. Back of beyond in the Welsh hills. Nothing but woodland and a few farms, lower down. The nearest one is six miles away." He had a distinctive, lilting Welsh accent, though his wife did not.

Edmund emptied his wine glass. "How do you communicate? I mean, how do you keep in touch with the Service? Phones don't work here, as I've discovered." He glanced at Mary Platt. "You should have told me."

She smiled. "You didn't ask."

"How far to the nearest place I can pick up a signal, Mal?"

"A long way. You'd need a compass, and walking boots."

"Surely you must have some way to contact London? What would you do if you had an emergency?"

Irene Morgan interjected, "We have ways." She stood up and looked around. "Now, who's ready for a piece of fruit flan?"

By late evening, Edmund realised that this peaceful place was beginning to work its magic on him. He was relaxing in the cosy, low-beamed living room with Mal Morgan and Mary Platt. The others had gone to their rooms. The Inspector seemed an altogether different person to the tough woman who had been so brusque with him earlier. She sat back in a cushioned armchair with her legs stretched out, a gin and tonic in her hand. Earlier she had changed her high-heeled shoes for soft flat ones that she had now slipped off. Her feet, in striped ankle socks, were crossed on a leather footstool. Edmund watched, fascinated, as she wiggled her toes contentedly.

"Back to the grindstone tomorrow?" he asked.

She grimaced. "Duty calls, unfortunately. But you'll have Alan for company." She looked across at her host. "You know, Mal, I think that given the chance, I could stay here forever."

"Do you?" he snorted. "You'd change your mind soon enough. Too quiet for anyone in a high-pressure job, if you ask me. Great for a break, but you'd be bored rigid, sooner or later."

Edmund saw the opportunity to broach the question that he had been burning to ask all day. "How long do you think I'll be here?"

She shrugged lightly. "I have no idea." Then she added, "That's not a stock answer, I really don't know. Are you worried about the isolation? I'm afraid there's no other way."

"It's not that, so much. But my family and friends will be concerned. They need to know I'm OK."

"Don't worry. Texts have been sent to the main contacts on your phone to tell them you're safe and that you won't be in touch for a while."

Edmund took a sip from his glass of scotch. "Any plans to move me on?"

"Not that I know of. Unlikely, in the short term. Right now you're a grade one target. The first priority is to get you safe and the second is to keep it that way."

Edmund had not really expected a straight answer. He raised his glass slowly and took another sip. "I was hoping you could give me some idea of how long it'll be before I can go back to my job."

"Sorry, I can't. Guarding you twenty-four seven would be impossible. The House of Commons is secure, but your Somerford office and your apartment are not. How could we protect you coming and going from there?"

Edmund's job was his life and he could not imagine doing anything else. The thought that he might have to give it up gave him a sick feeling. He sighed. "Looks like my career's hit the buffers, then."

Neither of the others spoke. The awkward silence was disturbed only by the antique wooden clock on the windowsill. It whirred for a few seconds, girding itself before delivering eleven melodic bongs.

Inspector Platt yawned and covered her mouth. "Sorry." She drew her legs in and sat up. "My bedtime, I think. What time's breakfast, Mal?"

"Seven thirty on the dot when we have guests who are leaving after."

"OK, see you then. Goodnight."

Mal Morgan appeared to be a man of few words. Not what Edmund had expected of an MI5 man, retired or otherwise. Mal recharged their glasses with whisky, one of the better single malts. Edmund had been thinking about whether there might be internet access available. This seemed like a good time to ask.

"Something I'm curious about, Mal."

"Uh-huh?"

"When Irene said you have ways to keep in touch with your base, did she mean by internet?"

"There's a satellite dish on the wall outside and we have a tablet and a laptop. Off limits to you, I'm afraid. We also have a sat phone."

Edmund perked up immediately. "A satellite phone?"

Mal nodded. "Mind you, it's useless indoors. Irene takes it out to the garden. And before you ask, I'm sorry but you won't be allowed to use it."

"But – Irene?"

"You didn't know? She was Irene Pickering before we married and came here."

"Irene Pickering?"

"I'm surprised you've not heard of her. Irene was with CTC, Counter Terrorist Command. Head of her department for six years before retiring."

"Really? I had no idea."

"She's quite well known, in certain circles." He took a sip of whisky. "She opted for early retirement. Well, sort of. This place used to be called Home Farm and it's actually owned by the Service. Mind you, we don't farm the land, though. Only some chickens. We're not farmers, you see. I was a maths lecturer at Cardiff University."

It all made sense. Edmund said, "Come to think of it, I don't remember seeing a sign on the gate."

"They took it down, first thing they did. It's just called

The Farm in the Service."

"I see."

They talked amiably for another ten minutes and then retired for the night.

In London earlier that evening, Commander Richard Bennett had been seated across the desk from his immediate superior, in her office. The Deputy Assistant Commissioner, the formidable Mrs Helen Aylmer, was clearly unhappy.

"It has to be a mole. There's no other explanation," she said. "What are you doing about it?"

"We're on it, ma'am. Lafitte made his speech on Wednesday. He was attacked on Saturday evening and he was at his club in between. He never went out, we checked. The restaurant's one of those places you have to book well in advance, normally. So who knew he would be there before the booking? Not the restaurant or the taxi firm. Maybe the club, but unlikely." He shook his head. "I think it was the woman, Naomi Porter."

The DAC's eyebrows lifted. "You're sure? Where's the connection?"

Bennett allowed himself a smile. "Javid Nasir. They've been in a relationship."

"Well, now." She sat back and her face lit up. "Has he finally made a mistake?"

"Nothing we can prove. I'll have to find a way to flush him out."

"That would be quite a coup, Dick. But you need to be careful."

"I know. It's a sensitive area. He's on committees to

combat radicalisation. Doesn't get more sensitive than that."

"Have you had much to do with him?"

"I've met him a few times. I interviewed him a couple of weeks ago. Informally, at the House. I wanted to find out if he could give us anything on the Donfield murder."

She nodded. "Of course. It happened in his constituency. How did you get on?"

"I got nothing, as you'd expect. Said he'd never heard of the Brotherhood." He snorted. "Like I'm going to believe *that*."

"He must know the hate preacher Mahmud. Was he mentioned?"

"He said his sermons are all hot air, not to be taken seriously." Bennett made a face. "Fake charm, that's all I got. But it wasn't a complete waste of time."

"How so?"

"He was lying and we both knew it."

She tilted her head. "A negative plus, then. Are you going to be seeing him again?"

"Sooner or later, but it'll be official. He's not someone I'd socialise with."

She nodded. "Let me know when you come up with something." She sat up and pulled forward a file that he had given her earlier that day. It was a two-page report on the proposed plan to deal with Lafitte's plight.

"I've looked through this; it all seems in order," she said.

"Coming together nicely, ma'am."

She picked up a highlighter pen and used it to mark a line. "So far. Remains to be seen if that's the case when the dust's settled." She raised her head and peered at him over her half-framed reading spectacles. "Between now and the release, I see you're putting out only two reported sightings. Is that enough?"

"Should be. You know what it's like, soon as one goes out, reports of sightings will come in from all over the place."

"Can we be certain it won't be cocked up?"

He shrugged. "Anything's possible." His mouth twisted to form a smile. "But I'm impressed with what I've seen. It'll be ready by the end of the week. Difficult to see what could go wrong."

"Hmm. I hope you're right."

"The FO's happy."

"Of course they are, they've got their political quid pro quo. Politicians!" She almost spat the word out. "This whole mess was caused by one whose mouth is bigger than his brain. A loose cannon," she sniffed. "If the security of their jobs depended on their integrity, the House of Commons would be an empty chamber."

Bennett smiled. "The politics don't concern us, fortunately."

"Amen to that." She removed her spectacles, folded them carefully and put them into a case. "We're done for now." She rose from behind her oak desk. "Sherry? I think we've earned it."

Bennett placed his file on the end of the desk. "Yes, thank you." The office was one of the privileged few that overlooked the Thames Embankment. He went over to the window while the lady moved to the drinks cabinet. The view over the river, now all the more enchanting in the gloaming, was one that never failed to impress him.

"It'll be yours one day," his superior said, returning with

two glasses. "All you have to do is to keep your nose clean. And always remember to kowtow to our political masters." She handed him a crystal sherry glass. "Even the ones who are intellectually challenged."

CHAPTER TWENTY-FOUR

In a speeding unmarked CID car the next morning, Inspector Royce glanced up at the rear-view mirror, an item routinely installed on the passenger's side in most police vehicles. A back-up patrol car was following, as arranged. Despite his years of experience, the detective was apprehensive. Extra muscle might be needed. In these situations one could never be sure. But there was no need for speed, a low-key approach would be better.

He said, "Slow down, Jimmy. You drive too fast, you could do with taking lessons from Brody."

Detective Sergeant Poulter apologised. "Sorry, sir. I thought you wanted to get there quick."

"No need to overdo it, we have plenty of time. He usually leaves the house around eight-fifteen. No hurry."

This was a special day. Poulter's adrenaline rush was understandable, Royce thought. The whole department was looking forward to seeing Kemal Abdullah pulled in. The constable sitting quietly in the back was probably also chafing at the bit.

Easing off, Poulter asked, "Expecting trouble, sir?"

"He should come quietly, but you never know. Whatever happens, don't mention the thumbprint. In fact, you two leave the talking to me. We're here to fetch him in. The questions can wait till we get him back to the nick."

From the rear seat Constable Swan observed, "He's a big guy but we've got enough to deal with him."

Royce had instructed the patrol car to park on the main road, out of sight. This pick-up needed to be carried out quickly and with as little fuss as possible. Abdullah was unlikely to cooperate willingly and a doorstep confrontation with him or his neighbours was best avoided.

As before, the narrow road was lined with vehicles on both sides. Royce checked the mirror again; no sign of the back-up vehicle. Wherever they had parked, they would be only minutes away if needed. He pointed ahead.

"End of the next terrace. The one with the white van outside. Pull up behind it."

From the look of astonishment on the big man's face, it was clear that he had been caught unawares. His bulk filled the doorway.

Royce came straight to the point. "Good morning, sir. We are here to ask you to come with us to the police station."

Abdullah's eyes narrowed. He squared his shoulders. "What for? I have to go to work."

"We need information from you."

"What information? I answered your questions already."

Royce lowered his voice slightly but there was an edge to it when he said, "There's been a new development in our investigations into the murder of Sayeed Iqbal. Now, if you're not prepared to come with us voluntarily, I'll have to arrest you." He stared at the suspect. "Which is it to be?"

The man looked unhappy and nervous. His eyes flicked briefly at Royce's companions. "What about my job?"

"I can call your employer from the station. You are helping

us with our enquiries and for now, that's all they need to know." Abdullah seemed to be considering this, until Royce added, "Unless I have to tell them you're under arrest."

Abdullah's face took on a resigned look. "No need, I'll come. I must tell my mother." He started to close the door, but Royce put out a hand to hold it open. "Bring whatever you need, but leave the door open, please."

Kemal Abdullah's shoulders dropped. He nodded, then turned and walked back down the hallway.

Poulter frowned. "Why don't we just arrest him?"

"Much better if we get a confession." Royce was relieved that it wasn't going to be messy. No need for doorstep back-up. He took out a radio communicator, pressed a button and said, quietly, "We'll be coming out with him shortly. Stand by and follow."

At every stage of the induction procedure Kemal Abdullah had acquiesced, reluctantly doing whatever was asked of him. He hesitated when asked to open his mouth to provide a DNA sample, but did not make an issue of it. Royce watched closely when he was being fingerprinted. The man seemed to accept the procedure, a sign that reinforced the detective's belief that he did not know about the thumbprint on the card.

However, there was a degree of tension in the air and the officers involved appeared nervous. This was no ordinary collar but Royce was confident that when the fingerprint evidence was revealed he would get a confession from the suspect. It was a done deed. He did not want to make an arrest on the evidence of the phone call alone; it was too risky.

Thirty minutes later, the Inspector made his way to the interview room, carrying a brown document file. A uniformed sergeant let him in and remained in the room, standing by the door. Abdullah and Poulter, on opposite sides of the table, looked up when he entered. Royce took the chair beside the sergeant.

"Your employers have been informed that you are helping us today, Mr Abdullah," he said. The suspect said nothing. Royce went on. "Thank you for agreeing to this interview."

Abdullah asked, "Am I under arrest?"

"Not at the moment." Royce removed a sheet of paper from the file and looked at it for a few long moments. "Do you know a Mr Salim al-Sana?"

The suspect reacted with a slight but noticeable snap of his head. He blinked and replied flatly, "No."

"Are you quite sure, Mr Abdullah?"

"Never heard of him."

"No? He's the suicide bomber who attempted to kill a Member of Parliament on Saturday. The night before last."

The man said nothing. Royce went on. "The Member of Parliament that you told me," he paused to riffle through the papers in the file, "you'd never heard of. That was on Wednesday, three days before. In fact, you said that you didn't know any MPs." The suspect's face paled and small beads of sweat appeared on his brow. Royce asked his leading question. "If you've never heard of Salim al-Sana, how do you explain the fact that you telephoned him the same night?"

Abdullah's mouth fell open and he looked away. Royce had him. All he needed now was confirmation of the thumbprint. The silence that followed was broken by two gentle knocks on the door. Royce stared at the suspect but said nothing. The uniformed constable opened the door and DC Helen Jason, one of the team, stepped forward. "A word, sir?"

Royce stood up, walked over to the door and went through. In the corridor the woman said, "I'm sorry to interrupt, but you need to know this. No joy with the print."

Royce was stunned. "Not Abdullah's? Are you sure?"

"Double checked."

"I can't believe it. How's that possible?" He sucked in a deep breath. "I reckon he doesn't know about the print on the card. But if he did, he'd know whose it is. Best keep it to ourselves for now. Tell the squad, Helen, this must not get out."

CHAPTER TWENTY-FIVE

Two days later in Somerford, Amir Hakim parked outside Edmund's constituency office. He had spoken to Stella and agreed to call in and check the mail. Normally the place was staffed by two part-timers on weekdays, but Rosie, the senior, was away that week. Teenager Laura would be there, but she was not allowed to open the post.

She was on the telephone when he entered, a notepad at her elbow. Amir nodded to her and picked up the pile of envelopes on the end of the desk. He was flicking through them as she concluded the call, saying, "Sorry but there's nothing I can do. You'll have to try later." She left the handset off the hook and made a note on the pad.

"Another newspaper. They just won't go away. Any news about Mr Lafitte?"

"No, nothing new." One item of post that stood out was a padded envelope addressed to Lafitte and marked 'Confidential'. Amir turned it over. No sign of where it had come from, and it bore no stamps. "Was this delivered by hand?"

"Don't know. It was on the mat when I came in." She added, "I've cleared the phone messages. Can I put it back on answer? I need to use the toilet."

"Yes, fine."

She stood up. "Do you want to see the list of calls?"

He was on his way to Edmund's office at the back. "No hurry, I'll be here until lunchtime."

Amir deposited the wad of post on the desk and sat down. The padded envelope intrigued him. He was about to tear it open when he stopped short and put it down. It was, after all, marked 'Confidential'. And hand delivered? Bloody hell! Suddenly he had not the slightest inclination to pick it up, let alone open the thing. He sat, staring at it and thinking about what he should do next.

After a few minutes' deliberation he took out his mobile and scrolled through the record of texts to find the one from Scotland Yard that he had received on the Sunday. He was relieved that he had not deleted it.

In Wales that afternoon, Edmund went into the kitchen, looking for Mal. Irene was at the sink, washing up the lunch dishes.

"Irene, is Mal around?"

She turned. "Just what I was wondering. He should be in here doing the drying." She put a plate into the drip tray. "What do you want him for?"

Edmund went over to stand beside her, looking out of the window. "Rain, just look at it. Has he got a pair of boots I can borrow?"

"You're not thinking of going out in this?"

"Tramping around outside is better than sitting watching TV all day. I'll wait until it eases off."

"I hope it does, we'll both be going out later. Commander Bennett wants a word with you and the sat phone doesn't work indoors. We're due to speak at five o'clock."

"What's it about?"

She hesitated. "Best if he tells you himself."

"Problem?"

"If there is, I'm sure he'll tell you." Nodding towards the cooker, she said, "Make yourself useful, there's a drying cloth on the rail."

Edmund went over and picked up the cloth. She had been evasive. Best not to push it; he could wait a couple of hours. He asked, "Do you have to set up your calls in advance?"

She had finished the washing and was emptying the bowl into the sink. "Only to him. He's a busy man."

By late afternoon the rain had eased and was scarcely a light drizzle under the leaden sky. Edmund followed Irene out to the garden. She made the call, speaking briefly before handing the instrument to Edmund. "Commander Bennett," she said.

"Lafitte here, Commander."

"Bad news, I'm afraid." He was brusque. "Peter Stanway's dead. They murdered him this morning."

"*What?*"

"Sorry to break it to you like this. They decapitated him, videoed it and put it on the internet."

The news hit Edmund like a hammer blow. "Bastards!"

"Irene will show you the clip on her laptop."

"Was there any sort of advance warning?"

"No, nothing. For what it's worth I think you may be right about wiping them out on the ground. I want you to call me back after you've seen the video. Can you put Mrs Morgan on again?"

"Yes." Edmund handed the phone to Irene. He turned and walked slowly back towards the house, feeling confused, sick and angry. He went to the kitchen and stood by the sink, staring bleakly at the dark skies outside. A minute later Irene came in.

"Edmund, I'm so sorry."

"Animals." He spat the word out. "The Stanways will be devastated. Decent people, they don't deserve this."

"The Commander wants you to see it now."

"Yes, I know."

Irene led him upstairs into the tiny spare room that she used as a study. It housed a single bed and a wooden table, upon which were a laptop and a printer. There were two plain chairs, one at the table and the other against the wall. She seated herself at the table and indicated towards the other chair.

"Do sit down. It's a bit cramped in here but this won't take long."

She started the laptop and selected a file. Within moments the screen was showing the IS video. Edmund moved his chair closer, leaning forward.

The image was not of the best quality but was clear enough. It showed two men in bright sunshine squatting in the open on brown, sun-baked earth. The rough terrain was stark under a clear blue sky, with low brown hills in the distance. The men were dressed in loose-fitting black robes with their faces covered, and one had a rifle across his knees. It was the other who spoke. He raised a hand and pointed his index finger at the camera.

"You will see how we deal with people who spread lies about us." The words were delivered in perfect, unaccented English. The man lowered his hand. *"This is a message to all who attack the State of Islam and condemn our cause. This*

man who will now meet his fate is one of those." He raised his hand and pointed to his right. *"Witness and take note, this is the price that will be paid by those who oppose us."*

The camera panned slowly to its left, where a figure clad in an orange robe was kneeling, the bowed head covered completely by a brown cloth hood. The hands were tied behind the arched back, the body shaking. Desperate sobbing could be heard clearly in the still air. The executioner stood alongside, holding aloft a large sword. He was clad entirely in black, with his legs spread apart.

The video fell silent, until a single word of command was shouted crisply in the background. The executioner looked down at his victim for a few seconds. Then he drew the weapon back and brought it down in a single violent sweep. The victim's severed head, still covered by the hood, fell to the ground, where it rolled for a few moments before settling. The camera lingered on the blood gushing out, slowly forming a red circle as it soaked into the hard, dry earth.

"My God!" Edmund's response was a spontaneous reaction. He turned away and shook his head mutely.

"That's it," Irene Morgan said flatly. "Barbaric."

The voice on the sat phone sounded metallic. "You've seen it?" And the Commander's mood did not appear to have improved.

"Yes."

"Inspector Platt will be visiting you tomorrow."

"Oh?"

"There's something we want you to see. She'll show it to you."

Edmund had a question. "Are you sure it was Peter Stanway?"

"Yes, unfortunately, no question. Can you put Mrs Morgan on?"

Without another word, Edmund handed the phone to Irene. He still wanted to find out how they knew that the victim was Stanway. Maybe he would be told the next day.

Another disturbed night for Edmund, but this time the nightmare was real. The four residents had watched the news channels throughout the evening. A sanitised clip of the video formed part of the lead story. It conveyed all the savage brutality of the incident without showing the bloody details. There was no mention of Peter Stanway. After viewing it again on the ten o'clock evening news they talked late into the night.

At breakfast the next morning the mood was sombre, with little conversation. Edmund toyed with his scrambled eggs in a desultory manner. Constable Alan Cosgrove's appetite, on the other hand, did not appear to be much affected by the prevalent gloom.

"Look at it this way," he said, shaking a second helping of cereal into his bowl. "That video is exactly the sort of thing that's bad for ISIS. They're always looking for publicity, but that's no good if it puts people's backs up. Stands to reason."

At the worktop Irene was refilling the coffee pot. Edmund asked, "Do we know why Mary Platt's coming today? The Commander said it's to show me something. Any idea what, Irene?"

She returned to the table with the coffee. "All I know is that there'll be two more for lunch. But they're not staying, they'll be going back today." She put the pot down. "Whatever it is, you'll know soon enough."

So, important enough for Platt to make a return day trip over a long distance, but too sensitive to be discussed on the phone?

Platt and her driver Briggs arrived shortly before noon. Mal took them into the kitchen, where Irene was preparing lunch. Edmund had been in his room and he hurried down to join them. They exchanged greetings and Edmund immediately broached the subject uppermost in his mind.

"Well," he asked, "what's all the fuss about?"

Mary Platt was seated at one end of the dining table, a document case by her elbow. She hesitated. "Can we deal with it after lunch? We've only just arrived and it's been a long morning." She looked away. "And it'll be a long day, by the time we get back."

He nodded. "Yes, OK." *Had she deliberately avoided eye contact?*

"We brought the things you wanted from your flat. They're in two suitcases in the car."

"Thanks, I'll get them."

At lunch the conversation around the table covered a variety of topics, but the infamous IS video was not mentioned, despite its prominence as the lead story in the news. Nor had there been any mention of the attempt on his life, Edmund reflected. It was all just small talk. Curious, and frustrating.

At the end of the meal, Mary Platt asked Irene, "Would you like some help with the washing up?"

"No need," she replied, rising. "I'll use the dishwasher. Mal says we don't use it enough."

"That's a fact," her husband muttered.

Irene said, "Well, you can load it, then. Mary and I need to sort out this business with Edmund and she'll want to get off back to London. We'll be in the living room."

Edmund followed the women out. Irene and Edmund settled into armchairs. Platt took a seat on the settee and removed a DVD-playing tablet from her document case.

"A DVD was delivered to your constituency office yesterday, apparently by hand," she said. "I have a copy. Why don't you sit here, by me?"

Irene's face was impassive. Edmund had an uncomfortable feeling. Was the atmosphere a little strained? He moved to the settee.

Platt turned the device on and slotted the disc into it. The screen came on showing the desert scene with the two black-clad men and the same introduction that he had seen the previous day. "We've already seen this," he protested, as the footage unfolded.

"Wait, there's more. Something added that was not shown before. We think that's why it was hand delivered through your letterbox."

Edmund's jaw tightened as he watched again in horror the collapse of the headless corpse gushing blood, and the close-up of the cloth-covered head staining the dry earth. As before, he experienced the sickening feeling of rising nausea.

"God," he muttered, "how can this be happening?"

But this time the scene did not end there. The camera panned slowly back to the narrator, whose face was still covered. Impossible to see what effect, if any, the barbaric act had upon him. He spoke again, directly to the camera.

"This is a message for Lafitte the English politician." Edmund froze. *"Look again, infidel."* The man pointed to his right and as the camera panned left again, his commentary continued. *"It was* your *choice to use this lying wretch as a pawn in your plans to further your interests by attacking the State of Islam. This is what you have achieved."* The executioner was now facing the camera and holding up by its hair the uncovered, severed, and still dripping head. Unmistakably the head of Peter Stanway. The narrator concluded, *"You are next, Lafitte. You were lucky before, but we will come for you and next time we will not fail."* The scene faded out.

The blood drained from Edmund's head.

CHAPTER TWENTY-SIX

Detective Sergeant Brody was on his desk phone, listening and making notes on a pad. "OK," he said, "I'll tell him." He put the handset back in its cradle and muttered, "He won't be a bit surprised."

Brody strode across the open-plan CID office, weaving his way around the desks at which his colleagues were working. He knocked twice on Inspector Royce's door, pushed it open and said, "We have the DNA info on the vomit at the scene, sir. It's not a match for Abdullah's."

Royce was at his desk. "Can't say I'm surprised." He waved his sergeant in. "We need to think about our next move."

Brody entered and the hinges squeaked as the door swung back. "What do you want to do?" He took the chair across the desk.

Royce pushed aside the file he had been working on. "What have we got? I mean, what have we *really* got?"

Brody could not see where this was going. "Bugger-all, sir?"

"Not quite." The DI seemed amused by his sergeant's reply. A small smile appeared on his face. "Not a lot, I'll grant you, but think on. We reckon it was Abdullah did the job. And the Imam was, like you say, pulling the strings." He spread his hands. "Who else was there? Must have been at least one more at the scene, maybe two. Who made the print? Who threw up?"

"Not Abdullah. We know that."

Royce leaned forward and cupped his face in his hands. "You know, Colin, most Muslims here are good, ordinary folk. Trouble is, there's a few nasty ones making the others clam up."

"What about your informer? Do you want to maybe lean on him a bit?"

Royce shook his head. "He's scared witless, I don't want to push him anymore, I could lose him altogether. But he did say there's a few fed up with the Imam's poison. Some even walk out when the guy starts ranting."

This was something that Brody had not heard before. "Is that a fact? Did he say who they were?"

"No way would he say. He's terrified. I know real fear when I smell it."

Brody's surge of hope passed. "The wall of silence, again."

"We've still got our ace. They don't know about the print, maybe now's the time." He tapped his fingers on the desk. "Let's go and see that nice Imam again. This evening, when he least expects us."

At Gulam's Techstore in Donfield there were three salesmen, the most junior of whom was Ibrahim. He had worked at the shop since his arrival from Pakistan two years earlier and he loved his job. His sharp mind quickly absorbed all he needed to know about mobile phones and other communication devices.

The amiable proprietor Gulam was the first to arrive every morning and the last to leave at night. Ibrahim liked to work late because he would rather be at the store than at home. Not that it was any sort of home. He was never in a hurry to leave the shop, but he knew that he had to be back before Salat al-Maghreb, the prayers to be said just after sunset. His tolerant employer knew it, too.

That evening, Ibrahim left the shop, heading as usual for the tram stop around the corner. After a journey of around fifteen minutes he would arrive at his destination, five minutes' walk from the house. His routine never varied and he had perfected its timing to the point where he knew exactly when to leave so that he would get to the house in time to go to the mosque with his uncle. As far as he was concerned, the later he left, the better. But on that evening it did not go to plan and he was kept waiting for his tram. When he finally boarded, he knew that he could not get to the house in time.

He had a second-hand mobile that had been a gift from his employer, but his uncle did not like him using it. Although the Imam had one himself, he abhorred all such devices and Ibrahim was not allowed to use his at home. Should he call to tell them that his tram was late? He took the mobile out, considered it for a few moments and then put it away again. He really did not want to speak to the Imam about being late.

When he arrived at the house his aunt scolded, "Where were you? Your uncle's angry. He left ten minutes ago."

"The tram didn't come," Ibrahim replied, breathless.

She waved him into the house. "Go, get your mat. Your uncle will deal with you when he comes back."

Without another word, Ibrahim hurried to his room to pray.

Later, his aunt came upstairs to tell him that his uncle wanted to see him in the living room. The message was delivered bluntly. Why did she have a smug look on her face? He went downstairs, feeling apprehensive.

The Imam was sitting in his armchair, holding open an Arabic newspaper. Ibrahim entered and remained standing, a few feet away. His uncle closed the paper slowly and put it on the floor. Taking his time, he removed his reading glasses, folded them and placed them carefully into the case that was on the arm of the chair.

Ibrahim could wait no longer. He blurted, "I'm sorry, Uncle, I..."

The Imam raised a hand to silence the boy. From his jacket he removed another pair of spectacles and put them on. Finally he looked up.

"Explain," he said, coldly.

Ibrahim's mouth was dry. His uncle always talked down to him and sometimes he raised his voice. But this time it seemed different. The boy swallowed and lowered his head. "I'm sorry, Uncle. The tram was late."

The Imam brought his hands together and locked his fingers. "Was it?" He stared, raising his head slightly. "Why did you not leave earlier? If you know the tram can be late, you should leave the shop in good time."

"I'm sorry, Uncle."

After a few moments' silence, the cleric said, "It is time you stopped being a child. You need to understand that your faith – Islam – is the most important thing in your life. Nothing else matters, nothing."

Ibrahim bit his lip and murmured, "Yes, Uncle."

"You need to become a man and do the things that our

faith demands of all true Islamic men." His eyes narrowed. "I have decided that you will go on another mission, very soon."

The words hit Ibrahim like a blow to his stomach. Another killing? Trying to control his terror, the boy stammered, "What – what do you mean?"

His uncle stood up and came over, a thin smile on his face. "You will know, soon." He put a hand on the boy's shoulder. "You will be a man, blessed by the Prophet. We will all have reason to be proud of you."

Ibrahim stood still, too shocked to move. The Imam said, "Come, our meal is ready."

To Inspector Royce's surprise, it was the Imam himself who came to the door that evening. He had been expecting to see the boy Ibrahim. For a few moments the cleric held the door partially open. Then he lifted his head, frowned and said, "Inspector? What is it now?"

Royce had instructed Brody to leave the talking to him. He answered evenly. "Sorry to trouble you again, sir, but we'd like to speak with you for a few minutes."

"You came a couple of weeks ago. I have nothing more to say."

"Just a few questions. We'll not keep you long."

"All right." The cleric opened the door fully, but with a show of reluctance. "I am a busy man, Inspector." He nodded towards the hallway. "I can spare a few minutes. Go in the living room."

"Thank you." Royce looked down at his feet. "Shoes?"

The Imam made a dismissive gesture. "No need." He shut the door and followed the policemen down the hall.

The room was dark but this time the man did not bother with the curtains. Instead, he turned the light on. "Sit, please."

When they were seated the cleric said, "This is the third time you have come to my house. What will you ask me that you did not ask before?"

Royce was surprised that the man was confident enough to fire an opening salvo. "For a start, Mr Mahmud, do you know the MP Edmund Lafitte?"

"You asked me that already. I told you I didn't know the man. But now he's in the news, I know who he is."

"Ah, of course." The inspector glanced at Brody, who had his notebook out. He leaned forward and said, "Do you know Mr Kemal Abdullah?"

The Imam made a show of annoyance. "What is this? Of course I know him, he's a good Muslim and he comes here often. You know that. Your people were across the road for two weeks with their cameras. Telling my neighbours they were students." He snorted. "What were they studying? Me? My visitors?"

Royce made a point of sounding apologetic. "I'm sorry but I had to ask, I wanted confirmation that you know him." He paused and tilted his head. "Can I ask if you know a man called Salim al-Sana?" This time there was a small but definite reaction.

The Imam's eyes widened. Then he frowned and said, "Who?"

"Salim al-Sana. The man who attempted to murder Lafitte."

"Of course I don't know him." The beady-eyed stare again. "What are you suggesting?"

"I am suggesting, Mr Mahmud, that not only do you know al-Sana, you also told him to kill Lafitte, using Abdullah to convey your instruction."

The Imam's expression changed instantly, as if a switch had been thrown. His face took on a look of surprise, but there was a momentary show of fear in the eyes. *Got him.* Royce was about to press home his advantage, when the door burst open. The youth Ibrahim stood in the doorway, holding a book.

"Oh, sorry," he mumbled, "I didn't..."

The Imam reacted instantly. His face contorted. He raised his voice almost to a shout, saying something in a language that Royce assumed was Urdu. He waved his hand to dismiss the boy, but Ibrahim stood rigidly still. For the briefest of moments his eyes locked onto the policeman's, almost as if he was about to speak. An unspoken plea? Then he scuttled out, hurriedly closing the door behind him.

The Imam seemed to have recovered his composure almost as suddenly as he had lost it. He brought his hands together and smiled awkwardly. "I am sorry, gentlemen. My nephew – I'm sure he didn't mean to disturb us. Now, what was your question?"

Royce was disappointed and annoyed. The moment had passed and it was a few seconds before he replied. The element of surprise had been lost and he would just have to do the best he could. Choosing his words carefully, he rose slowly and said, "I think that will be all, sir. Our enquiries into the Milford Park murder are on-going and it's likely that we may need to see you again."

Sergeant Brody looked astonished, apparently bursting to speak. Royce glanced at him and shook his head slightly.

To the Imam he said, "But let's leave it there. For now, anyway."

The comment had clearly come as a welcome surprise to the Imam, who appeared relieved. He stood up. "Always pleased to help, Inspector."

They made their way down the hallway. The cleric opened the front door and added, "No problem if you want to come again, but better if you make an appointment first."

Brody had stepped through. Royce, who was following, paused and turned. "Yes, Mr Mahmud, we'll do that." He stepped out. "If necessary."

In the car Brody was unable to contain his frustration. He slammed his hand onto the steering wheel. "We had him, sir. Why...?" He shook his head mutely.

Royce was calm. "You forget, we've no proof. I was fishing. Might have worked if the boy hadn't come in."

"But – you could've nailed him. You never even mentioned the print. We've got nothing." He fumed. "Again!" Brody had stopped the car at traffic lights.

Royce was gazing out of the side window at a busy Asian grocer's store, well-lit and full of people in colourful clothes. He turned his head to say, "Not exactly. We didn't get him this time, but maybe we got a bit more than I'd expected, Sergeant." He smiled to himself.

CHAPTER TWENTY-SEVEN

Early the following morning, Irene Morgan went into the kitchen to organize the breakfasts. Mal was at the table, watching the television that was fixed on a side wall. He looked up and pressed the remote to mute the sound.

"Tea?" he asked. Their routine was that Mal came down first to set the table and Irene followed shortly after.

"Make it a coffee this morning, love." She set about collecting the ingredients for the meal. Irene preferred a simple breakfast of toast and marmalade but Mal liked to start the day with a fry-up. Irene knew that Alan Cosgrove liked both, usually accompanied by cereal. She wondered briefly whether Edmund would be having breakfast that morning. Unlikely.

"Coming up," Mal replied. "Had a bad night, didn't you?"

She shrugged. "I did get some sleep, but not much."

"I noticed. You weren't the only one, lots of pacing around in number four." He was referring to Edmund's room.

"No sound from him when I came down. He must be asleep."

"Poor bugger. I don't suppose he'll be in any mood for breakfast."

Irene took a box of eggs and a pack of bacon from the fridge. "You're probably right. But it'll be here if he wants it."

"Don't worry, I'm sure Alan will keep you busy. Any sign of him?"

"I heard him pottering about. He's not one to be late for a meal." Mal went over to the worktop to load the coffee machine.

Constable Cosgrove strode in a few minutes later. "Morning, both," he said. "Something smells good."

"Well timed, Alan," Mal observed, as he poured water into the cafetière.

At the cooker Irene was holding a sizzling pan. She looked over her shoulder. "Nearly ready. Bacon and eggs, I'll bring it over."

Mal was about to join Cosgrove when his attention was grabbed by the television. A picture of Edmund Lafitte had flashed up on the screen. "What's this?" he said, stabbing at the remote to turn the sound on.

The presenter was speaking over the image: *"...the MP for Somerford, who is believed to be in a safe house, where he would have been taken after the attempt on his life last Saturday. It seems that the shocking video of a brutal killing that was aired on the internet two days ago was incomplete. A video disc showing the whole scene was received by the BBC early this morning and we understand that copies have been sent to other broadcasters and to newspapers..."*

Mal sat down heavily and muttered, "Oh shit."

Irene spun around and Cosgrove, his eyes fixed on the television, froze. The report went on, *"...concludes with a message addressed directly to Mr Lafitte threatening his life. It also provides what appears be clear evidence that the victim of the beheading scene was the newspaper reporter Peter Stanway, as had been speculated. Mr Stanway has been held hostage by the so-called Islamic State, and Edmund Lafitte has been prominent in negotiations seeking his release. There can be no doubt that this is a serious attempt to intimidate the MP whose recent explosive speech in the House of Commons condemning the so-called Islamic State and calling for its total eradication appears to be the root cause of the vendetta against him."*

They watched as the item went on to reveal that so far there had been no statement from the Foreign Office or the Secretary of State.

Irene moved towards the door. "I'd better call the Department."

Mal asked, "If Edmund appears, should we tell him?"

"Better not, not yet. If he comes in, turn it off."

Irene Morgan was not one for pacing. She stood in the garden, muttering, "Come on, come on." Nearly a minute and there was no reply from Commander Bennett. She was about to give up when he came through.

"I was just about to call you," he said. "You've seen the news?"

"Yes, just now."

"Has Lafitte seen it?"

"No. He had a bad night and isn't down yet."

"Good. We have to do something, but right now I'm not sure what. Give me thirty minutes – no, better make that an hour, then call me again."

Irene walked slowly back to the house. It was difficult to see what they could do. Heavier protection? Maybe, but not here. They'll have to move him again, she thought. On balance she did not rate too highly his chances of survival. She felt sorry for him. Altruistic, misguided, reckless – *and now a sitting duck*. She shook her head and sighed.

Some forty-five minutes and several brews of coffee later, the three were still at the table, talking quietly. The fact that the whole video had been made public was a brutal twist that should be revealed to Edmund gently, they agreed. Irene said that she would do it, better for him than hearing it in a news bulletin. The television was on, but the sound was muted.

Mal checked his watch. "Do you want me to give him a call?"

"No, best leave him. He needs all the rest he can get." She stood up and started collecting the dishes. "You can give me a hand with the washing up. Just time to get that done before I call the boss."

At that moment Edmund walked in, stooping slightly. His face was pale and unshaven and his hair awry. He was wearing the jeans, trainers and sloppy tee-shirt that he used when out walking. He glanced around, speaking quietly. "Good morning. Sorry I'm late."

Mal immediately switched off the television and he and Cosgrove murmured their responses. Irene smiled brightly. "Good morning, Edmund. Sit yourself down. What would you like for breakfast?"

Edmund moved to the place that he normally occupied at the table and drew out the chair. "Uh, just a cup of coffee, please, Irene."

"You should eat something. How about a piece of toast? It won't take a minute."

"No, really, I'm fine." He smiled. "I promise I'll make up for it at lunch. Can we put the TV on? I'd like to catch the news."

Irene took the stack of plates over to the sink. "It's not too good this morning." She turned and spoke gently. "It's on the news. The video."

His expression changed instantly. "All of it?"

Irene nodded. "The full version. I'm really sorry."

Edmund looked from one to the other. "But – why?"

She shrugged. "Maybe to reveal it was Stanway? To show their power over the hostages, I suppose. And to put more pressure on you. In my opinion, they want you to think that there'll be loonies everywhere looking for you. Not true, of course."

Edmund's expression softened. "I hope you're right."

"Anyway, this place isn't shown on any map. There's no reference to it anywhere except as a normal farmhouse."

Mal said, "That's a fact."

Irene moved to the sideboard and picked up her sat phone. "I'm due to call the boss about now. I'm sure the Department will be working on it." She smiled. "Try not to worry."

This time she did not have to wait longer than a few seconds. Commander Bennett answered immediately.

"Has he surfaced?"

"He came down a few minutes ago. I told him it's on the news."

"How did he take it?" The question was rattled out.

"Better than I thought. I said just because it's on TV doesn't mean the risk is worse."

The Commander snorted. "Actually, it rocketed today."

"What? Why?"

"They've put a price on his head, a big one. It's on their Arabic websites. Five million US in cash, to anyone who can tell them where he is."

Irene groaned. "Oh, God, that's awful. He's already at rock bottom. What are you going to do?"

"Have you gone soft in your retirement, Pickering? Of course we want to save his neck but our first priority is to ensure that whatever happens, IS doesn't win."

It had been some time since anyone had used her maiden surname. Irene ignored that and responded testily, "I thought our first priority was to protect British citizens, and this one is an MP."

"I'm right, you have gone soft. We're working on a plan, just a few details to sort out. Call back in, say, two hours and I'll bring you up to speed." He ended the call.

Pickering? Was that deliberate, or a slip? She had no wish to go back to all that. If he thought otherwise, he could think again. She went back to the house. She had lunch to prepare.

The men were in the living room, watching the TV news. Irene leaned in from the doorway. Edmund was seated in an armchair and he seemed more relaxed.

"Anything new?" she asked.

Alan Cosgrove said, "Not a lot. They got the number of the bomber's bike off the CCTV. Enhanced the image, but it was a fake. There's been some raids in north London but no trace of the man who drove the bike."

Edmund looked up. "Did Commander Bennett say what they're going to do with me?"

"They're working on a plan, just a few details to be sorted, as he put it."

"What sort of plan?"

"He didn't say, but I have to call him back in a couple of hours. He's not one for giving anything away, not until it's all buttoned up." She looked at Mal. "I've got the lunch to prepare, can you give me a hand, Mal?"

"OK," he replied, getting up.

Irene spoke to Edmund. "Don't worry, I'm sure they'll come up with something good." She knew better than to say anything about the price on his head. Bennett was a cynic, but he was good at his job. No need to alarm Edmund. Not yet, anyway.

Lunch over, Irene loaded the dishwasher. The men were still at the table, finishing a bottle of wine. It was nearly two hours since the last call. She picked up her sat phone and went to the door.

Edmund said, "Can I tag along?"

"If you want to."

He stood up and followed her out to the garden. Irene made the connection and Commander Bennett answered.

"Punctual as usual, Pickering."

Her immediate reaction was to question his use of the name, but she didn't. It could wait. "We're here," she replied, hoping he would pick up the hint.

"You're not alone?"

Irene hunched slightly. Edmund was watching her. "No, I'm not," she replied.

"Who's with you? Lafitte?"

"Yes, that's correct."

"Right. We have a plan and with luck and a fair wind, it could work."

"Uh-huh."

"We're going to use Chameleon."

"I see." She knew immediately that he was referring to Philip Grant, one of the world's best in his field.

"But don't say anything to Lafitte."

"That won't be easy. Surely there must be something I can say?"

"All right. Tell him there's a good plan and that Platt will be coming over tomorrow with the details. But say nothing else." There was a brief pause. "He doesn't know about the open contract on him, does he?"

"No."

"Good, that's what it's all about. Phil Grant will be with her, just so you know. But don't tell Lafitte that either. Understood?"

"Yes. Will she be staying over?"

"Not necessary, neither will he. OK, now you can give him the good news. And remember to smile."

"Yes, I will," she said, but the line clicked. He had already gone. She turned the phone off and smiled.

Edmund looked disappointed. "I was hoping to have a word."

"Sorry, he rang off. But they have a plan, a good one, he said."

"What is it? What will they do?"

They started to walk back to the house. "He didn't give me details, but Inspector Platt will be coming tomorrow to go through it with you."

Edmund looked relieved. "Never a dull moment."

They arrived at eleven the following morning. Edmund wondered why he had not been told that Inspector Platt would be accompanied by a colleague. No matter. After the introductions, Irene ushered them into the living room.

"It's quiet in here," she said. "You won't be disturbed.

Would you like some coffee, or tea?" The two from London asked for coffee. Irene left, saying, "Three coffees, then."

Mary Platt settled into an armchair and put her document case on her lap. Grant was holding a tablet. He was below average height, a slim, dapper man with a thin face, wearing rimless spectacles. He was staring at Edmund, something that the MP found unsettling.

Platt said, "Phil's an expert in his field, the best."

Grant nodded.

"What do you do?" Edmund asked.

"We'll come to that."

Mary Platt opened her case and removed a file. "First, I have to tell you something that isn't good."

"What is it? I've had enough bad news lately."

Her grey eyes fixed on his. "I'm really sorry, but I have to tell you that IS are offering a reward for information about you."

"Information?"

"Specifically, anything that will reveal where you are."

Edmund got it immediately. "Wait a minute. Are you saying that they're offering money to anyone who can tell them where I am?"

"In a word, yes." She added hastily, "But the plan will take care of that."

Edmund shut his eyes and leaned back. "Oh–my–God. They said they were coming after me. Irene thought they were just saying that to wind up the pressure. Christ! They really mean it. Bastards." He shook his head. "What do they call it? A contract? Open season on Lafitte."

Platt said, "Look, Edmund. You stuck your neck out when you made that speech. Ten, eleven days ago? And you're still here, though you had a close call outside that restaurant. Right now you're safe and alive, so we're doing our job." She held her hands up. "You have to admit that none of this would have happened if you hadn't started it."

Edmund bristled. "All right, I know." He clenched his jaw. "I made a mistake and I'm sorry. I know I was right to go for them, but I could have done it differently."

Grant had said very little. Now he spoke, quietly and with conviction. "You will have to trust us, but I'm telling you, they will not win. There's a lot going on to support you. These people have publicly threatened a British MP and they won't get away with it."

There was a brief silence, before Edmund asked, "Where did they make this statement? In a newspaper? And how much are they offering? Just curious, I'd like to know what they think I'm worth."

Mary Platt answered, "It appeared on two of their websites yesterday. The amount's not important because it's not going to work anyway."

"Websites? Why are they allowed to have websites? Surely they can just be taken down?"

"Very difficult. A site appears, puts out the propaganda and then, just as suddenly, disappears. Sometimes they're only there for a few hours."

"But how..."

"They change the URLs as often as they want. Their key people in cells all over the world are told when and where to log on."

"That's the bad news out of the way," Grant said. He looked down at his tablet. "Time to tell you what we're going to do."

The meeting lasted no more than forty minutes, leaving Edmund feeling much better. There was something he had to do before the guests left. A letter to Naomi that Mary Platt agreed to post. Nothing sensitive in terms of security but as it was unlikely that he would be seeing her for a while, there were things he wanted to say. The least he could do. Impossible to say what might have been, but she was fun and he would miss her.

For the first time since the nightmare began, Edmund had started to believe that maybe, just maybe, there really was a way out.

CHAPTER TWENTY-EIGHT

Stella peered through the net curtains of her living room window to check the road. Would they be there? *Bloody reporters.* Unlikely, she hoped, at eight o'clock on a Saturday morning. But there were two unfamiliar cars parked just outside her gate, one with only the driver visible and the other with two men in it. Damn. Why didn't they believe her? She had no idea where Edmund was and if she did, she certainly wouldn't tell them. Why couldn't they leave her alone? Bad enough that she had been harassed by press and media people all week but this was getting to be too much. She had been looking forward to some privacy at the weekend. It seemed that it was not to be.

Amir had phoned the previous night to ask her if she could help out that morning. He was covering for Ed at the constituency office. She agreed but now felt that it might have been better if she hadn't.

The reporters were still there when Stella left the house later. She eased her car out of her garage, determined to ignore them. They scrambled towards the open gateway but she did not even glance at them as she drove through, forcing them to step aside. She drove off rapidly. On the main road her phone buzzed.

"Are you on your way in?" On the hands-free Amir's falsetto sounded metallic.

"Be with you in five minutes. Traffic's not too bad."

"The place is full of people. Just thought you should know."

Stella was not surprised. Edmund had not been seen since the day after his close call. "It's to be expected, I suppose. Are they all locals?"

"I doubt it. We need your help, Stella. Rosie's not back until Monday. Young Laura's doing her best but she's out of her depth."

"OK, be with you in a few minutes."

It took much longer than a few minutes for Stella to get to the office. She had to cruise around to find a parking space and then walk from there. Holding her briefcase she eased her way through a clutch of smokers on the pavement outside and entered. The reception area was full of people. The dozen or so chairs placed around the perimeter of the room were occupied, with more people milling around in the centre. Behind the desk Laura, looking stressed, was attempting to deal with a large, imperious woman who appeared to be giving her a hard time.

Laura looked up. "Ah, good morning, Mrs Tudor," she said, clearly relieved to see Stella. "I was just explaining to this lady that Mr Lafitte..."

The woman interrupted. "Stop telling me he isn't here. I know that," she snapped. She turned to Stella. "What I want to know is when is he coming back? My landlord..."

Stella forced a smile. "I'm sorry, but we don't know. I'm a lawyer and I'm here to help out. Please give your details to Laura here and I'll see you as soon as I can."

Laura said, "Mr Hakim's in the office. There's someone with him."

Stella nodded. "I'll go in now."

She was about to make her way to the door when a man in one of the chairs stood up and came forward, smiling brightly as he said, "Stella? Can I have a little word, please?"

Stella did not know him. She took in the designer jeans, leather jacket and expensive trainers but could not recall ever having met him.

"Yes?"

The man put his hand out. "Gerry Dawson, Global Press. I won't keep you..."

Stella answered bluntly. "Excuse me, but I'm expected in the office. I have no idea where Mr Lafitte is." Ignoring his extended hand, she added, "And it's Mrs Tudor."

She knocked on the inner door and entered. Amir Hakim was sitting at Edmund's desk, speaking to an elderly couple seated across from him.

Stella apologised. "I'm really sorry to barge in like this, but young Laura outside has her hands full."

Amir stood up. "Ah, Stella. Glad you could make it." He gestured towards the couple. "Mr and Mrs Williams had a problem but we've sorted it." To the couple he said, "This is Mrs Tudor, a lawyer who's come in specially to help out." They exchanged brief greetings with Stella before Amir escorted them out.

He turned at the door. "Am I glad to see you! It's been a madhouse all morning. Any news?"

Stella put her briefcase on the desk and sat down. "I've heard nothing. You?"

"No. Not since I told them about the envelope. Thank God it wasn't what I first thought."

She snorted, "That would have been messy. What about the Stanways? Have they called?"

Amir sat down heavily. "No, and I've not tried to contact them. Dreadful business." He placed his elbows on the desk. "At least we know Ed's safe for now." He drew forward a notepad. "Let's get on. There's a queue waiting."

"I wonder how many have a good reason for being here?"

"Probably some time-wasters," Amir replied. "But I suppose we'll have to see them all."

"There's at least one reporter. He's not going to go away unless he gets something. Why don't I make some sort of announcement? The locals know the Stanways. I'd like to offer condolences to the family. Then I can say that as far as we know Ed's safe but there's no new information. That should help."

"Good idea. Maybe get rid of the time-wasters."

Stella moved to the door and opened it. There was a short queue immediately outside, with a couple at the front.

The man said, "We're next. My wife and me."

"We're sorry you had to wait. I'll be with you in a minute; I just need to say a few words first." She looked up, lifted a hand and raised her voice. "Ladies and gentlemen." The hubbub diminished but apparently not everyone had heard. She raised her voice. "Ladies and gentlemen, may I have your attention for a moment, please?" The room fell silent. "My name is Stella Tudor and I'm Mr Lafitte's partner. I'm a lawyer and I'm here to help while he's away."

A voice from the back asked, "Where is he?" Another said, "Yeah, tell us. We need to know." There were murmurs of assent and muttered comments.

Stella raised a hand and waited until the room was quiet

again. "Thank you. Thank you for your patience. Since the attempt on his life last week, Mr Lafitte has been taken to a safe place by the authorities. I know that I speak for him and for all here, to send the Stanway family our sincere condolences for their tragic loss. Peter Stanway was a fine man, a good journalist just doing his job. As you see, this is not a large office and we are short-staffed. If you wish to ask for advice on any specific issue, we will do our best to help. If you are here to show support for Edmund, thank you. However, I have to tell you that we have no idea where he is at present and we do not know when he will be back. So if you have no other reason to be here, please help us by coming back another day. Thank you for your patience."

There was some shuffling of feet as a few rose to leave, when the man who had identified himself as a press reporter said, "But surely you must have some idea where he is? I'm a journalist and our readers want to know what's going on." He had used an aggressive tone.

Stella replied, "So do we, Mr..."

"Dawson, Gerry Dawson."

"Mr Dawson. We don't know any more than you. Edmund Lafitte's life is under threat and he is in a place where he has close personal protection. That much we know. Nobody's told us where he is or how long he'll be away." The man appeared to be about to speak again, so Stella raised a hand and shook her head. "I've nothing more to say. Now if you don't mind, there are people here who have been waiting for advice on local matters." She turned her back and moved over to the couple at the head of the queue. "Would you like to come in now?"

The constituency office usually closed around noon on a Saturday but Stella and Amir stayed until everyone had been seen. It was nearly two o'clock in the afternoon when she finally arrived home, tired and hungry. Parked at the roadside near her house was another unfamiliar car. Her heart sank. *Oh God, not another damned reporter?*

She steered straight onto the drive without pausing and pulled up in front of the garage. Without a backward glance she opened her front door, went in and put her briefcase and handbag on the hall table. She was in the kitchen surveying the contents of her fridge when her doorbell chimed.

Stella stiffened. This was a Saturday, she was in her own house, tired after a morning's stressful work and she was hungry. How dare they disturb her? She strode down the hall to the front door, steaming inwardly, ready to unload a piece of her mind. Through the frosted glass panel in the door she saw the form of a tall man.

She yanked the door open and blurted, "Who the hell do you think..." She realised that she knew the man standing there. "Oh, sorry, I thought..."

The man smiled. "No apology needed, Mrs Tudor."

"It's Sergeant...?"

The tall man in the police uniform said, "Lavery, ma'am. Steve Lavery, Somerford station. I'm sorry to disturb you."

"Yes, of course. Sergeant Lavery." She moved aside. "Come in, Sergeant. Have you brought news about Edmund?"

Lavery stepped inside, shaking his head. "Sorry, no. Actually I'm only here to deliver a message. From Scotland Yard, Commander Bennett. It'll only take a minute."

Stella closed the door. "What's it about?"

"I honestly don't know. We've only been asked to tell you that two officers will be coming to see you tomorrow morning, if it's all right with you."

She felt a sudden tightening in her chest. "What do they want to see me for? Why don't they just call?"

"We weren't told what it's about, but they said that Mr Lafitte is fine and that you weren't to worry."

"Why didn't they phone?"

"My boss asked the same question. They said that face-to-face is more secure. I'm here in person only to deliver the message but if tomorrow's not convenient, we have to tell them."

Stella relaxed. "Is that all? Well, it's fine, Sergeant, you can tell them I'll be here."

Lavery left and she shut the door behind him.

CHAPTER TWENTY-NINE

Imam Zulfikar Ali Mahmud was sitting in his armchair, his spectacles in his hand. He frowned as he peered at his visitor, Rafiq al-Ghani.

"Kemal won't be going. Just now he needs to be rested. But he did well, and you also. The troublemakers have been silenced; they won't be a problem any more. It's a good result." He raised the spectacles to his mouth, breathed on the lenses and wiped them with a handkerchief. "This one is different, a small task that does not require Kemal's skills. But he will be using them again, soon." His eyes narrowed. "The mission after this one will be the biggest ever. Authorised at the highest level, to be carried out here in England, by us. The money will be paid to us. It will make a big difference to our recruiting fund." He polished the lenses and held the frame up to the light to peer through them. Satisfied, he put the spectacles on, leaned back and brought his hands together. "Our enemies will be left in no doubt about the power of the Caliphate." Behind the round lenses the cleric's eyes were shining. "That will happen soon. But for now, all we wish is to make a man of the boy." He shrugged. "A small task, but necessary. What does it matter if there are one or two fewer soldiers in the British army?"

"I understand, Ustad." His visitor had used the term of respect, as he always did when speaking to the Imam.

"Have you told him?"

"He knows he will be going on active duty soon, but nothing more."

"Is it far?"

"The town is in Wiltshire. There are three inns where the soldiers go to drink and the one we've chosen is perfect. You'll be able to work swiftly and quietly. It will be easy, they will be full of alcohol. Savages!" He spat the word out. "God's justice, delivered by your hand."

"For me it is better at the weekend but if it must be in the week, so be it. There are more important things than my job."

"Don't worry, it's on a Saturday, this week or next. You will go to the town in the evening to meet the brother from London. It is all planned. He'll have the transport and the implements that you need. They will be sharp, and quiet. Just keep to the plan. No mistakes and you'll be back here with nothing to connect you with the mission."

"Do you want the boy to be involved? Using a weapon?"

"Of course, that's the most important thing. Last time he was with you to learn, this time he will take part and become a man. He is weak, it is time for him to change."

In Somerford, Stella was ready for her visitors. She had prepared and loaded a tray with the items she would need to offer tea or coffee, and biscuits.

She checked the road. There were no unfamiliar cars parked near the end of the drive. Probably because it was Sunday. Good. She went to the living room to read her *Sunday Times*. Edmund was still on the front page and she was anxious to learn what the political columnists had to say.

Stella trawled through the columns of news and opinions with mixed feelings. This was the biggest story in months and Edmund, *her* Edmund, was bang at the centre. Her eyes danced across the pages, her mind scooping up and filtering the information. Above all, she only wanted him safe so that they could return to normal life again. But she had realised days ago that was now impossible. What was to become of them? She loved him but he was on the run, perhaps for the rest of his life. She did not think she could spend her life in hiding. He had started something that had taken over their lives, changing them forever. Why the *hell* couldn't he have done the sensible thing and just backed off? She sighed. Because he's Edmund, of course. The impulsive do-gooder, champion of the underdog, the crusader against evil. *Stupid sod!*

The doorbell chimed. She folded the paper and went to the window. A large dark saloon car with tinted windows was parked on the drive.

Stella took her visitors, a thick-set man and a smartly-dressed woman, to the living room. When they were seated, it was the woman who spoke.

"We're here to tell you about the Department's plan to deal with the threat to Mr Lafitte, Mrs Tudor. I was with him yesterday and I'm pleased to tell you that he's safe and well."

"Any chance I can see him?"

"I'm afraid that won't be possible just now, but he's written you a letter. Perhaps you'd like to read it before we begin?" She withdrew an envelope from her briefcase.

The woman seemed to be the one in charge; the man had said nothing so far. She was of average height but surprisingly slight stature, given her credentials. Stella had asked for and checked their warrant cards. Inspector Mary Platt of the counter-terrorism unit looked more like a secretary than a high-ranking cop.

"A letter from Edmund? That'll be a first." Stella reached out and took the envelope.

The man, a detective constable called Thorne, leaned forward and said, "The plan requires your cooperation, Mrs Tudor." He had a deep, gravelly voice. "So we need your approval before we go on."

Stella turned the envelope over, noting that the flap was loose. "It's open." She looked up. "Did you read it?"

Inspector Platt shook her head. "No, of course not. It's personal, from him to you, and it's not been out of my briefcase."

The letter was hand written, on a single sheet of paper. It said:

My darling Stella,
I miss you, more than you could imagine. I'm OK and unharmed, but to stay that way I had to make a difficult decision, one that will change my life. Not being able to talk it over with you has been sheer agony. Inspector Platt will give you details of the plan to get me out of this mess. It could involve you or not, as you wish. The choice will be yours and I shall go with whatever you decide. You have worked hard to earn the partnership in your law firm and I cannot ask you to throw it away. You are young, intelligent and beautiful, with a great future, not to be dismissed lightly. I love you and always will, whatever happens.
Edmund.

She read it again, more slowly. They were looking at her, apparently waiting for her reaction. Stella said, "He says that I have a decision to make. I don't understand."

"You will when we tell you the plan," Platt answered. "It will be easier for us to pull it off if you can help. But if you can't, we think it'll still work."

Stella listened as they spent the next few minutes going over the details. She did not interrupt; it all made perfect sense. The only problem was that if she agreed to cooperate, her life as she knew it would cease. She now understood what Edmund meant in the letter. Platt concluded by asking, "What do you think?"

Stella took her time. It was too big a decision to be taken instantly. "When do you need my answer?"

Platt seemed uncomfortable with the question. Strange, for someone who was presumably a hard-nosed professional.

"Well," she replied, "as soon as possible and preferably right now. And there's something else. Mr Lafitte insisted that we provide you with close personal protection until the plan has been carried out."

"Personal protection? What does that mean?"

"In this case, we would ask that a local police officer stays with you."

"What? Here in my house? Absolutely not."

"I believe that you know her? WPS Jan Wainwright of the Wiltshire force."

Stella was not happy. "I don't think I can agree to that. She's a good officer but with all due respect, that's not the point."

Platt nodded. "I understand. But I have to tell you that Mr Lafitte insisted. He said that you are the most important person in his life. He said that if we can't protect you," she paused, "he'd be on the next train to London and take his chances, as he put it."

Stella was stunned and appalled. She was in effect being asked to put a value on her relationship with Edmund. And what did he mean? Was 'take his chances' a threat? Unthinkable that he would resort to blackmail. So were these people lying? She certainly did not want a police officer living in her house but if she refused to go with it and he went back to London, whose fault would it be if he was killed? Hers? The very thought stuck her like a blow to the stomach. She felt sick.

Surely, *surely*, they must be lying. And they wanted a decision right now. Impossible, she needed more time. She and Edmund had been comfortable together for years, never feeling the need to rush into marriage. She loved him and she did not doubt that he loved her, too.

After a short awkward silence, she stood up and said, "Let me get you some tea, or coffee, if you prefer. What would you like?"

They had their coffees and biscuits and left ten minutes later, with her decision. She had decided to go with the plan. It was clearly what Edmund wanted her to do.

CHAPTER THIRTY

By the Friday evening of the following week, Stella was getting to know her bodyguard. She had at first felt lukewarm about having to share her home with a stranger. Not the policewoman's fault, of course, but not hers either. Nothing to do but make the best of it and they had settled into a routine. Her guardian stayed in the house at night but Stella was unaccompanied during the day while she was in her office. It worked and there were no problems.

As a legal professional, Stella had met Police Sergeant Jan Wainwright a few times previously. She knew her to be a reliable, straight-talking officer who was respected and liked by her colleagues. The policewoman wore her uniform when she went out but at Stella's she dressed casually. They were relaxing in the living room, with mugs of fresh coffee.

"You're married aren't you?" Stella asked.

She nodded. "Gary's a sergeant, too. Uniform, not CID. We met in the force just after I joined. A long time ago."

"So what does he think of you moving in with me?"

She shrugged. "Comes with the job, he knows that."

"And you, what do you think? It's interfering with your life, surely?"

"Not really. Anyway it's not going to be for long, is it?"

Stella took a sip of coffee. She was curious. "Did you

volunteer for this, or could you have said no?"

"I could've said 'no', but I didn't. Being here is a bit of a change from my routine. Actually, they don't think you're in danger, but they said you need to have someone around. I reckon that's 'cos you're on your own."

"Didn't they tell you? Edmund insisted that I have police protection. I don't think I'm in any danger either, but that's what he wanted."

Jan seemed about to say something, when her mobile rang. "Sorry," she said. She took the instrument out. "It's Gary. Do you mind...?"

"No, go ahead."

The policewoman turned her head so speak. "Yes, love." Seconds later her expression darkened. "*What?* Right now? I'll tell her." She rang off. "Mr Lafitte's gone missing. It's on the news."

The television remote was on the table between them. Stella lunged forward and grabbed it. "Which channel?" She jabbed at the device to switch it on.

"Breaking news. They interrupted what he was watching."

Stella's television was tuned to the news channel. The presenter was saying, *"... believed to have been in an isolated location, so it is difficult to understand how this could have happened. The report has come in from a reliable source but so far there has been no confirmation from the authorities. There is speculation that Mr Lafitte may have been abducted, because it is believed that Daesh or Islamic State as it is known, has recently put out an appeal to their followers, seeking information as to his whereabouts."* The broadcast went on to describe how

Edmund had become involved with the rogue state and referred to the attempt on his life and the brutal murder by Daesh of the journalist Peter Stanway.

Stella was standing with her eyes locked onto the screen. She muted the sound, put the remote down and said, "Well, that's that," before calmly resuming her seat.

Jan Wainwright seemed astonished. Her eyes saucered and she gestured at the television. "But..."

"What?"

"He's supposed to be in a safe house, a counter terrorism place. How could he just disappear?"

"Actually I don't think he's been abducted. I know Edmund Lafitte. My guess is that he's just left, taken off."

"You're not worried?"

"Not really. I'm sure he'll be in touch, sooner or later." She smiled. "Another coffee?"

Naomi Porter bit her lip and frowned. She was trying to call Martin Houseman, editor of *The Sentinel*. Was he still using the same mobile number, she wondered? The one he used when she was working at the newspaper five years earlier. She and the editor had been close for a short time.

On her way home that evening on the Underground, Naomi checked her Twitter feed and was horrified to learn of Edmund's disappearance. She trawled the social media and news feeds but learned no more. He was simply reported as missing. As editor of *The Sentinel*, Houseman was likely to have some idea about what was going on behind the scenes. But she had to get home first to find his number.

"Come on, pick up," she muttered.

"Martin Houseman." He had answered sharply, his tone impatient. She could hear the bustle of a busy office.

"Martin? Thank God. I was hoping you're still using this number. It's Naomi Porter."

"Naomi? Have you spoken to Becky?"

The question stopped her train of thought instantly. "Becky? Becky who?"

"Becky Newman, one of our reporters. I asked her to give you a call."

"Oh? No, I haven't heard from her. What's it about?"

"Edmund Lafitte. What else? What have they done with him?" He was speaking rapidly.

"I have no idea. Actually that's why I'm calling you. I thought that if anyone knew, you would."

"Ah. Sorry, I don't." He sounded calmer, but disappointed. He added, "You sure?"

What a question! "Sure? What the hell do you mean? Why would I be calling you if I already knew?" She realised immediately that she had been rude. "Sorry I snapped, I'm a bit upset."

"No probs, I understand. We saw the footage; the Doogie's incident. Must have been a bugger for you."

"Yes, at the time. Look, Martin, I'm sorry I troubled you, I'll..."

"It's OK, it's OK. Let's talk for a minute. It's been quite a while." That sounded more like the Martin Houseman she had known. Probably stalling to see what he could get out of her. Calm, persuasive and single-mindedly ruthless in his pursuit of a possible scoop. She decided to humour him, he might still prove useful.

"OK, but like I said, I don't know where he is."

"Has he been in touch lately? I mean, since they put him on ice."

There was the letter she had received from Edmund. "Not really," she replied.

"Not really? Is that a yes?"

"No. I haven't heard from him." Best say nothing about the letter.

"If you say so. But you were dating him, weren't you?"

None of your bloody business! What she said was, "Rubbish! We had dinner once, it was business."

"Yeah, whatever."

The bastard was patronising her. "I have to go," she snapped, "I've got some calls to make."

"No, wait, there's something I want you to know."

She had been about to ring off. "What?"

"You know the drill, how we operate."

"So?"

"The Yard says Lafitte's missing. I don't buy that, it's crap. I'm guessing they've lost him, one way or another. And now they're running around like headless chickens. Could be he's taken off, or more likely, he's been abducted. Only they're not going to admit it while there's a chance they can find him."

"Is there a point to all this, Martin?"

"I've got an idea. Why don't you do a piece for us? From the inside, if you see what I mean. Anyone who knows something might see it and come forward. Worth a try."

She was not sure she would be comfortable with that. "I'm not on the inside, as you put it, so I don't know anything."

He snorted. "Not like you to sell yourself short. You were there when they tried to blow him up, for Christ's sake. In fact, there's our headline, right there: *Missing MP. I was with him at Doogie's,* by Naomi Porter. And a 'have you seen him' tag with a mug shot of the man."

"I don't know..."

"Listen to me. You called me because you're worried about him. Well, we can help. You do the piece, we run it. I'm guessing there'll be loads of possible sightings. We'll check them out. Every one, I guarantee that. And if we get a result, I promise you'll be the first to know."

She felt that it could be worth considering. "Let me think about it. I'll get back to you."

"You need to do it now, before the situation changes."

"All right. When do you want the copy?"

"As soon as possible. Get it to us by Sunday afternoon and we'll run it Monday morning. No point in hanging around, the situation could change at any moment."

"By Sunday? That's not enough time. I don't..."

"It's more than enough. You've beaten much tighter deadlines than that."

"That was a long time ago."

"Not really. I don't see a problem. Your stuff usually went straight in, no need for much tidying. But if it helps, get a draft to me by tomorrow evening and we'll check it out. I'll text you my email address now. And you've got my number, you can call me."

"OK, I'll give it a go."

"Good girl. Between us we'll find him, so stop worrying. And Naomi..."

She heard him chuckle. "What?"

"Get on with it. What are you waiting for?"

The following morning Stella Tudor arrived at her office an hour early. She settled at her desk with a polystyrene cup of coffee from the dispenser in the corridor, relieved to have avoided the media scrum whose persistence had ruined her weekend.

When her PA Rachel came in later, she was holding a folded copy of a newspaper. "I know you don't take *The Sentinel*," she said, "so I brought my copy in for you."

"Why? Is there something interesting in it?"

Rachel put the paper down in front of Stella and moved to her own desk. She said, "Edmund's the lead story today."

Stella stared at the headline. **MISSING MP: I WAS WITH HIM AT BOMB ATTEMPT.** Alongside was a photo of Edmund Lafitte.

"Oh, no!" Stella picked up the paper. Her eyes scanned the text, slowly at first and then increasingly quickly as she devoured the item. Written in the first person, it read like a dime novel, she thought, littered with hyperbole. Not at all like the incident described to her by Edmund. Stella checked the byline, her anger rising. Naomi Porter. Who was this woman?

CHAPTER THIRTY-ONE

"OK, let's break for lunch." Harry Mason, CEO of Tolgate Films, looked around the boardroom table. "Resume at two o'clock. Sharp." He snapped his document case shut. As the seven people at the meeting rose to leave, he added, "Naomi, a word, please?"

Naomi guessed what was coming. She had taken little part in the proceedings. All morning her mind had been preoccupied with Edmund's disappearance. It had been three days since her article appeared in *The Sentinel* and she had heard nothing. Harry was about to tell her off, she thought. Fair enough.

He waited until the others had left. Then he folded his arms on the table and leaned forward. "Do you want to talk about it?" he asked.

No, she didn't. "Talk about what?"

"OK, let's see. You did that piece in the paper on Monday?" Naomi did not reply.

He added, "Would I be right in thinking you've heard nothing since?"

Her mouth turned down. "Not a word. It's been on my mind. Sorry."

Harry sat up. "Call the paper. Or go do your worrying at home, if that helps. You need to get it sorted. Right now you're no use to us, or yourself."

She answered quietly, "Thanks. I'll call them from my office." She collected her papers. "I don't need to go home. I'll be back at two."

Ten minutes later Naomi called Martin Houseman on his mobile.

He answered, "Naomi. You OK?"

"I'm good. Can you talk? I need to know if there's any news about Edmund." The chatter and background sounded like he was in a restaurant.

"No probs. I'm in the canteen, having lunch. We've had a few sightings, but nothing that looks promising. We're chasing them up anyway."

"Nothing at all?"

"Not yet. Give it a little longer. I said you'd be the first to know, and I meant it."

Naomi could not hide her disappointment. "OK." She had a sudden thought. "What about his partner? Do you think she might know something?"

"Stella Tudor? Can't get near her. Her law firm won't let anyone in and they're stonewalling calls. There's a media scrum outside her house and – get this: a WPC's taken up station inside. Unbelievable! OTT or what?"

"What about your contacts at the Met?"

He snorted. "No joy. Same story; nobody knows anything. Or so they say."

Naomi's spirits sank. Martin Houseman had a reputation for ruthless pursuit of news stories. Maybe she should just give up. "I guess that's it, then."

"No, hang on a minute. Like I said, this disappearance thing, I just don't buy it. There's something going on and my instinct is that the Tudor woman's in on it. You know what I think?"

"What?"

"You should try to get to her. Think about it. You wrote the article, front page. If you meet her, you could get a result. Find out where Lafitte is. It'll be the scoop of the year, a great follow-up to your piece."

"Uh, not sure I want to do another article."

"Listen to me. You're better placed than anyone to winkle out the truth. Just find a way to get to her."

She considered this briefly, then said, "OK. I'll try. Can you send me contact details? Home, where she works, email and phone numbers. What about the constituency office?"

"No chance. You won't find her there. And the Saturday surgeries are being handled by the agent."

Naomi's brain had moved up a gear. "Send me his details too. And all you've got on the office." As an afterthought she added, "Have you got anyone there?"

"At the moment, only a stringer. I'll be sending someone to cover the office on Saturday, probably Julie Meadows."

"I don't know her, but that suits me. I don't want to be recognized if I go there."

She heard him chuckle again. "OK, it's a deal. And keep at it, kid, you're a winner."

On the following Saturday morning, Naomi rose early. She had a plan. She would drive to Somerford and go to Edmund's constituency office. Unlikely that Stella Tudor herself would be there, but Naomi believed that she had the means to engineer a meeting with the lady.

Just after eleven o'clock she parked in an adjacent street

and made her way on foot to the office, carrying a document case and holding an umbrella against the light drizzle. There was a knot of people outside and to her dismay some of their umbrellas were shielding cameras and recording equipment. Media people. *Damn!* Would any of them know her? With her coat collar turned up and her head lowered she strode forward, making for the door. She had an uncomfortable feeling that she was being observed, but nobody spoke to her. She paused to close her umbrella, opened the half-glazed door and entered.

The room looked like it could do with a decorative makeover. It was tidy, but low key to the point of being drab. There were posters on the walls and a few framed photos, the most prominent of which was one of Margaret Thatcher looking stern. The Iron Lady. People were seated in wooden chairs around the perimeter and a young woman with lank, shoulder-length hair sat behind a pine reception desk. She was on the telephone. While Naomi stood by, she finished her call and made a note on a clipboard, before looking up. She pushed a strand of hair back behind an ear and said, "Can I help you?"

"Naomi Porter. I spoke to Mr Hakim earlier, he's expecting me."

She nodded. "Yes, Miss Porter, he told me. He's got someone with him at the moment. I'll let him know you've arrived." She gestured, saying, "Please take a seat."

The door to the inner office opened a few minutes later. A young couple emerged, shepherded out by a stocky, dark-skinned man wearing casual trousers and a smart leather jacket. He looked at the receptionist. She nodded towards Naomi, who stood up and moved forward. "Mr Hakim? Naomi Porter."

"Ah, Miss Porter." He looked her up and down, briefly but thoroughly. "This way, please." He ushered her towards the inner office.

The room was sparsely furnished. Behind a simple pine desk there was an office armchair and on the desk were a landline phone, an open laptop, an A4 notepad and two document trays. On the opposite side were two plastic chairs, with another two placed against the wall. An untidy wooden book case and a steel filing cabinet adorned the opposite wall. Not the sort of office one might expect a high-flying Member of Parliament to have.

Hakim indicated, moving to take the armchair. "Please take a seat, Miss Porter."

Naomi took a chair, placing her document case on her lap and her umbrella on the floor. "Actually it's Mrs, I'm divorced but I kept the name. Just Naomi's fine."

Amir Hakim nodded. "OK, Naomi." He put his elbows on the desk and leaned forward. "You said you're a film producer? What can we do for you?" He was polite but brusque.

"I make documentary TV programmes. I met Mr Lafitte a few times; he's helping us with research into a project on Islamic State." Instantly, Hakim's demeanour sharpened. She had his full attention.

The man's eyebrows arched. "Islamic State? Have you got some news? About where he is?" The questions were stabbed out rapidly in an urgent falsetto.

Naomi took a folded copy of the previous Monday's *Sentinel* out of her document case and dropped it, face up, onto the desk. "No. But I'd like to meet Mrs Tudor. I wrote this article to help smoke out the truth and..."

"You're a *journalist?*"

"Not now, but I used to be."

Hakim sat up at once, clearly angry. His jaw set as he said, "I know all about that article, Mrs Porter." He pushed his chair back, saying, "I don't know whether you're a film producer or a reporter, but you know what? I don't care. Mrs Tudor isn't here and thanks to the media her life's been hell recently." He stood up and said, coldly, "Now if you don't mind, I've got people waiting."

Naomi stayed seated and answered calmly. "All I want to do is to help find Mr Lafitte. That was the purpose of the article. If Mrs Tudor knows I'm here, I think she'll want to see me."

Hakim stared at her. "I can assure you, that's most unlikely."

Naomi maintained a reasonable tone. "You may be right Mr Hakim and I understand that you're doing your best to protect Mrs Tudor. But since I'm here, why not let her decide for herself? Please, call her. It'll only take a minute."

For a few moments he did nothing, apparently thinking. Then he sat down and reached for his mobile. "I'll call her but there's no way she'll see you. For your information she's even had to change her number, thanks to you people." He tapped the phone. "You're wasting your time and the only reason I'm doing this is that it's the quickest way to stop you wasting mine."

Hakim drummed his fingers on the desk, waiting for a response. Moments later he raised his head and said, "Stella? Can you spare a minute?" After a brief pause he said, "Good. I'm at the office and we have a visitor. She called earlier to make an appointment and she's here now." He listened and then turned his head to look at Naomi. "A Mrs Porter. When she called she said she was a TV film maker. Now I've learned that she's the person who wrote the *Sentinel* article." He paused again before saying, "Yes, that one. Here in my office, she wants to meet you." Then his face took on a look of surprise. "What? Are you sure?" He shrugged, turned to Naomi and handed her the phone, saying, "She wants to talk to you."

In her living room, Stella clenched her jaw. Yes, she definitely wanted to speak to that woman. Suddenly aware that she had tensed, she made a conscious effort to relax. Important that she stayed calm. She took a deep breath and listened as the woman spoke.

"Good morning, Mrs Tudor. It's Naomi Porter here..."

Stella interjected. "I understand you want to meet me?"

"Yes, I'd like to do that, if possible." She sounded calm.

"Can you tell me why?" Stella replied, sharply.

"I want to see if there is anything I can do to help find Edmund. And I've come a long way, Mrs Tudor."

Edmund? Was she close enough to use his first name? *Bloody cheek!* But Stella had to stay composed. She loved Edmund and trusted him, but he was weak. Especially around pretty women who fed his ego. She wanted to know more about this one. "Very well," she said, "I'll see you."

"Great, thank you. Can I buy you lunch somewhere?"

"No," Stella replied. "They follow me everywhere; the press people."

"I understand. Shall I pick you up?"

"That won't work, either. We'd have an audience

wherever we go." After a brief pause, she added, "You can come here, to the house. Amir will give you directions. Don't park on the road, you'll be hassled. Come up the drive and park in front of the garage, the gate is open."

"Thank you. I'll come straight over."

"It'll take you about fifteen minutes to get here. Now, can you put Amir on again?"

"Right."

Moments later, Stella heard Hakim's falsetto. "Yes, Stella?"

"Amir, she's coming over. Can you give her directions? If she comes on her own I'll let her in. Please tell her that if she's not alone or if she tries anything, I won't open the door."

"OK, will do."

Stella put the phone down. She did not really believe that there was anything going on between Edmund and this Porter woman, but it was just possible. She would find out, she felt sure. But she would need to be careful. She was certain that Ed's disappearance was contrived, probably a lie deliberately leaked by the security people for reasons she did not yet know. Just as well that she had insisted on sending Jan Wainwright back to her normal duties. This was a meeting she preferred to conduct in private. With Edmund missing, there was no reason for continuing with the police protection, she had argued.

Stella made her way to the kitchen. She would need to gain the woman's confidence, she felt. Had she been too harsh? Best lighten up. Apologise, perhaps on the grounds of being distraught? Yes, she could do that. And she'd make them both a light lunch. There was cheese and some sliced ham in the fridge, she could make a salad.

Naomi arrived at Stella's house some twenty minutes later and Stella took her into the living room. After a few minutes' innocuous small talk, Stella suggested that they move to the kitchen for the cold lunch that she had prepared. She had already set the table. There was a television on the wall with its sound muted. It appeared to be showing a cookery programme.

"It's so kind of you to go to all this trouble," Naomi said.

Stella shrugged. "You've come a long way, least I could do,"

Naomi took a seat. "To be honest, I took a chance. I wasn't sure you'd want to meet me."

Stella moved to the worktop and picked up a bottle of wine that she had opened earlier. "This is a Napa Valley red," she said. "Or I have a bottle of Riesling in the fridge. Would you prefer that?"

"A glass of red would be fine, thank you. But just the one; I'm driving."

"Of course." Stella poured wine into their glasses. She put the bottle down. "Do you know Edmund well?"

Naomi was helping herself to salad. "Not really; it's just business."

"Business? He never mentioned it."

"No reason why he should, I guess. We met only three times."

"You make films for television, I believe?"

"Yes, that's right. He's been giving us a bit of background on Islamic State."

Stella's lips curled into a smile. "Are you a full-time film producer and part-time journalist, or is it the other way around?"

Naomi hesitated. A loaded question and Stella's lips were smiling but her steady gaze seemed cold. Naomi answered, quietly. "I haven't been a newspaper reporter for years. My job in films keeps me fully occupied."

Stella had her head down as she helped herself to food. "There can't be many people in your business who get to write front page articles in a national daily."

This is turning into a verbal tennis match, Naomi thought. *Stay calm.* "I expect you've read it, so you must know that it's an attempt to find Edmund, or rather to flush out information about where he is. I was with Edmund when the suicide bomber tried to kill him and I used to be with *The Sentinel*. It was the editor's idea to ask me to do the piece. I'm trying to help because I'm worried about him. Aren't you?"

"Is that why you've come? To find out if I know where he is?"

"Actually, yes. And also to tell you that the paper's willing to keep trying."

Stella smiled and this time it looked genuine. "OK, and since you ask, of course I'm worried he's missing. But I don't believe he's in danger."

Naomi took a sip of wine and put the glass down. "Why do you say that?"

"The anti-terrorist people are saying that he's disappeared. Nothing else. Not a word about how that's happened, or where he is. Not good enough and they know it."

"So what do you think?"

Stella did not reply immediately. She seemed to be deliberating. "Well, there's definitely something going on. Maybe they've moved him to another safe house. Or maybe he's just taken off. That's possible. I know Edmund; he's bright and resourceful." She shrugged. "Who knows? I wouldn't be surprised if he walked through the door." She didn't seem too worried. *Was Edmund really missing?*

Stella glanced at the television and pushed her chair back. The programme had just ended and the closing credits were rolling. She stood up. "Time for the one o'clock news. Let's see if he's turned up." She moved to the worktop and picked up the remote.

The news channel came on with the presenter at his desk. The headline banner scrolling across the bottom of the screen screamed: **BREAKING NEWS - Missing MP - Shocking new IS video on Internet**. Instantly it grabbed the attention of both women. Stella was holding her wine glass, staring at the screen. The presenter's bearing and delivery conveyed a tone of the utmost gravity.

"Within the last hour a shocking video purporting to be from so-called Islamic State has been put on the internet. It is alleged to portray the assassination of Edmund Lafitte, Member of Parliament for the Somerford constituency..."

Horrified, Naomi muttered, "Oh God, no!"

Stella's face went white and the wine glass slipped from her hand. It smashed on the tiled floor with a tinkling crash, scattering fragments in every direction.

On her way back to London an hour later, Naomi waited until she was close to the M4 motorway before she pulled off the road to make her phone call. The one that she was bursting to make. It had not been easy but she had forced herself to wait. Just as well, it had given her time to think; the forty-minute drive had served to crystallise her thoughts.

She clenched her jaw while tapping the displayed number on her mobile. How dare they? What the hell was going on? Clearly, Stella really did not know where Lafitte was. That was no act. That much was obvious from the woman's reaction.

"Yes, Naomi?" The question was stabbed out. Javid Nasir sounded stressed.

She was fuming. "What's going on?"

"I have no idea. Where are you?"

"Where do you think?" she snorted. "I've just left Somerford, been there the whole bloody day. What was the point of sending me there?"

"Look, I told you. I don't know what happened, but I'll find out. I'm tied up tomorrow; we can talk on Monday but not now. Where will you be?"

"At work. My office at Tolgate."

"I'll come over at lunchtime. Meet me in La Baguette. It's on..."

"On the high street, I know. I can be there for half past twelve."

"Right." He rang off.

Still fuming, Naomi shoved her mobile back into her handbag. She had more questions but discussing the issue on the phone was not an option.

CHAPTER THIRTY-TWO

Amir Hakim was heading to his home in the West Midlands. The Saturday traffic had been slow leaving Somerford but he would be on the motorway shortly. Then he could relax for two hours or so, with his radio already tuned to his favourite classic music station.

He was listening to a Beethoven symphony as he approached the motorway junction, about to peel off onto the slip road when the music stopped suddenly. In terse, clipped tones, the presenter said, *"We interrupt this programme with a special news announcement. The missing Member of Parliament Edmund Lafitte is alleged to have been assassinated. A video posted on the internet appears to show him being murdered in the most brutal fashion. It is believed that so-called Islamic State has claimed responsibility for the act, although that has not yet been confirmed..."*

"Bloody hell!" Amir braked and swung away from the slip road, nearly colliding with a lorry that blared its horn in anger as it swished past. For a few seconds he concentrated on re-joining the flow of traffic, shutting his ears to the broadcast still on the radio. A few hundred yards further he pulled up in a lay-by, cut the engine and scrambled for his laptop. It took him less than thirty seconds to find the video. The obscene footage of the bloody decapitation was followed immediately by the raising of the severed, dripping head by the assassin. The head of his close friend Edmund Lafitte. Amir gagged and flung open the door. He leaned over and was violently sick.

The news broadcast was still on. He sat back, breathing deeply. Then he closed the laptop, wiped his mouth and turned the sound up on the radio. The presenter was going through the main points again, saying, *"...precise location was recognized and Yorkshire Constabulary has confirmed that swift action was taken to locate and safeguard the body. It is to be taken to London for examination and a post mortem that will be carried out by senior Home Office pathologists."* There followed an interview at the scene with Detective Chief Superintendent Flack of Donfield CID, who said that all was in hand at the crime scene. He was not prepared to name the exact location but urged the public to stay away from Denndale Moor.

Amir had recovered enough to take out his mobile and call Stella.

In Donfield, Sergeant Brody was on duty. He had just seen the video and immediately called Royce, who was at home.

His superior was not pleased. "My first Saturday off in weeks and you can't leave me alone?"

"Sorry, sir, you have to know this. Have you heard about the MP Lafitte?"

"They've found him?"

"No, he's dead. They've killed him."

"What?"

"It was on the news. They put a video on the internet. I've just watched it."

"OK, email me the link. Give me five minutes and..."

"Sir, I think you should know, it wasn't in the desert, they did it here."

"What, here in Donfield? Again?"

"No, not in the city. On Denndale Moor, I recognize the place, there's Camel Rock in the background."

"*What?*" Royce was plainly astonished. He said, "We need to get over there, fast. Have you called the Super?"

"Not yet, would you like me to?"

"No, I'll do that. Get your skates on and pick me up as soon as you can." Royce ended the call.

What the hell was going on? Royce's laptop was in the living room and he wanted to see the video for himself. But first, better get hold of his boss. With a bit of luck the superintendent's phones wouldn't be switched off. Denndale Moor? He knew the place too, with its distinctive double-humped rock. Why had they chosen to do the job there, right on his patch? This did not sound good. Royce felt that he and his staff would be hung out to dry. Again. He called Superintendent Flack's mobile.

"Yes, Charlie?" His superior had responded immediately, his manner terse.

"Sorry to bother you, sir. Colin's just called about the MP, Lafitte. Seems..."

"Yes, I know, he's dead. It's all in hand, Charlie."

"In hand? But there's a video..."

"On the internet, yeah. A copy on DVD was couriered to the Met six hours ago. They saw it before it went on the net."

Royce was stunned. "Why weren't we told?"

"We were. Actually, I was. The ACC called me and told me to meet him at the scene. Just me on my own, nobody else and no uniforms."

"When was that?"

"About one o'clock. I got here thirty minutes later." He growled, "Missed my fucking lunch."

"What's going on, sir? Who's securing the scene?"

"Them. The Met. And they're taking the body to London. Sooner the better, far as I'm concerned. Like I say, it's all in hand. No action needed by us."

Royce felt his blood rising. "So we're not good enough to do our own policing?"

"Not the point, Charlie. They said it's being handled on a need to know. I'll fill you in tomorrow. Unless I fucking starve to death first."

OK, Royce thought. So be it. "You'll be coming in to the office tomorrow, then?"

"Ah, Sunday. No, I'll be busy, Charlie. Got something planned. It'll have to keep till Monday. Anyway, it's out of our hands. The guy's dead, the Met's taken charge, end of story."

CHAPTER THIRTY-THREE

Ibrahim left the house that Saturday afternoon with his uncle's words echoing in his head. Over and over, burning into his brain: *"Use your weapon with pride."* What sort of weapon? He had not been told and he did not ask. Not a gun, he fervently hoped, because he had never used one. A sword? Probably. The very thought made him shrink in fear as he saw again in his mind's eye the severed head of the last victim rolling away from the body. He had been violently sick. Would that happen again?

Sitting in the passenger seat of Rafiq's battered Renault, which ratted with every bump, he agonized. The isolation that he had felt when he arrived in England worsened with every passing month. And now, locked into a nightmare not of his making, he had nowhere to turn. He felt desolate, abandoned and trapped. Of one thing he was certain: he could not and would not kill anyone. Somehow, he had to get away. No chance while he was locked in this uncomfortable, oil-smelly car on the motorway.

"Do you want the toilet?" Rafiq's question cut through his thoughts. The man had said very little during the journey and Ibrahim had no inclination to make small talk.

"No."

"Service area coming, I'm pulling off. I need to go." Rafiq steered the old car onto the slip road. "Also, we can eat."

Ibrahim was not hungry. But if Rafiq left the car, maybe there was a chance that he could get away. But how? And where could he go?

Rafiq drove slowly past the main building and serried ranks of stationary vehicles slotted neatly in their marked spaces. A motorway patrol van was parked right outside the entrance. Ibrahim caught his breath. Yellow, with red stripes and a blue light on top. A police van? There was a man at the wheel. But Rafiq did not stop; he headed for the part of the parking area that was furthest from the main complex. In that area there were no other vehicles and he pulled up.

"Better here," he said. "We can eat in peace."

Ibrahim had never been to a motorway service place before. Eat? Did that mean that they would be buying food? They would need to wash if they were going to eat. He was thinking quickly. He would wait until Rafiq went to the toilet and then make a dash for the patrol van. Any minute now the nightmare would be over. He tensed, scarcely able to contain his excitement.

Rafiq undid his seatbelt. "Come. If you don't need the toilet, just wash. I brought food, enough for us both."

Deflated, Ibrahim trudged behind Rafiq as they made their way along the pathway towards the main building. People were entering and leaving through the glass-enclosed area that surrounded the entrance. The patrol van was parked at the kerb and Ibrahim had his eyes fixed on it, his heart pounding. He could still do it. Now or never, he might not get another chance. Just a bit closer and he would dash across. A few more metres. His mouth went dry. What would he say to them? No matter; he craved safety, above everything. He was ready.

Rafiq stopped abruptly and spun around. Ibrahim's pace brought him alongside and Rafiq was now standing between him and the patrol vehicle. He ordered, "Keep close. Speak to nobody."

Ibrahim was staring past his captor. A patrolman holding a bulging brown paper bag climbed into the van. To Ibrahim's dismay, it pulled away and drove off.

The supermarket on the outskirts of the town of Bursdon was well signposted from the main ring road, but Ibrahim had no idea where they were. All he knew was that this was the day he had been dreading. The store's car park was still light when they arrived and Rafiq drove slowly past the entrance, an area that was busy with shoppers emerging, pushing laden trolleys out against the stream of people entering.

"A white Ford Transit. Look out for it," Rafiq said, swivelling his head to check the rows of vehicles parked to the left and right. Ibrahim had retreated into himself, arms folded against his chest. He said nothing, mentally willing the rendezvous to fail so that the mission would be aborted.

Rafiq steered the Renault along the periphery road until they reached the outer edge of the parking area. He nodded forward. "There. Against the hedge," he said, heading for a white van that was conspicuous in its isolation, with no other vehicle nearby. He flashed the car's headlamps and there was a momentary flash in response from the van. Ibrahim's depression deepened as he realised that this was not a place where he could attempt to get away. He should have acted when they stopped. Now he was really trapped.

Ten minutes later, they were on their way again, this time in the Ford van. A stocky, full-bearded Londoner called Hassan was driving. Rafiq's car had been left where it was parked. The van had a twin-seat bench adjacent to the driver's, so the three were sitting line abreast. Rafiq had taken the end seat near the passenger door. Ibrahim was in the middle, where he felt helpless, trapped again with no chance of flight.

Hassan kept the speed down while they made their way past signs showing the way to the town centre.

"Why are we going slow?" Rafiq complained. "We don't want to be noticed."

Hassan growled, "If I go fast we will definitely be noticed." The man had crooked teeth and seriously bad breath. Ibrahim recoiled involuntarily. The driver added, "Plenty of time. The place is called the White Horse. It's in the middle of the town, near to the square."

They made their way into the centre of the town at a steady pace, pulling up at a set of traffic lights at one corner of the square. The area within the perimeter roads of the square was laid out as a car park, with a barrier at the entrance, the bar of which was in the raised position.

Hassan pointed ahead. "I'll show you the place, it's not far. Then we'll come back here and park in the middle, until the time is right."

Rafiq said, "Why can't we wait at the inn?"

"It closes at eleven o'clock. There's a car park at the back, but the best time to do the mission is between ten and eleven. We'll go there and choose our targets when the men come out."

The van moved along on the perimeter road, past the

square. Fear gripped Ibrahim, who glanced around, desperately looking for some way in which he could escape. There seemed to be no way out. The car park was about a quarter full. Most of the perimeter area facing the square was taken up by retail stores, now closed, their window displays ignored by pedestrians who seemed to be gravitating to and from a fast-food burger bar and a kebab shop.

The opposite side of the square was dominated by the Miramar hotel with its glass-fronted entrance, behind which the reception lobby was clearly visible. Ibrahim was now sweating. He would have given anything to be able to dash into that hotel for sanctuary. The van stayed on the main road and went on through traffic lights, heading away from the square. Hassan said, "Next turning, it's on the corner."

Shortly after, they reached the junction. Hassan slowed the van and nodded towards the Victorian building on the opposite corner. "That's the place."

Hanging from a metal bracket above the double doors at the front was a sign declaring it to be *The White Horse Hotel,* with the image of a rampant equine painted in white under the script. Hassan slowed the van, indicated and turned left into the side road. They moved forward slowly down the narrow road, past the rear of the building. Hassan nodded towards the right. "Car park," he said.

Ibrahim wasn't listening. He stared straight ahead, his mind locked into finding a way to escape at any cost. Rafiq leaned forward to peer past him. "There's lots of space. Why can't we park here and wait?"

Hassan snorted. "I told you. We go back to the square and wait until the time is right. If we sit here for three hours before we do the job it will be a risk. Not necessary."

Rafiq grunted. "Whatever you say, brother."

They drove around the block, emerging onto the main road again, heading back into the square. The traffic light was red and Hassan pulled up. Ibrahim's heart leapt instantly. There, parked at the kerb outside the burger bar, was a police patrol car! White, with fluorescent orange stripes on its sides and lights on the roof. *A real police car.* He could scarcely believe his eyes. He tried to suppress his excitement as he took in the scene. A uniformed policeman was on the pavement, talking to a group of youths. Another was in the driving seat in the car.

Hassan steered the van into the car park, passing under the raised barrier. He pulled up in a space away from other vehicles. "No need to pay. Parking is free after hours," he explained.

Ibrahim's gaze was locked onto the police car. It was in plain sight, about sixty metres away. His heart was pounding. He had to find a way to get out. But he was trapped between the other two men. Oh God, help me, help me, he pleaded mentally.

Rafiq shifted on the seat. "How long will we wait?"

"A couple of hours at least," Hassan replied.

"I'll need the toilet."

Ibrahim held his breath. Was Rafiq about to get out? At last, a chance.

Hassan said, "In a minute. First, I want to show you something." He spun around and reached behind his seat. Ibrahim winced as he was assailed by a waft of foul breath. Hassan straightened, swinging a canvas sports bag over the seat and onto his lap.

"This is our present to the British soldiers," he said,

displaying his crooked teeth in a wide grin. He unzipped the bag, took out a bundle wrapped in a stained towelling rag and placed it on his lap. He looked across at his companions and flipped open the towel.

"Here, look." His face broke into a grin again.

The two men peered at the bundle. Rafiq gasped. Ibrahim was instantly appalled and frightened. Lying on the towel were several large, shiny, steel knives. Hassan picked one up.

"Look at this. Beautiful, is it not?" He twisted his wrist, turning the ten-inch blade that tapered to a point. "See, double edge, both as sharp as razors."

Ibrahim struggled to control his emotions. Oh God, did they expect him to use one of these? On a total stranger? Hassan held the knife out at arm's length and turned suddenly, feinting a thrust at the young man. Ibrahim shrank back, terrified.

Hassan laughed. "Did I scare you, boy?"

Ibrahim was frightened and angry. He sat up and mumbled, "It's not funny."

Rafiq said, "Give him time, this is only his second mission. His first in action."

Hassan's eyes narrowed. "Then I'll show him the right way to use this." He held the knife up in his right hand. Then he placed the palm of the other hand on Ibrahim's chest and pressed his fingers gently against it. His eyes burned into Ibrahim's. "Here. You strike *here*, between the ribs, upwards. Quick and hard, into the heart."

Ibrahim struggled to stem the urge to be physically sick. These people were mad. His head buzzed and he felt dizzy. Nobody spoke, until Rafiq broke the silence. "I'm going to the hotel to use the toilet."

Hassan was carefully wrapping the towel around the knives. He indicated by nodding to the side. "Go," he said. Rafiq opened the passenger door, stepped down and slammed it shut. The clang echoed through the cabin. Quite suddenly, with nobody between himself and the door, Ibrahim's spirits soared, he was nearly free. Not yet released, but no longer shackled between the two men he had come to hate. For a few seconds his eyes followed Rafiq's progress towards the hotel. *Steady*, he cautioned himself. A quick glance confirmed that the policemen were still there, but the officer on the pavement seemed to be stepping away from the youths. It was now or never. Ibrahim's mouth went dry. Now, he must act *now*.

Without looking at Hassan he blurted, "I'll go with him." He shuffled his backside along the seat, gripped the handle and flung the door open. With his head down he jumped out, his legs feeling like jelly when his feet hit the tarmac.

Behind him Hassan shouted, "Hey!" But Ibrahim ignored him. He had to get to the police car. He quickened his pace, breaking into a run when he saw the policeman opening his door. Ibrahim raised an arm, calling out, "Wait, wait!"

They had not heard him. With rising panic he saw the patrol car indicating and starting to pull out. Ibrahim had reached the edge of the car park. He needed to cross the road, but there was a car approaching. He took a deep breath and sprinted across, throwing himself over the bonnet of the police car. It lurched and stopped, tossing him onto the road.

For a few seconds Ibrahim lay on his back, stunned. The first sensation he felt was pain in his left knee, followed immediately by a feeling of immense relief. He had done it!

"Are you all right?" The anxious voice of the face leaning

over him. It was one of the policemen, a beefy individual kneeling at his side. The other was standing behind.

Ibrahim sat up. "Yes, I'm OK..." An urgent nearby screech of tyres on tarmac interrupted. The noise had come from the white Ford van. It lurched out of the car park at speed, with the passenger side door swinging loose as the vehicle rounded the opposite corner, heading past the hotel.

"That van," Ibrahim exclaimed, pointing. "Those men want to kill the soldiers."

The policeman's head spun around. "What? What soldiers, where?"

"Stop them. They want to kill the soldiers," Ibrahim blurted. "In the *White Horse*."

The second policeman reacted more quickly. He sprinted into the road, his eyes staring at the rear of the van as he spoke into the phone on his lapel.

"Can you stand up?" the patrolman asked.

Ibrahim nodded and with the man's help he stood up. Two of the youths who had been on the pavement came forward. One said, "Do you want me to call an ambulance?"

Ibrahim shook his head. "No, I'm OK."

The patrolman said, "Come on, let's get you in the car."

The other policeman hurried over. "I called in the number," he said. "You all right?" he asked Ibrahim, who nodded.

"I'm OK."

The patrolman put his hand on Ibrahim's shoulder. "I suppose we'd better get you back to the station and find out what this is about."

An hour later the phone on Chief Inspector Royce's desk rang. He picked up. "Royce."

"Charlie? Bernard Milner here. I have some news for you."

The Assistant Chief Constable did not make a habit of by-passing the chain of command. Probably something to do with the fact that it was a Saturday. Royce smiled at his own cynicism. He replied, "Sir?"

"It's about a man named Ibrahim Asif Mahmud. Do you know him?"

Ibrahim? Royce was instantly alert. "He's Imam Mahmud's nephew. I've met him a couple of times. What's this about?"

"Oh bugger! That could be a problem." The ACC's reaction spoke volumes. "He's been picked up in Wiltshire. He and two others were on their way to attack off-duty soldiers from an army camp. Do you know anything about that?"

Royce's immediate feeling was one of dismay. He smelt trouble. "No, we don't, sir."

"Must have been planned here in our patch. I don't like nasty surprises, Charlie."

"We've heard nothing. Impossible to get any info about jihadists around here. What happened?"

"In the end, nothing, they were all picked up. I've had a call from the Met, CTC unit, Commander Bennett. Seems Mahmud chickened out, did a runner and gave himself up."

Tension flowed out of the Chief Inspector like water from a burst dam. He took a deep breath. "Well now, that's interesting."

"He gave up the other two straight away. One's a Donfield local, he and Mahmud drove to Bursdon, a garrison town. The other guy's a Londoner, met up with them in a Transit that was nicked a few days ago."

Royce asked the burning question. "Has he given us anything about the killing of the MP? Or the Milford Park murder?"

"Not a word from him or the other Donfield man. They've clammed up. But here's the thing: Mahmud told them he would speak to you."

"He did?"

"Yes, to you and no one else. He insisted. Sounds like you've cracked it, Charlie."

Royce took a few seconds to savour the moment. Fantastic! He felt ecstatic, but toned down his reply. "Maybe so, sir. Best not count the chickens yet. What do you want to do?"

"Mahmud's on his way to us, special delivery. SO15 wanted them both in London but we persuaded them to send him here, on the grounds he's insisting on only talking to you. They'll be sitting in, but it'll be your interview. Let him cool off in the nick overnight, you can take your time questioning him tomorrow. The Met people want to do it tomorrow in any case."

"Shouldn't we be on him straight away, sir? I'm thinking about all the grief we'll be getting from the media about the MP. It's started already."

"A fair point. OK, speak to Mahmud when he arrives. He's likely to be more cooperative if it's just you. You never know, you could wrap it up quickly. All of it."

"I'll do my best, sir. What about the other man?"

"Wiltshire's got enough to hang on to him for now. But if Mahmud fingers him for the other jobs, we'll get him back, fast. Keep me in the loop."

"Yes, sir." Royce was still elated. There was a good chance that he'd be able to clear out the whole filthy gang. From Donfield, at least. Abdullah and the other monkeys, and maybe the organ grinder too. Sometimes he felt that he had the best job in the world.

CHAPTER THIRTY-FOUR

The door hinge squealed. Chief Inspector Royce looked up from the papers he had been studying. "You didn't have to come in tonight, Colin."

Sergeant Brody demurred. "Yes, I did, sir. Came as soon as I heard. You don't mind, do you?"

"Course not. The lad's in a holding cell but I won't be doing a formal interview until tomorrow." He rolled his eyes. "SO15 want to sit in."

"You'll be talking to him first?"

"Whatever gave you that idea?" He smiled crookedly. "Yes, but I don't think you'll be in with me. Seems he's insisting he wants to speak to me on my own."

Brody looked crestfallen. "Oh. A bit dodgy, though? Unless you mean off the record."

"That's exactly what I mean. I'll talk to him informally. I think this boy's been through hell. He took a huge risk when he gave himself up. Seems he threw himself on the bonnet of a patrol car. Not the behaviour of a criminal, is that."

"I see what you mean."

"I want to hear from him what happened yesterday. Also if he knows anything about the murder of the MP. Now *that* would be interesting. And I reckon he was at the Middle Meadows murder, but not willingly. If I do it right, he'll open up to me. More likely than in the interview room, with others there and the recorder running."

"But if you want to use what he tells you..."

"The lad's just a kid, scared out of his wits. I can help him to get it right tomorrow, when it'll be formal. If I don't talk to him before, he could feel pressured. Likely he'll clam up. That'd be no good for him, or us."

Brody nodded. "Anything I can do?"

"Yes. Go have a word with him, make sure he's comfortable. But no questions."

"OK."

"And if he's hungry, we'll order a take-out for him." Brody was at the door as Royce added, "And Colin..."

"Sir?"

"Tell him I'm paying and make sure you say that you're not supposed to be telling him that I am."

Brody grinned. "Will do."

Royce went down to the holding cell shortly after, with Brody following. The boy had declined food when seen by the sergeant, asking only for water. *And to see me*, Royce reflected. He tried to imagine how the lad was feeling. An outsider in a strange land, where he'd been forced by a deranged obsessive in his own family to be a party to unspeakable brutality. Now he was incarcerated in police custody, while knowing that he was innocent of any wrong-doing. Probably. That was the first thing he would need to establish. A holding cell is still a cell. A nightmare for anyone who had never experienced any sort of prison before.

He was deep in thought when Brody asked, "Wouldn't it be better if you went in on your own, sir?"

"What?" Royce paused before replying, "I'll see him on my own, but I want you there so that he can see me dismissing you."

On the ground floor, a uniformed constable took them to Ibrahim's cell and unlocked the door. In the adjacent room a man was ranting, demanding to be let out.

The constable bellowed, "Shut up, Jamie." To Royce he said, "Sorry, sir. Jamie's a regular overnighter. Far as he's concerned, we're the Donfield Hilton." He opened the door and stood back.

The two detectives went in. The room was narrow, no more than eight feet across and about ten deep. In one corner were a stainless steel toilet and hand basin. The only natural light came from the barred window set in the back wall, across which was a narrow single bed. Ibrahim was on the bed on his haunches, his arms wrapped around his folded legs and his head bowed on his knees. He looked up, his face a picture of relief.

Royce was the first to speak. "Now then, young feller, what have you been up to?"

The lad tilted his head, a sickly smile on his face. "Nothing, sir."

Royce smiled. "Then let's talk about what you've not been doing."

"Thank you, sir." He shot a glance at Brody and then looked at Royce again. In a voice barely above a whisper, he said, "Only you."

Behind him the uniformed constable who was standing in the doorway, said, "Do you want me to get you a couple of chairs, sir?"

Royce turned. "We're OK, Constable. I want Sergeant

Brody to leave." He took a short step forward. "And if this young man doesn't mind, I'll just sit here, on the end of the bed."

The constable had closed the door but left it unlocked. Royce felt it important that they should be sitting together, side by side, and that he should not speak first.

After a few moments' uncomfortable silence and without looking at the detective, Ibrahim asked, "How long will I go to jail for?" His tone was apprehensive, the words spoken quietly.

Royce glanced at the boy. "I really can't say." He shrugged. "Depends on what you've done, I suppose."

"I haven't done anything, sir."

Royce stretched his legs out. "If that's true, you won't go to jail. But if you know about things that other people did," he turned again to look directly at Ibrahim, "you need to tell us."

"Oh."

"Have you committed any crimes yourself?"

The young man shook his head. "No. I haven't done anything; I told you."

Royce drew his legs in and sat up. He slapped his thighs. "Good. That's what I thought. But there's something called aiding and abetting, which basically means helping. You need to tell us everything that you know, or even suspect, about crimes committed by other people. It's no good keeping quiet, you're already involved. At the moment it looks like you've been forced to do things that you knew were wrong. We call that acting under duress. And that basically means it probably isn't your fault." He put a hand lightly on the young man's shoulder. "But you need to speak up now. If you don't, when the truth comes out they'll say you've been aiding and abetting criminal activity. You can't conceal evidence, that's an offence. And the truth will come out sooner or later, make no mistake." He drew his hand back and shifted his position, the better to observe the boy's face and mannerisms. He said no more, he wanted to leave the young man to work it out for himself.

A leaden silence followed until Ibrahim asked, "Can I go back to Pakistan?"

The question caught the Chief Inspector off balance. He had not given that a thought. He took a moment, clearing his throat before responding. "To be honest, I don't know. Far as I'm concerned, it won't be a problem, but it's not going to be possible if you're in jail. You really don't want to get a criminal record."

Royce thought that Ibrahim looked the picture of misery, his face and manner clearly reflecting the torment going on in his mind.

Speaking quietly, the detective asked, "When did you leave your house?"

"Yesterday."

"You know what I don't understand?" Without waiting for a reply, he went on. "I can't think why we've not heard from your uncle. You spent last night in Wiltshire, but nobody's reported you missing. Weren't you supposed to be home last night?"

Ibrahim's head dropped. He said, "Can I make a phone call?"

Royce was surprised. Had he misread the situation? "You want to call him?"

"No, no! I want to call Pakistan. My mother. I don't want

to see my uncle again."

"I may be able to arrange for you to speak to your mother. Actually I'm sure I can, if you tell me all that you know about the incident in Milford Park five weeks ago. Specially what your uncle had to do with it."

Ibrahim Mahmud did exactly that. He spoke hesitantly at first, but more easily as the story unfolded. Royce listened carefully, needing to prompt only when the young man forgot to mention the MP's business card. Ibrahim confirmed that there had been blood on his hands at the time and agreed to provide fingerprints and a DNA sample voluntarily.

Finally the detective said, "I think you'll be all right, lad. You're not under arrest at the moment but it's possible that you could be charged with being an accessory to the crime. But to my mind that's not likely, seeing as you're a hero."

Ibrahim sat up, a look of pure astonishment on his face. "A hero?"

Royce smiled. "You prevented a major terrorist crime. Saved the lives of soldiers, didn't you? But we need to keep you here until we get the record straight. That'll happen tomorrow. You must tell your side again in the interview room. Plus anything else that you think can help. There'll be a couple of other policemen there but you'll be OK, just tell the truth. The conversation will be recorded. That's normal and it's done to protect you."

"Thank you, sir." Relief lit up the young man's face.

"Meantime, if you need anything – food, change of clothes or suchlike, just tell the duty constable. I'll send him in now." Royce took two steps toward the door and turned suddenly. "Oh, I nearly forgot." Certain that he had

Ibrahim's full attention, he asked, "What do you know about the murder of the MP not far from here?"

"Murder, sir?" No question about it, he was plainly astonished. "Nothing. What MP?"

"Never mind." The look on Ibrahim's face was enough to convince Royce immediately that he was telling the truth. The Inspector did not explain. Important that the boy reacted the same way when asked the question again. And that would certainly happen the following day.

In his modest semi-detached house late that night, Inspector Charles Royce left his shoes on the landing and quietly opened his bedroom door. He had phoned his wife Brenda earlier to tell her that he would be late home and as expected, now found that she was already in bed.

Light from the street lamp outside the window cast a dim orange glow over the room. Royce entered and waited a few moments for his eyes to adjust to the gloom. On her side of the bed, the snugly-wrapped figure under the double duvet stirred. She reached out and switched on her bedside lamp.

"Have you eaten anything?" her muffled voice asked.

"Hello, love. Sorry I disturbed you."

She eased herself up. "You didn't. I hadn't got off yet. I did sausage and mash for tea, when you phoned I turned the oven off. There's fresh cheese sandwiches on the worktop."

"Yes, I found them."

"I didn't hear the kettle."

"It's OK, I had a beer." He switched on his bedside light. "I'll not be long; I've already used the bathroom."

She switched her light off and lay down again. "You on early shift tomorrow?"

"Yes."

Brenda dragged the duvet around herself. "Best get your head down, then."

Royce changed into his pyjamas and opened the drawer of his bedside cabinet, where he kept his second mobile. He had established a routine of checking it every night. He switched it on, not expecting to see anything on the display, but on this night there was a message. Royce tapped to view it. All is said was: *"Meet Greyfriars nr ticket office 9 am tomorrow V. urgent."*

Anwar! Greyfriars was the name of the main train station in Donfield. Tomorrow? He checked quickly. The message had come in that afternoon.

CHAPTER THIRTY-FIVE

I'm getting old, Inspector Royce thought wryly. Time was when six hours' sleep would have been plenty. Not anymore. That morning the ticket office in the Victorian building that was Greyfriars Station was busy with commuters streaming through. Some with heads bowed, tapping at their mobiles, others had their phones flattened to their ears. He looked around.

There were benches placed along the wall opposite the ticket office. Anwar was seated at the end of one and beside him were a canvas sports bag and a wheeled suitcase. Royce was surprised to see the luggage. He strode forward and the young man stood up.

"Going on holiday, Anwar?" the detective asked.

"I wish, Mr Royce." He sat down again. The Inspector took a seat beside him.

Anwar said, "I've got a job abroad. A relative in Canada."

"Uh, huh. Doing what?"

"He's got two restaurants and wants to expand. He needs staff."

"Well, good luck, you deserve a break." He changed the subject. "You wanted to see me? What's so urgent?"

The informant reached into his anorak and took out a mobile. "I want to return this. I used it to take some photos that you may be interested in."

"Photos? Of what?"

"Documents, from the office in the mosque. You know I worked there as a volunteer."

The detective's fatigue disappeared instantly. "What sort of documents?"

"There's some lists. Looks like the contributions from businesses. In the Imam's handwriting."

"Contributions?"

Anwar shrugged. "You know what I mean." He smiled thinly. "Also a couple of letters to the Imam from Pakistan."

"What do they say?"

The young man's mouth formed a wide smile. "I'll show you." He tapped the display and a picture of a document appeared.

Royce could scarcely contain his excitement, until Anwar expanded the image. "Oh, it's all in Arabic?"

"Urdu. But I can tell you what it says." He scrolled through a few pages, briefly explaining what the text of each meant.

Royce was staggered, and elated. "Bloody hell! This is fantastic." Then he frowned. "Why are you doing this?"

"When I was in a bad place, you helped me. I never forgot. Now I'm helping you."

The detective shook his head. "But..."

"And I'm leaving the country. A good time to pass this to you. Don't worry, I'll be OK. They won't be looking for me, even if they figure out how you got the stuff. And you're going to put that man where he belongs, aren't you? For a long time, I hope."

Royce lowered his head. "Yes, with luck, a very long time. I'm really grateful, lad." After a few moments' silence, he added, "How can I reach you, in case...?"

"My brother knows what I'm doing and where I'll be." In a determined tone he added, "If you're asking if I'd be prepared to corroborate, yes, I can do that."

Royce struggled with a mix of emotions, all positive. "I don't know what to say."

Anwar reached down and zipped open the sports bag beside him. He withdrew an envelope. "You'll need this; the originals." He stood up. "I have to go, my train leaves in five minutes."

CHAPTER THIRTY-SIX

Naomi checked her watch. He was late. Typical of the man, arrogant and thoughtless. Not for the first time, she wondered what she had ever seen in him. How different from Edmund. Both were Members of Parliament and of similar age. Ed the Conservative and Javid, who was with the party in opposition. The former born into a wealthy English family and the other, the son of a dirt-poor hotel porter in Pakistan. Now, one was dead, and the other? Responsible, in part at the very least, for Edmund's brutal assassination. How could she have been so stupid? But enough was enough. She wanted out.

Another ten minutes and she would leave, regardless. Mondays were manic in her office and she had work to get on with. She finished her egg-and-cress sandwich, wiped her mouth with a tissue and drained her coffee cup. At the table across the aisle, two young couples were noisily comparing photographs on their mobile phones, apparently taken at a party that they had all attended together. Good. Her conversation with the man would not be overheard.

Shortly after, Javid Nasir entered and stood still, framed in the doorway, his tall figure silhouetted by the bright sunlight outside. He removed his designer shades, put them away and looked around. Seeing Naomi, he raised a hand before moving to the counter. She watched as he placed his order, handsome in his bespoke grey suit, his dark beard neatly trimmed. He appeared to be exuding charm, as usual. Then he turned to look at her, pointing at the coffee machine and mouthing "Coffee?" She merely nodded.

A minute later he came over, bearing a tray. He put it down and leaned forward. Naomi shrank away. She did not want his kiss.

"Oh," he said, backing off. "Having a bad day?"

"I am now," she snapped.

"OK." He shrugged and sat down.

Naomi glared at him tight-lipped, as he started on his sandwich, apparently unconcerned. He was munching, his full cheeks bulging.

He swallowed, raised his eyebrows and said, "Problem?" before taking another large bite.

Is he serious? Barely controlling her rising anger, she hissed, "Yes, there's a sodding problem. Why did you send me on a bloody wild goose chase?"

Still munching, he shook his head. Then he raised a hand. "I didn't know, I swear."

"What?" she sputtered. "I don't believe you. They were quick enough to claim responsibility. You *must* have known. Are you telling me you knew nothing about the killing?"

He frowned and swivelled his head, glancing around quickly. "Keep it down," he snarled quietly, adding, "No I didn't. And for your information, neither did Donfield. They reckon it was a rogue element. Not that it matters, even loose cannons work."

She glared at him. "Crap! Since when are there loose

cannons in Donfield? It's where they control your lot from. And you're sitting here stuffing your face and telling me they've got loose cannons?"

He shrugged. "It's true." He picked up his cup.

"I don't believe that. Anyway, I've had enough. I delivered Lafitte to the restaurant like you wanted, against my better judgement. And you screwed up."

"It happens sometimes. Doesn't matter now, anyway. We got him, he's history."

She made a show of looking at her watch. "I have to go," she said. "I meant it; I've had enough. I won't be doing anything else for you." She pushed her chair back.

Javid Nasir was wiping his hands on a tissue. Without looking at her he said, "Have you forgotten who gave you your job and your fat salary?" He balled the tissue and tossed it onto the table.

She was half expecting some such comment. Nasir was a director of Tolgate and he owned a minority shareholding. "Makes no difference. I'm good at what I do. The company needs me and there's nothing you can do about that." Her chair scraped as she stood up.

"You sure?" He was looking up and grinning. "The thing is, sweetheart, I bought Harry's shares. As of last week, I own Tolgate. One hundred per cent." The grin vanished as he paused, seemingly for effect. "So you will continue to do *exactly* as you're told."

It was a turn of events that Naomi had not seen coming. The threat of being fired hit her like a slap in the face. But she was not prepared to be bullied just to keep her job. She stooped so that she was closer to him and she stared into his eyes.

"Is that a fact?" Her simmering anger was taking control.

She hissed, "I know enough to get you banged up in jail for a long time. A very long time, you bastard. Stick your job up your arse."

The rush of adrenalin was a heady tonic. She straightened and turned to leave, but he grabbed her wrist and stood up. "Before you go," he said in a tone dripping with menace, "Remember this – we can get to you anywhere and anytime we want." He tapped her cheek with a finger. "Think about that. What would surgery do to your pretty face, eh?"

CHAPTER THIRTY-SEVEN

Despite the ungodly hour the following morning in Donfield, Detective Chief Inspector Royce was fully alert. He had been waiting weeks for this day and it was here at last. There was no better feeling. Years of patient policing occasionally provided the heady reward of bringing to justice felons whose criminal behaviour was an affront to decent, law-abiding folk. People whom it was his job to protect. This was to be one of those times. The joy of its anticipation was so strong it was positively delicious.

"No cock-ups, Charlie." Chief Superintendent Flack was hunched over, scowling and twirling a pencil in his fingers. He was clearly not happy to be there at that hour. In his unshaven face his tired, bloodshot eyes blinked. His manner was brusque. "The biggest collar this nick's ever had," he growled.

Seated across the desk, Royce agreed. "Yes, sir."

Flack pointed with the pencil. "Run through it one more time, from the top."

Royce checked his notes. "Sunrise today was at four fifty-seven. First prayers had to be before that and they take about ten minutes. Allowing fifteen minutes for them to get back from the mosque, both should've been home by five twenty-five, give or take." He checked his watch. "It's five forty-seven now."

Flack groaned, pushed the pencil aside and wiped his face with his hands. "Yeah, I know."

Royce glanced up, then back to his notes. He went on. "Simultaneous pick-ups, six-thirty on the dot. Two squads: I'll go for Mahmud. Colin and Jimmy will pick up Abdullah. Uniformed back-up out of sight for both."

"Communication?"

"Continuous, from the moment we leave. Abdullah's in Bridge Lane. The Imam's house is in Middle Meadows, Kitchener Road."

Flack nodded. "I know. Make sure the pick-ups are low key. No marked vehicles in sight. Don't even think about sirens or lights. Any bugger doing that will find himself on dog-shit patrol, pronto."

"We need to leave at six-ten, latest," Royce observed.

"Everybody here?"

"Ready and waiting for the off, sir."

"Better get on, then." The Chief Super sat back and as Royce rose to leave he added, "Oh, before you go. Tell Jenny to fetch me a coffee, Charlie. Two sugars."

In Kitchener Road shortly after, Inspector Royce said quietly, "It's this one, number fifty-five."

Some of the houses on the street were showing lights, but only in their upstairs windows. The pavement was deserted and the air smelt clean and fresh, glowing in the early morning light. Royce radio checked his back-up and the status of the second squad outside Abdullah's house. All were poised and ready. It was six-thirty and he gave the order to proceed. The operation was on.

With all seventeen stone of the six-foot-four frame of

Detective Constable Swan at his back, Royce stepped forward and rang the bell. They were kept waiting a full minute before the door jerked open to reveal the face of Imam Mahmud. He seemed astonished, but only for a split second. The man's face briefly displayed amazement and then a flash of anger, before becoming a blank mask.

The cleric was not wearing his spectacles. His collarless shirt was undone and his hair was awry. He was clearly not as composed as he might have wished to appear. Slowly, he pushed the door to a partly closed position.

"Inspector? What can you want at this hour?"

Royce took his time. "Oh, I think you know the answer to that, Mr Mahmud."

The Imam looked up. "You know I am a busy man. I have duties to perform." His eyes flickered, taking in the considerable presence of the man behind Royce. He shook his head. "This is intolerable," he said, his voice a tone higher than normal. "Please explain yourself."

Got him! Over the years the detective had used the statutory warning hundreds of times, but never before had he felt such intense satisfaction at the anticipation of doing so. He took his time, savouring every word.

"Zulfikar Ali Mahmud, I am arresting you on suspicion of complicity in the murder of Sayeed Iqbal in the early hours of Sunday, March seventh of this year. You do not have to say anything, but it may harm your defence if you do not mention, when questioned, something which you later rely on in court. Anything you do say may be given in evidence."

The cleric's inscrutable mask slipped. His eyes rounded and his mouth fell open. Then he tried to close the door, but the detective's foot was firmly in place to prevent that.

The Imam blurted, "You can't do this. I'm not going."

"Yes, I can, sir." Royce held up his warrant card. "You know who I am. My colleague here is Detective Constable Swan. We have a valid warrant empowering me to arrest you." He put the card away, adding calmly in a firm tone, "We require you to accompany us to the police station. Right now, please."

The man opened the door fully. His body shook and his eyes were bulging. "I know what this is about. You are discriminating against me because I am a Muslim. I will not stand for it." He was breathing heavily, a distinct note of fear in his response. "My people will not stand for it. You are forcing me to go with you. I want to call my lawyer and I am saying nothing until he comes."

The Chief Inspector allowed himself a small smile. He replied quietly, "I have already told you sir, that you do not need to say anything at this stage. You can contact your legal representative from the police station, but I must insist that you come with us now. Please bear in mind that if you resist, we have the right to use any necessary force to do what we need to."

That did it. The man acquiesced, his reluctance to cooperate made clear with every measured, slow step. He had nothing to say.

Back in his superior's office, Royce watched as the Chief Superintendent reached for a chocolate-covered biscuit from the packet on his desk, saying, "Which one will you interview first?"

"Abdullah," Royce replied. "Mahmud's not ready; his

solicitor's only just arrived."

Flack snorted. "Took his time, didn't he? It's been an hour since he called them." He took a bite and pushed the packet across. "Have a biscuit."

"Thank you, sir." Royce took one. "It's a woman. Colin's taken her to see him. I'm guessing that's one Imam who's not a happy man."

"A woman?"

"Amina Datta."

The Chief's eyebrows arched. "Unusual."

"She's with the Younis law firm." Royce's mouth formed a twisted smile. "The way I see it, could be the senior partners are making a point."

Flack swallowed, reaching for another biscuit. "Such as?"

"I know the firm. Good people, respected by the Muslim community." Royce bit into his biscuit, gesturing as he munched. "Haroun Younis loathes Mahmud, calls him a hate-peddling jihadist."

"So why hasn't he shopped him?"

Royce shrugged. "I'm guessing he can't unless he's got proof of something criminal. Unlikely, is that."

"So what's her being a woman got to do with it?"

"Men like the Imam have no respect for women. It's not in their nature, or creed. They treat them like slaves. Sending a bright, educated woman to advise him says it all. In Mahmud's eyes, it'd be an insult. Likely he'll think they sent her on purpose."

Flack snorted. "Well, now. There's a thought." He reached for another biscuit. "All in all, a great result, Charlie. We've done well."

We? Royce stifled the urge to comment. No matter, he

was right and it really was a good result. Everyone knew about the Chief's weakness for chocolate biscuits and the fact that there was always a packet in his desk drawer. But Royce could not remember him ever passing them around before. No doubt about it, his boss was well pleased. He replied, "Yes, sir. And with the documents translated now, we should be able to wrap it up."

"Should be? I'm betting it's all over. The Chief will be crowing to the press tomorrow, you mark my words."

"I'm not so sure. The problem is that it's still all circumstantial. We've nothing that links Mahmud directly to any crime. But the documents may make a difference. We'll see."

A double knock on the door prompted Royce to look up. It was Brody. Flack put the biscuits away in a drawer and waved him in. "Come in, Colin."

The Detective Sergeant was holding a file. He put it on the end of the desk. "There's a problem, sir," he said. "Mahmud refused to speak to the solicitor. Went ballistic, in fact, shouting at her."

Royce asked, "What did he say?"

"No idea. It was all in Arabic or something. He waved his arms around like a lunatic."

Royce said, "Where's the lady?"

"She left, said something about sending someone else. I felt really sorry for her."

Flack made a dismissive gesture. "OK, no rush. You can get on with interviewing Abdullah, then, Charlie. I'll be down to watch."

Royce stood up. "Right, let's do it. You coming, Colin?"

On the way to the interview room, Brody said, "When we picked him up, it was like he was expecting us."

"What do you mean?"

"He was no problem. I mean, he didn't seem surprised. And he never gave us a moment's trouble. Just came along."

"He wasn't bothered? Interesting," Royce replied. So, was the big man resigned to his fate? Or was he so confident that he believed that there was no proof of his guilt? *Soon find out.* They paused outside the interview room and Royce nodded to the uniformed constable at the door.

"Any problems, Constable?"

"Quiet as a lamb, sir. The Sarge told him he could have a brief, but he said no." The man opened the door and the detectives entered.

Standing near the door was another uniformed constable. Kemal Abdullah was seated at the interview table, hunched over with his arms crossed. Royce and Brody placed their files on the table and took the chairs opposite him.

Royce began. "This is a formal interview, Mr Abdullah. We'll be recording it but before we start I need to ask if you want to call in a solicitor. If you don't have one, we can arrange for one to be called for you."

Abdullah looked up. "No need."

"As you wish." Royce started the recorder, checked his watch and said, "Tuesday twenty-first April, interview of Mr Kemal Abdullah by Detective Chief Inspector Royce and Detective Sergeant Brody. Interview commenced at oh-nine-twelve hours. Mr Abdullah has been offered legal representation and declined."

The Inspector opened his file and spoke in a measured

tone. "Mr Abdullah, can you tell us where you were between the hours of midnight on Saturday the sixth and the early hours of Sunday the seventh of March this year?"

Abdullah scowled. "At home."

"We believe that you were directly involved in the murder of Mr Sayeed Iqbal in Milford Park on that day and at that time. There were two others involved, Rafiq al-Ghani and Ibrahim Mahmud. What do you have to say to that?"

Abdullah took a deep breath and sat back. His face bore a tired, resigned look and he did not reply. Royce waited for half a minute before saying, "You have not answered. Would you like me to repeat the question?"

Again there was a stony silence. Kemal Abdullah did not respond, merely shutting his eyes. After another half minute, the Chief Inspector said, "Mr Abdullah has not replied or responded to the question. For the record, he has shut his eyes." He paused for a few seconds before continuing. "Mr Abdullah, I shall ask you once more to confirm that you were present at the murder of Sayeed Iqbal. If you do not reply I shall have to terminate this interview."

Abdullah opened his eyes, stared at Royce for a few seconds and then closed them again. Royce said, "Mr Abdullah has not replied or responded in any way." He glanced at his watch. "This interview is suspended at oh-nine-fifteen, to be resumed later." He switched the recorder off and spoke to the uniformed policeman. "Take Mr Abdullah back to his cell, please, Constable."

Chief Superintendent Flack seemed disappointed. He, Royce and Brody were making their way back to the CID offices. "You've got the boy's statement. You could have used that to open him up. Or the bloody print on the card." He had watched the interview from the adjacent room through the one-way glass window. "Sooner he cracks, the better."

"It didn't feel right. He's still a long way off confessing. Let him cool his heels for a while. Likely he'll spend the time worrying. Then I'll go back and use what we have. I'm certain he doesn't know about the thumbprint."

The superintendent said, "Mahmud's solicitor's here; he's with him at the moment. Do you want to tackle him now?"

"Has the interpreter arrived? I asked for Urdu."

"On the way, I believe," Flack replied.

"I'll wait till he gets here. Gives me time to go through my notes."

The interpreter was a short woman wearing a hijab. She arrived shortly after and was shown into Royce's office. He was at his desk, a file open before him. Brody was seated opposite. At the Inspector's invitation she took a seat.

Royce said, "We've not met before, Miss."

"I'm Jamila Khan, Inspector. I'm on your list." She had a round, open face. She was wearing heavy spectacles and holding a document case.

"Do you do Urdu?" Royce asked.

She nodded. "Yes, and Punjabi."

"It has to be Urdu. Do you read it?"

"Yes."

"Good. There are documents involved, they were translated yesterday. By your firm, I believe. Sorry I had to ask, it's important."

"They use different scripts, sir. The spoken languages are pretty similar and I'm fluent in both. I read Urdu but not Punjabi."

"I know they're different. The documents are in Urdu." He asked, "Do you know Imam Zulfikar Mahmud?"

"I know who he is but I've not met him."

Royce asked, evenly, "I believe he has strong views about certain things. Have you heard him preach?"

She smiled slightly before answering, "You don't need to worry, Chief Inspector. I just do my job, my personal feelings are not relevant."

Royce decided that he liked this woman. "Thank you. No offence, but I have to be sure."

"None taken. I just interpret and I do it without bias. But for your information, I can't stand the man."

Yes, he definitely liked her. Good, there should be no problems taking on the Imam. Not with the language, anyway. He said, "Thank you. If you're ready, we'll go down now." He picked up his file and added, "If you don't mind my asking, what's your first language?"

"English, Chief Inspector."

CHAPTER THIRTY-EIGHT

When Royce, Brody and the interpreter entered the interview room, the Imam and his solicitor were seated on one side of the table. The solicitor was a thin man whose lightly pock-marked brown face bore a neat moustache. He and his client had their heads together, speaking quietly. The cleric looked up and instantly his face darkened.

He nodded dismissively towards the interpreter. "Who is this woman?" he demanded.

Royce did not answer immediately. He turned to her and said, "Please take a seat, Miss Khan." Taking his time, he placed his file on the table and looked directly at Mahmud.

"Miss Khan is a professional linguist who works for the accredited service provider appointed by West Yorkshire police. She is here to act as interpreter, in your interests as much as ours, Mr Mahmud."

The cleric reacted by turning sharply to his solicitor and making a comment. The language was foreign but there was no mistaking the man's anger.

Jamila Khan spoke. "Mr Mahmud said that he objects to my presence, Chief Inspector. He said that if I do not leave, he will not agree to be interviewed." She added, drily, "To be perfectly accurate, what he actually said was that he would not agree to be interviewed unless I am dismissed."

Royce looked at the Imam. "You are entitled to choose

your own legal representative, Mr Mahmud. That concession does not extend to specialists employed by the police. I am now about to commence the interview and start the recording machine. I must ask you to use English, please. Miss Khan is here, so you do not have to, but I suggest that you do because it will be a lot easier for us all."

The Imam sat stony-faced. He did not reply. Royce switched on the machine. After setting the scene, he said, "Mr Mahmud, you have been arrested on suspicion of complicity in the murder of Sayeed Iqbal in the early hours of Sunday seventh of March this year, in Milford Park. A formal statement has been taken from one of the three people who carried out the murder. He has named you as the person who planned and organized the crime. What do you say to that?"

The man replied, deadpan. "I am innocent. You have no proof. What statement? Who made it?"

It was Sergeant Brody who replied. "Your nephew Ibrahim."

Mahmud snorted. "Huh, I should have known. Anything he says is not evidence, it is worthless."

Royce asked, "Why do you say that?"

"I know the boy. You cannot believe a word he says; he's a dysfunctional teenager." The words came out easily, but the man looked uncomfortable.

"Are you saying that he has a mental health problem?"

"Absolutely. He is naive, easily led." Mahmud seemed to be regaining his confidence. "If he was involved, he must have been forced into it." He glanced at his lawyer, and then went on. "Whoever did it must have bullied him. It's nothing to do with me."

Brody appeared about to say something, but Royce intervened. "You're saying that he's mentally unstable? He's been living with you for two or three years so I suppose you should know."

"Yes, I do." Mahmud made a dismissive gesture. "The boy is not insane, you understand, but as I say, naive and easily led. Maybe he's been keeping bad company."

"You seem to be quite concerned about him."

"Of course I'm concerned; I'm his uncle."

Royce nodded. "Understandable. So why didn't you report him missing?"

Mahmud sat up. The shocked look on his face showed that he had not seen that coming. He shrugged. "I didn't know he was missing. He has friends. If he's away for a day or two, why should I think he was missing?"

"He's not been home since Saturday, has he? I put it to you that you've not reported him missing because you know where he is and you almost certainly know that he gave himself up. You didn't report him missing because you knew he was in police custody. Isn't that so?" Royce looked down at his notes. The Imam did not reply and the Inspector added, "He says that you ordered him and another person to attack soldiers from a British army base in Wiltshire that night."

Beads of sweat had appeared on the cleric's brow. He turned to glance briefly at his lawyer, whose eyebrows arched as he shook his head lightly. Now clearly in some distress, Mahmud blurted, "I know nothing about that. He's lying, you have no proof." He was breathing heavily. "I want to confer with my lawyer."

Chief Inspector Royce leaned forward, placing his elbows

on the table. He locked his fingers and rested his chin on them, glaring at the man. Several long moments later he said, "Very well. We'll take a break. I'm suspending this interview and we'll resume in twenty minutes."

In Superintendent Flack's office Royce was staring pensively into his coffee cup. His superior had asked him why he had not pushed Mahmud harder.

"I thought it was the right moment to give him time with his solicitor. I want him to know that he's in trouble. His brief will tell him how bad it is."

"What about the MP's card?"

"I'm sure he knows about it, but there's no direct link to him. Not yet." He drained the cup. "After the card, the documents; one thing at a time. That way he gets to feel the net tightening. Better chance of him slipping up."

A double knock on the door announced Sergeant Brody's arrival. He bustled in, holding papers that he handed to Flack. "This has just come in, sir. Email from the Met. Rafiq al-whatever's folded. A confession and a full statement."

Flack took it and began reading. Royce could not wait. "Has he given up Mahmud?"

Brody beamed. "Nailed him, good and proper."

The interview with Mahmud was resumed shortly after. The Imam seemed to be trying to put on his inscrutable mask, but he was plainly anxious. He frowned and his eyes were not still. Beside him, the solicitor was flicking through papers, looking far from relaxed.

Royce took his time starting the recorder and going

through the formalities involved in resuming the interview. He began with a question.

"Mr Mahmud, with reference to the murder of Sayeed Iqbal on the seventh of March, is it not the case that you ordered Kemal Abdullah, Rafiq al-Ghani and Ibrahim Mahmud to lure Mr Iqbal out and kill him? Did you not order Kemal Abdullah to decapitate him?"

The Imam's head jerked back. He looked as if he had been slapped in the face. He passed his tongue around his lips, blinked and then replied, his voice quavering, "I had nothing to do with it. If they killed him it must have been Abdullah who planned it." The man was breathing heavily again. "You have no proof that I was involved. No proof."

"Are you saying it was Kemal Abdullah who was responsible for planning the murder?"

"I don't know for sure."

"We know that there were three them. If it wasn't Abdullah, was it planned by Rafiq al-Ghani?"

"I don't know," Mahmud mumbled.

"It surely wasn't your nephew Ibrahim?"

"No, not possible."

"So it must have been Abdullah?"

Mahmud's distress was clearly showing. "I told you, I don't know. But it wasn't me. I had nothing to do with it." He whined, "You have no proof that I was involved."

"So it must have been Abdullah? Is that what you're saying?"

"Yes."

Again the Chief Inspector paused. The Imam had a hunted look on his face and his brow was damp. Royce could almost smell his fear.

Beside him, the solicitor was checking through his papers.

Finally the Chief Inspector spoke again. "We now have statements from two of the three individuals who carried out the murder. The statements were taken separately and at different locations. Both name you as the person who planned and ordered the crime. Do you have anything to say about that?"

"They're lying. I was not involved. You have no proof that I was." The words tumbled out rapidly. The man was clearly under severe stress.

Royce said nothing. After a few long moments, the solicitor broke the silence. "My client is right, Chief Inspector. The statements are not actual proof that he was involved. If you have nothing stronger I don't think you can charge him and I must ask you to release him. As you know, he has duties in the mosque at mid-day."

Royce checked his watch. He shut the file and said, "We're not finished yet, I have some more questions. This interview is suspended, to be resumed shortly." He checked his watch. "The time is ten forty-seven." Without waiting for a response he switched off the recorder. "We'll resume in twenty minutes."

Sergeant Brody and the interpreter followed Royce out of the room. The Chief Inspector strode forward purposefully and despite being taller Brody had to make an effort to keep up. Miss Khan followed. Brody had seldom seen Royce so intensely focused.

His superior turned in mid-stride. "Colin, I want you to get Abdullah and bring him to interview room two. Right now, please. I'll go on and meet you there." To the interpreter he said, "Miss Khan, you can take a break if you like. The coffee machine's in the corridor outside the main office. Please meet us back here in twenty minutes."

Brody replied to the retreating figure of his boss, saying, "Yes, sir." Then he turned to the interpreter.

"Are you OK to find the machine, Miss?"

"I'll manage, thank you, Sergeant."

"Sorry I have to leave you on your own."

"No problem."

"See you later," he replied. "And by the way, the coffee's awful."

Royce was waiting at the table when the duty constable let Brody and Abdullah in. A uniformed officer stood quietly by the door.

When they were seated, Royce said, "We'll be formally interviewing you again, Mr Abdullah. This won't take long, but before we start there's something you should know." Abdullah did not reply.

Royce said, "First, I must ask you if you still wish to proceed without a solicitor to represent you. I shall be revealing to you new evidence that may place you in a worse position. There is a substantial case against you now and you are facing a long prison term. Very long."

The man frowned and shook his head. "No solicitor."

There was no doubt that Royce had his full attention as he continued. "The reason I am telling you this before we start is that the best thing that you can do for yourself is to try to reduce the length of the sentence you will receive. I know that you care deeply about your mother's welfare. You will certainly go to prison and you won't be able to help her from there. I cannot make any promises but if you cooperate fully there is a chance that it could make a difference to the length of time that you are away." The detective paused, deliberately. In a softer tone, he said, "Do you understand?"

Abdullah's expression was bleak. He nodded and answered, quietly, "Yes."

Relieved that the man had abandoned his silent stonewalling, Royce said, "Good. Let's get on with it." He started the recorder and set the scene, concluding with the words, "Mr Abdullah has been offered legal representation but has again declined."

Royce opened his file, withdrew the plastic envelope containing the blood-stained calling card and held it up. "Do you recognize this?"

Sergeant Brody said, "For the record, Chief Inspector Royce is showing the suspect the envelope marked Exhibit D4."

There was a clearly audible sharp intake of breath from Kemal Abdullah as his face froze in a look of total surprise. He stammered, "I... yes."

"It's a business card, one of those used by Member of Parliament Edmund Lafitte. It has a clear thumbprint on it and it was found on the body of Sayeed Iqbal, the man who was killed on the seventh of March. You have admitted that you recognize it. Can you confirm that?"

Abdullah lowered his head. In a voice barely above a whisper he said, "Yes."

Royce put the envelope down and leaned back. In an easy, relaxed manner he said, "Thank you, Mr Abdullah. You know what I don't understand?" He waited for a moment before continuing, adopting a conversational tone. "Why did you put it back?"

Now seemingly off guard, the big man responded. "It wasn't my idea, I was..." He blinked and stopped abruptly.

"You were instructed to put it back on the victim, weren't you? After you'd removed everything else? Who ordered you to put it back?" Abdullah did not reply.

Royce shook his head. "It would have been better for you if you'd removed it. But everything comes out, in the end. The truth will out, as they say."

The suspect's face seemed drained of all emotion. His eyes locked into a stare. Royce placed his arms on the table and leaned forward. "We know the print isn't yours. It was made by Ibrahim. He's told us that he was ordered to take part. Do you really want to incriminate that young man more than he deserves to be?"

In that small, enclosed room, the silence that followed generated an overpowering tension. Finally, Abdullah admitted in a flat monotone, "I was told to put it back. I handed it to Ibrahim to do that. It was not his fault."

Royce asked, "Who ordered you?" The man did not reply. The Chief Inspector said, "You're protecting someone. We both know who that person is." There was another brief silence. Royce leaned back again and spoke more quietly. "Mr Abdullah, we have just interviewed Imam Mahmud." The suspect looked up. Royce had his full attention. "I have to tell you that he stated that the murder was nothing to do with him and that it was planned and implemented by you."

Abdullah's eyebrows arched. He did not need to say a thing; the disbelief was evident in his face. Royce went on, "And that is now on record. If you wish to cooperate with us, now is the time to set the record straight. Are you ready to give us a statement?"

Abdullah wiped his face with his hands. "Will it help me?"

"Probably. Like I said, I cannot make you any promises, but I do believe it will."

The man nodded his head slowly. "I will make the statement."

Royce replied, "Thank you." A sense of relief flooded through him. Three down, one to go. He looked at his watch. It had taken just seven minutes.

The Chief Inspector left Sergeant Brody to take Abdullah's statement. A few minutes later he and Sergeant Jimmy Poulter met the interpreter Jamila Khan outside the other interview room. Before entering, Royce looked through the one-way window in the adjacent observation room. Mahmud and his solicitor were seated at the table. The lawyer was looking down at his notes. The Imam was frowning and he had his arms folded across his chest. A defiant stance? No matter, Royce was ready.

The three went in and took chairs opposite. Royce placed his file on the table. The solicitor made eye contact and nodded briefly but the Imam sat still, his impassive face registering no emotion.

The Chief Inspector said, "We are about to resume the formal interview, Mr Mahmud. Before we start, is there anything you may wish to say to me?"

The Imam ignored the question, staring straight ahead. His solicitor answered, "My client is ready, Chief Inspector. But he wishes to make it clear that he needs to get to the mosque for mid-day prayers."

"I don't think that's going to happen. Your client is under arrest and this is a murder enquiry, as you know."

The man replied, "He is certain that it's a mistake. Please proceed if you must."

Royce nodded. "Thank you." He started the recorder and began by stating the date and time, setting the scene, naming all present and noting the substitution of Sergeant Brody with Sergeant Poulter. Then he opened his file and removed three sheets of paper. He handed one to the interpreter and placed another on the table between Mahmud and the solicitor, who both looked down, scanning it.

"These are photocopies of a document that has come into our possession," Royce said, placing the third on the table between himself and Poulter. "We have some questions..."

Mahmud interrupted sharply. "Where did you get this? It's private, nothing to do with the murder. Where did you get it?" His manner was belligerent, but with a hint of rising panic in his voice.

Royce ignored the question. "This document was written by hand. Is it your handwriting, Mr Mahmud?"

The Imam slammed his fist onto the table and turned to make an angry comment to the solicitor in his own language.

Jamila Khan said, "Mr Mahmud asked his lawyer how the police have acquired a copy of one of his personal documents."

Royce intervened. "That's not the issue here. I have to ask you again Mr Mahmud, is that your handwriting?"

The Imam spoke directly to Royce, raising his voice. "I will not answer that. It's a page from a business file from the mosque. You have no right to go to my office there."

"You refuse to answer? Very well. For the record, I will

state that the document is handwritten in Urdu. It appears to be a ledger detailing names of Muslim businesses and persons who have been making payments to you. The amounts and dates are recorded on the document. You will note that three of the names have been struck through. We believe it is no coincidence that they are the names of three persons who have died recently." Looking directly at the cleric, he added, "In questionable circumstances that we shall be looking into again."

The Imam's chair fell over and clattered to the floor. He had shoved it back and stood up, clearly very angry. He shook his fist, his face contorted in fury as he raised his voice to a near-shout. "I told you that's nothing to do with you. I do not wish to proceed with this farce any longer. You must release me *now*." The man was leaning forward, glaring at the Chief Inspector. Droplets of white spittle had appeared at the edges of his mouth.

In the silence that followed this outburst, the solicitor's face betrayed his shock. He said something rapidly in a foreign tongue.

Beside Royce, the interpreter remarked, "Mr Mahmud's lawyer has asked him to be calm. He said that they will contest this intrusion of privacy later."

The Chief Inspector said, "Good advice, Mr Mahmud." The constable at the door stepped forward and picked up the Imam's chair.

Royce said, "Thank you, Constable." To Mahmud he said, "Please sit down, we are not finished and this interview will terminate when I decide that it should."

Imam Mahmud glanced behind to check his chair. Then he sat down heavily and brought his hands together, locking his fingers. He hunched his shoulders and his brow knitted as he lowered his head, glaring through the round spectacles at his adversary.

The Chief Inspector opened his file again and removed some papers. Using a calm and deliberate tone he said, "I have here photocopies of a document that appears to be a printout of an email letter sent to you, Mr Mahmud, together with an accredited translation into English." He separated the papers. There were three sets, each of two pages stapled together. He handed one to the interpreter and placed another on the table between the Imam and his solicitor. Their heads swivelled as they began to scan to top page.

Putting the third copy down, he continued, "You will note that the email was sent on Thursday the eleventh of March. It has been identified as coming from a known terrorist cell in Pakistan and was addressed to you personally, Mr Mahmud." The Imam's eyes rounded and his mouth fell open.

Royce went on. "The letter congratulates you, sir, on what is described as your successful operation to carry out the assassination that served to put down dissenters who refused to pay your organization. It also tells you to carry out operations against the British Army and suggests that several small attacks at different locations would be more effective than a single large one. It refers specifically to the Wembley bomb as an example." Imam Mahmud's head dropped and he covered his face with his hands.

Once again the room fell silent. Royce felt a tightening in his chest. Curiously, he reflected, he felt more relieved than triumphant. A good moment, nevertheless. He went on, "Like the other, this document was gifted to us. We are satisfied that no crime was committed by the donor." He could not resist twisting the knife. "The only surprise is that the email was copied and not destroyed." He looked directly at the Imam. "Vanity? Perhaps from your viewpoint an unfortunate error of judgement? No matter. For the record, I have to tell you that the three persons who carried out the murder of Sayeed Iqbal have now all made statements to that effect, naming you as the instigator who planned it. I must now ask you if you have any comment that you wish to put on record."

The Imam leaned towards his solicitor and whispered something. The solicitor nodded, saying, "My client has nothing to add at this time. He declines to make a statement."

The Chief Inspector nodded. "Understood. Interview concluded at," he checked his watch, "eleven thirty-one." He switched off the recorder.

Superintendent Flack had a huge smile on his face as he passed the chocolate biscuits around. Seated with him in his office were Royce and his two sergeants.

Flack enthused, "I told you, Charlie. Didn't I tell you? The Chief'll be crowing to the media. He said he's organizing a press conference for this evening."

Royce allowed himself a smile. "Pity we didn't get a confession from the bastard." He bit into a biscuit. "But with the three statements stitching him up and the incriminating documents, I can't see any jury acquitting him."

Brody said, "You can bet on that. No chance." He leaned forward and took another biscuit.

Superintendent Flack beamed. "A great result. Well done,

all of you." He picked up the packet of biscuits, placing it carefully in an open drawer, which he pushed shut.

Sergeant Poulter's eyes were shining as he said to Royce, "Fantastic, sir. You're a genius."

"You think so? Do me a favour, Sergeant."

"What?"

Royce smiled. "Tell my wife."

CHAPTER THIRTY-NINE

Naomi Porter felt quite out of place at the funeral. Apart from Stella and Hakim, there was nobody present whom she knew. Not that she had expected anything different. She did a quick head count. Only fourteen people were at the cremation service. She would not have been there, she reflected, had Stella not invited her. It was to be a 'low key' ceremony, a friends and family-only service. No publicity, absolutely no press or media presence. And that bastard Nasir had insisted that she should attend. She was invited, so that would be what was expected. Everything had to be normal and seen to be so.

Amir Hakim had delivered the eulogy. He kept it short and dignified. As the coffin moved slowly on noiseless rollers towards its fiery end, Naomi wondered who had chosen the music playing softly in the background. It was the Sanctus from Fauré's *Requiem*. Soothing, sublime and totally appropriate.

Ed would have approved.

Immediately following the ceremony, the mourners lingered in the porch outside the building. Stella was at the centre of a small knot of people. Naomi stood alone, waiting. Amir Hakim was standing to one side.

He saw her and came over. "Stella's glad you came."

"He was my friend," she replied, "although we'd met only

three times. Pity the coffin was closed, I'd like to have seen him just once more."

"Actually the lid was secured and the undertaker told Stella that it would be better left that way. Fortunately she didn't mind."

"A bit unusual, don't you think? Why was it sealed?"

He made a face. "The body was identified by DNA and fingerprint checks. It was Edmund, all right. Could be the undertaker botched the repair. A difficult job I should think, considering how he was killed." He shook his head. "Ghastly business."

Stella's guests were leaving and she could be seen making her goodbyes. When only one person remained, Stella brought her over. They made slow progress because her companion, an elderly lady, was leaning on a stick.

Stella introduced her as an aunt who had come to stay for a few days. To Naomi she said, "Thank you for coming. I think Edmund would have been glad that you did."

"We hadn't known each other long, but he was a good friend. I'll miss him."

They turned to walk to the car park. Stella replied, "We've been together eight years. We should have married, really."

"I get the impression that you were perfectly suited to each other," Naomi said.

"We were. The house seems so empty without him around." She glanced behind to see that her aunt and Amir were dropping back. "But life goes on." After a few moments they started walking again, more slowly, the gravel crunching beneath their feet.

"They sealed his coffin," Stella said. "You know, I'd like

to have seen him, just once more. But they advised against it. I should have insisted."

"Perhaps it was for the best." Naomi nearly made a reference to the manner of his death, but checked herself.

Stella seemed relieved to be talking frankly. "I had my doubts at first. About the identification, I mean. Despite the test results, I still wasn't sure, you know. Didn't want to believe it, I suppose." She smiled. "Until they mentioned the birthmark."

"Birthmark?"

"Yes, a distinctly star-shaped one. Didn't you know?"

Naomi shook her head. "He never mentioned it. Well, not the sort of thing that comes up in conversation. Where was it?"

Stella smiled. "Let's just say I'm glad you have to ask."

CHAPTER FORTY

"What?" Edmund could not believe what he was hearing. "You've got it wrong. Absolutely no way!"

Commander Richard Bennett's face was impassive. "I deal in facts," he snapped. "Whether you like it or not, the evidence is clear. I'm telling you, Nasir is a jihadist and Porter is under his control."

Bennett was older than Edmund had expected. In his fifties, he surmised. He had a shock of grey hair above a lightly lined, square-jawed face. Now he looked up, his eyes boring into Edmund's. No question, this was a man who exuded authority and knew how to use it.

They were seated opposite each other at the long dining table at the Farm. It was only that morning that Edmund had been told that Bennett and Platt were on their way to see him, but not why. Now he knew. He was being asked – no, told – to take part in an outrageous scheme to undermine Naomi. Did these people really believe that she was a puppet and that an IS operative was pulling the strings? A *jihadist?*

Edmund shook his head. "I'm sorry, but I just don't buy it. No way."

Seated beside Bennett, Inspector Mary Platt had been silent. She was looking down, stirring her coffee as she said, quietly, "We can understand why you find it difficult to believe, Edmund, but the evidence is pretty convincing. You believed us when we told you about her affair with Nasir, so look at the facts." She raised her head and her grey eyes rounded as she added, "She lured you to that restaurant. You were supposed to stay in your club, but she persuaded you to go. Nobody else knew in advance where you would be, at precisely that time."

Bennett interjected, his manner sharp and businesslike. "We know that the bomber was ordered by the Brotherhood people to kill you. Less than three days later, he turns up in the right place at exactly the right moment. And Porter was still in the cab; not a bad place to be when the bomb went off." He spread his hands. "Coincidence? I don't think so."

Edmund put his elbows on the table and covered his face with his hands. Could they be right? It certainly seemed possible. He sighed.

After a brief silence, Platt spoke again. "All we're asking you to do is to make a phone call. You don't have to go there, it'll be a man in our squad, disguised as you. If we're wrong, what's the worst that can happen? Nothing, because if she's not what we think, it'll be a no show. No one will turn up."

Bennett cut in. "But if we're right, we'll know for certain that Nasir is working for IS. In itself not direct proof, but we know how we can use it to get the proof we need."

Edmund felt hollow inside. He had to make a decision, but they were right about one thing. If the scheme failed, it would prove that they were wrong about Naomi. "All right, he said, wearily, "I'll do it."

Bennett nodded. He opened his document case, took out two pieces of paper and handed one to Edmund. "This is the gist.

Important that you relax and sound upbeat." He put the other sheet down and peered at it through his half-framed reading spectacles. "I've got a copy, we'll go through it together."

Edmund scanned the document. There were two horizontal bullet-pointed columns of print, one headed 'Mention' and below it, another titled 'Do not mention'. What the hell was all this?

He asked, "Why don't you just give me a script to follow? I mean, she's bright; she could see through this."

Bennett answered, "Not if you do it right. Just be yourself." He was clearly making an effort to be persuasive. "We'll do a few dry runs first, to get you relaxed and in the mood." Turning towards Platt he said, "Is there any more coffee, Mary?"

An hour later, Edmund felt ready to go ahead. They were at the table and Bennett and Platt each had blank sheets of paper and ballpoints to hand. Both were wearing ear-pieces that were connected to small electronic devices that Edmund was told were receivers that would allow them to listen in.

Commander Bennett asked, "Are we ready?" He was holding a mobile phone that he placed in front of Edmund. "Here's the mobile, pre-loaded with the number. Just tap the image on the screen."

Edmund hesitated. "There's something worrying me." It was a question that had been nagging at the back of his mind. "I'm supposed to be dead, right?"

"Yes."

"If they think I'm dead, why are we doing something that will show them I'm not?"

A smile appeared slowly on the Commander's face. "Don't worry about it. The people we're dealing with probably already know you're alive."

"But they claimed responsibility for killing me, right?"

"They would have done that anyway. Publicity is meat and drink to them. As far as they're concerned, you're history."

"So why bother coming after me again?"

Bennett closed his eyes briefly, displaying a look as if explaining something to a child. He spoke slowly. "Because if it comes out that you aren't really dead, they'd get the wrong sort of publicity. They'd look foolish and incompetent. Does that make sense?"

Edmund nodded. "I suppose so."

"Good." He pointed at the phone. "Actually, this is about nailing Nasir. A British MP who's spent years working himself into a position of trust. The truth is very different, he's with ISIS. We've known that for some time, but we can't prove it. The man is clever. Ruthless, he'll do anything to protect the image he's cultivated." He grimaced. "We have a real chance to expose him and that's exactly what I intend to do."

The penny finally dropped. They were using him as bait! Edmund said, "I get it. So I'm the sacrificial goat."

Bennett shrugged. "Not quite how I'd put it."

Platt said, "Goats don't wear body armour or carry guns. Anyway, it won't be you. The man taking your place is a professional. He'll be well covered."

Edmund picked up the mobile and took a deep breath. A thought occurred. "What do I do if it's a recorded message?"

Bennett checked his watch. "Good point. Sorry, I should have said. If that happens, just say you'll call again later. This phone won't leave a traceable number. Anyway, you should get a reply. She'll be on her lunch break."

Edmund checked the prompt sheet one more time and then tapped the display. After four rings, she answered.

"Naomi Porter."

"Are you sitting down?"

No immediate response. After a brief pause he heard an angry, querulous, *"Who is this?"*

"It's me, Edmund. Don't panic, don't..."

"Edmund? Edmund's dead. I don't know who you are but if this is your idea of a joke..."

"Sweetie, *listen*." He spoke rapidly, but calmly. "It's me, really. The video was faked. I'm alive and I'm OK. Don't hang up, don't go away."

In the background he heard a clattering noise against the general hubbub. It sounded like she had dropped a piece of cutlery. He went on, his voice still calm. "Yes, it's me. Just try to relax and listen."

"Is it really...?"

"It is. Are you alone?"

"What? Yes, as it happens. But..."

"It's me, believe it. All good news, but listen, please. I can't talk long; it's not safe. I'm OK, it was all faked. But that's got to stay a secret. I'll explain it all soon as I can, but it's important that you keep it to yourself for now."

"Where are you?" She sounded in control again.

"I can't say, but I'm being moved again. Today." He glanced at the paper. "I just wanted you to know I'm OK. The bad guys think I'm dead, so the heat's off for now."

"I can't believe this. It's wonderful! Can we meet?"

"Not yet, but maybe soon. I'm on my way to a houseboat, would you believe? In the Midlands, I think. They said I'll be getting a new identity soon."

"Shame. I quite liked the old one, actually."

"Got to go; I'll get back to you. Soon, I hope."

"Can I call you back?" She sounded anxious.

"No, it's not possible. I'm not supposed to be using this phone."

"The Midlands isn't far. Surely we can get together?"

"I haven't the faintest idea where I'll be. I overheard someone say that the boat's called Jenny May. I remember that because it was my mother's name, Jenny. Anyway, it's only a stopover for a couple of nights. I'll call you again when the coast is clear."

"Wait, don't go..."

"Sorry. Take care, see you soon." Edmund tapped the call off and slowly put the phone down. His shoulders sagged and his head dropped. He became aware immediately that his armpits were damp with sweat.

Commander Bennett leaned over and picked up the mobile. "Well done," he said. His eyebrows arched. "Was Jenny May really your mother's name?"

"No. It was Constance."

Bennett seemed impressed. "You had me fooled. Well done."

Edmund did not agree. In fact he felt deflated, downbeat, spent. Naomi's reactions weren't what he had expected. Before making the call he remained convinced that SO15 were wrong and that she was innocent. Now it seemed probable that she was not.

CHAPTER FORTY-ONE

Gravel scrunched under the wheels of the black limousine as it turned slowly into the car park of the Mariner's Arms hotel. The journey from Wales to the town of Eastdale had taken just over three hours. Seated in the back with Commander Blake, Edmund was tired. He was also ready for a good meal.

Blake leaned forward to speak to the driver and pointed ahead. "There it is. On the left, against the hedge."

The man turned the wheel. "I'll pull up alongside." He headed for a large white motorhome. In the passenger seat beside him, Inspector Platt clicked off her seatbelt.

"A camper van?" Edmund said. "I thought we were going to a houseboat."

"We are," Bennett replied. "Or rather, you are." The car pulled up beside the camper.

Bennett, Platt and Edmund were seated in the motorhome at a U-shaped bench with a rectangular table in the middle. An illustrated map of the immediate area was spread out before them. The driver of the motorhome, Constable Steve Scrivener, was a stocky man whose muscled torso stretched the white tee-shirt he was wearing. He was in the galley at the rear of the vehicle, making coffees.

Bennett looked up. "Where did you get the map?"

"From the marina office, sir. I marked Jenny May's mooring; it's at the end nearest the entrance to the basin from the canal. On the opposite side from the hotel. Monroe's already on board." He was referring to Sergeant Mike Monroe, whom Edmund had met in London. He added, "And the SRO teams are in place."

Edmund's curiosity got the better of his discretion. "What's SRO?"

Platt answered. "Specialist Rifle Officers. Snipers."

With just a hint of sarcasm, Bennett said, "Thank you, Inspector." Then he put his finger on the highlighted mooring mark. "The boat's been booked by a Mr and Mrs Saunders for the May Day weekend. That's you two," he said, looking at Platt and Edmund. "It's booked from today, Tuesday."

"We're not expecting any visitors tonight, are we?" Platt asked.

"Unlikely, they've not had enough time. Odds-on they'll try something tomorrow for sure. Friday is May Day, so the holiday weekend starts on Thursday evening, the day after tomorrow. That makes it a near cert that the attack will be tomorrow." He looked up again, addressing Scrivener. "Did you check the equipment, Constable?"

Scrivener came across with three mugs and placed them on the table. "All here and checked, sir." He nodded towards a monitor screen on the worktop. "And the hub's plugged in and working."

"I'll check that myself."

Edmund had assumed that it was a television set. "A hub?"

Bennett explained, patiently, "It's an interactive MS hub,

a communications device. I'll be able to direct the operation from here." He inclined his head. "Anything else?"

"Not that I can think of," Edmund murmured.

"Good," the commander snorted. "When you leave, Lafitte, you'll be wearing Challoner's protective vest. Bloody inconsiderate of him, pulling out at the last minute."

Platt smiled. "I don't think he got appendicitis on purpose, sir."

"His bad luck," Bennett growled. "He'll miss the fun." He looked at Edmund. "Unfortunately it was too late to get another man who could pass for you. And it has to be you, or someone who looks like you." His brow furrowed as he glared. "Listen to me. You are to go to your cabin and stay there. Do *not* go out on deck for any reason. You stay below until it's all over. Is that clear?"

Edmund nodded. "Yes." The man was rude but he could put up with that. He placed his elbows on the table. "Sorry, I should have said, I do have a question."

"Fire away."

"The boat's the nearest one to the entrance?" He pointed on the map. "What's to stop someone coming down the towpath from the canal side and lobbing a bomb onto it?"

The commander's mouth twisted into a smile. "We have all approaches covered. See these apartments fronting the wharf on each side of the basin?" He pointed. "Here and here. Our people are in them. Watching both sides as of this afternoon. Anyone perceived as an immediate threat will be taken out."

Edmund was startled. "Shot?"

"Immediately."

Edmund sat up and took a deep breath. "So Mary and I

will be at risk when we board the boat now? From snipers like yours."

"Technically, yes. But unlikely." He checked his watch. "You made the phone call five hours ago. Monitoring of all visitors to the complex began just before then, at noon. That includes the hotel and this car park. Nobody without a legitimate reason for being here will get past."

Edmund was not happy; there was still a risk. "Can you be certain of that?"

"Ah," Bennett said. "We've been planning this operation for a while and we usually know what we're doing." He shrugged lightly. "But I suppose nothing's *absolutely* foolproof." He had a small smile on his face. "Your presence here is proof of that. Should have been the unfortunate Constable Challoner."

Edmund's lips felt dry. He wiped them with his tongue. "OK," he mumbled.

Bennett continued, using a more moderate tone. "Good. You and 'Mrs Saunders' here will walk around the wharf," he said, tracing the route with an index finger on the map, "and board the Jenny May. She'll be the last one, at the end. Stroll – remember you're supposed to be on a holiday break. We're not expecting an attack tonight, but could be somebody watching. They wouldn't go ahead at all unless they thought you were here."

"Somebody watching? You said no-one can get through."

"Touché." The wicked smile appeared again. "I also said nothing's totally fool-proof."

It was an observation that did not exactly inspire confidence. The hollow feeling returned.

Edmund was finding it difficult to maintain a steady pace. The distance from the hotel car park to the wharf could not have been more than a hundred yards but in the soft twilight it seemed like a mile. He was dragging a wheeled suitcase, feeling exposed and anxious to get under cover. Vulnerable, a target. He was hot and had begun to sweat. The body armour didn't help. Beside him, Inspector Platt was carrying a sports bag.

"Take it easy," she said under her breath. "And for Christ's sake, relax."

"Sorry." He glanced down at her and checked his pace. "That bag looks heavy. Would you like me to carry it?"

"Thanks for the offer, but I'm OK. I'm stronger than I look."

A thought occurred. "Are you armed?"

"Of course."

"That'll be the weight in the bag, then."

She did not reply. He said, "I hate firearms, especially hand guns. No way would I ever use one."

"You've never fired a gun?"

"Only a shotgun. Clay pigeons, when I was a boy."

They were approaching the quay. Edmund took in the two blocks of low-rise apartments, one to his right and the other on the opposite side of the basin. In between was the expanse of water called Collier Basin, with vessels moored along the perimeter, many with their internal lights switched on. All were narrow boats of the type sometimes called barges.

A sign on the wall of the apartment block to the right declared that it was 'Waterfront North'. The wharf extended beyond, terminating at the Malcut Canal, the link to the basin from the River Deene. To their immediate left was the hotel, with its restaurant dining area and balcony.

"The boat's on the other side," Platt said. "We have to go around."

"I know. It's a long walk."

"Not really," she replied. "Five or six minutes, at most."

"Five or six minutes too long," he muttered, aware that they were overlooked by diners on the balcony above. He did not realise that he had increased his pace again.

Mary Platt put her arm through his and locked her elbow. She looked up at him, speaking through teeth clenched within an apparently broad smile. "Slow down, darling," she said. "Plenty of time."

"Sorry. It's the smell of food being grilled. I'm starving."

"And here's me thinking it's because you're scared shitless."

Edmund managed a nervous grin. "Come to think of it, I do feel a bit like a shitting duck. Any minute now you're going to notice a brown smell."

She spluttered and laughed out loud. A few of the diners' heads turned. Edmund said, "Shush, I'm trying to keep a low profile here."

"You're relaxing, that's good."

"Don't believe it. It's an act," he muttered, smiling and nodding as they passed a couple boarding a boat. They turned the corner and headed past the second block of apartments towards the entrance to the basin.

The vessel at the end must be the Jenny May, Edmund thought, suppressing the urge to break into a run. Mary Platt was doing a good job of holding him back but his eyes were busy, constantly scanning the area. Two young couples on the canal towpath beyond the basin were approaching, talking animatedly. Holidaymakers, no threat. Probably. He knew he was tense. *Get a grip*, he chided himself mentally. Only a few more metres to the boat's mooring point. Inside, the lights were on. No sign of Monroe.

"You're hungry?" Mary Platt asked, interrupting his thoughts.

Edmund's attention snapped back. They were approaching the aluminium boarding ramp. "I was," he replied. "Right now I think I've lost my appetite. It'll be back as soon as we're on board and out of sight."

"We'll be OK. Mike likes his food and he loves cooking. It's his hobby."

"You mean Sergeant Monroe?" Edmund recalled the only time he had met the man.

"Uh-huh."

"Any chance I can sneak back to the restaurant? I'm no fan of bread and water."

"Don't even think about it. We'll lock you in your cabin if we have to." He did not respond and she added, "I mean it," as she stepped onto the boarding ramp.

The following morning Edmund was lying on the bunk in his cabin, trying to read a book on his tablet. No good, it was impossible to concentrate, or to relax properly. He put the tablet aside, moved to the door and opened it slightly.

"I need a break. I'm going stir crazy here. Can I come out?"

"OK," Mary Platt answered. She was seated in the dining enclosure, using lightweight headphones with her tablet propped up on the table. "You can make some coffee."

Bright sunlight streamed in across the steps that led up to the deck but the interior was in shade. Cloth blinds had been drawn down over the windows on both sides of the vessel. Edmund moved to the kitchen and set about making coffees.

"Didn't seem to be much happening last night," he said. "Is Mike catching up on his sleep?" The two police persons had taken turns on watch overnight.

"He's outside, probably dozing. Hard to say; he's wearing shades."

"You're not expecting trouble during the day, then?"

"It's possible, but unlikely." She looked up. "I know what you're thinking, but don't worry. We've got the whole area covered. Surveillance." She pointed to the tablet and touched her earpiece. "Anything suspicious, we'll know at once."

He took two mugs of coffee over and stooped to set them down on the table. Platt was wearing shorts, he noticed. Her handbag was on the bench beside her. It was lying open, with the butt of a businesslike handgun clearly visible. Edmund slid onto the bench across from her.

"Can that gun go off by accident?" he asked.

"Impossible."

"How impossible? Guns make me nervous."

"Relax. It won't go off, it's a Glock."

He picked up his mug, "So?"

"The safety's built in. It's a double trigger mechanism. Doesn't matter, anyway. I don't think I'll be using it. And you certainly won't."

"That's for sure." Edmund took a sip from his mug. The sound of heavy thuds clumping down the steps prompted him to look over. Sergeant Mike Monroe entered, shrinking his large frame by ducking under the lintel.

"All quiet out there," he declared, pushing his sunglasses up onto his head. He rubbed his hands together. "I smelled coffee."

"You know where it is," Platt nodded, indicating the kitchen.

"I would've made you one," Edmund said, "but we thought you were dozing."

"Nah. Mind you, sitting in the sun can take your mind off the job."

"Shouldn't one of you be out there?" Edmund asked.

Monroe was at the worktop with his back to them. "Right little worrier, aren't you?" He swivelled his head, grinning. "Like you were when you missed out on stuffing your face at that restaurant."

Platt looked up sharply. "Enough of that," she snapped.

Monroe switched the kettle on. "OK." He shrugged. "The whole place is covered, so you can stop worrying. The only reason I was on deck is in case we have to move quickly." He patted the bulge in the pocket of the denim jacket he was wearing. "Me and my German friend here are ready for that."

Not if you're asleep, Edmund thought. He kept his feelings to himself.

In the 'Waterfront South' block that evening, at a panoramic window overlooking the darkening view of the basin, Sergeant Bob Evans put down his binoculars and peeled off his headphones.

"Nothing," he said. "Waste of time. My eyes hurt, time to

switch to night lenses."

Beside him, Specialist Rifle Officer Constable Glen Hogg drawled, "Too many punters around. My guess is they'll come after dark. If they're coming at all." He sat up and slapped his thighs.

"You hungry? The gaffer said we'd be getting something delivered from the restaurant."

"Sandwiches, I reckon. Prefer a fillet steak, I would," Evans replied in his pronounced Welsh accent.

The tablet on the table between them beeped. In the corner of the screen the image of Commander Bennett appeared. Evans tapped it.

Bennett's voice came through, relaxed and unhurried. "The quay lights are on, everyone. They don't look too bright. Sort of conditions that make an attack likely. Be on your toes for the next hour or so, dusk. If it doesn't happen now it'll be a late-night job. Anybody need anything?"

Evans was the only one who replied. He picked up his headphones and spoke into the microphone. "A bit of food would be good, sir."

"OK, we'll get that organized now." The image disappeared.

"I hope he's right," Glen Hogg said. "About the attack coming at dusk. Sooner the better, I say. I don't fancy another night in this place." His Heckler and Koch MSG rifle was on a tripod by his chair and he set about changing its telescopic sight for a night vision one.

CHAPTER FORTY-TWO

"The coffee's awful," Sergeant Bob Evans complained. He sank his teeth into a sandwich and then wiped a smear of mayo off his lips with the back of his hand. With bulging cheeks he added, "Beer would've been better."

"Yeah," Glen Hogg replied. "But as they say, rules is rules."

Hogg was the one watching the scene below when their tablet beeped. The image that appeared in the corner of the screen was that of WPC Philomena D'Souza, who was with another SRO marksman in the 'Waterfront North' apartment block. Evans tapped the screen.

The WPC's voice came through. "Suspicious male approaching from the canal towpath. Looks like a jogger, but I think he's wearing a backpack."

From the motorhome Commander Bennett responded immediately, his face appearing in another pane alongside the policewoman's. "Right, Phil. Full alert, everyone."

Bob Evans tossed his sandwich onto its plate. "Shit," he muttered, grabbing his binoculars.

SRO Hogg moved quickly to the wooden chair behind his rifle and wrapped his arms around the gun. He leaned forward, steadying himself to peer through the sight.

Bennett's voice came through again. "You're right, Phil. That's a backpack."

On the boat, Mary Platt was hunched over her tablet, staring intently at the screen. The image was a hazy view of the quay, the Jenny May at its mooring and the canal junction beyond. A figure on the towpath was approaching through the gloom, seemingly in no hurry. Platt straightened, scrambled over to the bathroom door and hammered on it. She bellowed, "Mike, out. *Now!*" Then she turned to Edmund, saying, "Get into your cabin. And stay there."

They heard Monroe's voice from inside the bathroom. "Just coming."

Platt picked up her bag and hurriedly fished out her Glock. Edmund hesitated, moving only when Platt swivelled her head to yell at him. "Go, *now!*" He reacted to the urgent tone and slipped into his cabin. His heart was thumping.

In the motorhome, Bennett touched the screen of the hub. Spreading a thumb and forefinger, he enlarged the image of the jogger, peering at it. The man seemed to be in no hurry. When he reached the corner of the quay where the canal joined the basin, he was about five metres from the Jenny May. He paused at the edge and glanced around briefly. Then he slid the pack off his back and lowered it to the ground. He stooped to kneel, as if re-tying a shoelace, but drew the bag forward instead.

The moment the bag was open, Commander Bennett barked, "Steady on the target. Fire only on my command."

The jogger removed from the bag a packet the size of a brick. He stood up, facing the boat, and raised his arm. He was holding the packet, his arm bent and poised to hurl it forward.

"Fire!" The single word was snapped out sharply.

Instantly, but not quite simultaneously, two rifle cracks echoed around the basin. Evans thought it was the first that shattered the terrorist's head. Almost immediately, the second one slammed into the torso, throwing the man backwards to the ground. The package fell from his hand and rolled over the edge into the water. Moments later it exploded with a muffled bang, spewing a column of water high into the air. *"Christ,"* Evans exclaimed, distracting Hogg, whose head turned.

"Two more," the Commander warned urgently. *"On the wharf. Take them out."*

Evans leaned forward, pointing. "There, coming out of the bushes. Get them."

Two men in battle fatigues and carrying stubby machine pistols were scuttling across the wharf towards the boat. By the time Hogg spotted them, one had been dropped in his tracks, felled with the crump of a rifle shot echoing around the basin. The other made it to the water's edge and jumped onto the deck of the boat.

Inside, Mary Platt was crouched against the rear bulkhead with her knees drawn up. She was holding the Glock with both hands, raised at arm's length. It was trained on the steps. She shouted, *"Mike, get out here."*

A staccato burst of gunfire shattered the wall panels of the staircase. The bathroom door burst open and Monroe lunged out and reached for his jacket. He had left it on the back of a chair and he scrabbled at the pocket, frantically trying to get to his pistol. A man in battle fatigues scrambled down the stairs, ducking under the lintel. He swung his machine gun around, spraying bullets in a deadly arc across the enclosure.

One struck Monroe, who collapsed to the floor.

Mary Platt fired her Glock twice at the assailant before she was hit by a round in her shoulder. She screamed and rolled over, still holding the weapon. The terrorist fell forward, flat to the floor with blood spurting from his chest. His gun slipped from his grasp, clattered and slid away, coming to rest against Monroe's inert body.

A metre away, the door to Edmund's room swung open. He emerged, a look of horror on his face as he scanned the narrow cabin. The terrorist had not given up. He was grunting, crawling on his belly towards his machine pistol. His fingers clawed at the deck, inching towards the gun.

Mary Platt, her left hand pressed against the wound in her shoulder, still had the Glock in her right hand. She was unable to raise it. In frustration she screamed at Edmund, "*Stop him.*" But Edmund did not move. He stood rooted to the spot, his face bearing a look of horrified incredulity.

The terrorist's hand was now close to his gun. He was breathing hard, his eyes narrowed, staring at Platt. Blood and spittle trickled from his mouth into his dark beard.

She shouted again, looking up at Edmund. "Stop him! *Take my gun, I can't use it.*"

At last, Edmund seemed to snap into the reality before him. He stooped, easing the Glock out of Platt's hand. Then he straightened, his body trembling as he pointed the gun. But nothing was happening; Edmund seemed to be rigid with shock, apparently unable or unwilling to do any more.

Mary Platt was appalled. "Shoot," she screamed. "*Pull the trigger, you fucking wimp!*"

Edmund Lafitte's hand was shaking like a sapling in a gale. He shut his eyes and squeezed the trigger.

CHAPTER FORTY-THREE

Deputy Chief Commissioner Helen Aylmer had insisted on watching the interview that morning. Not something that the DCC of the Met police had done often, as far as Commander Bennett knew. They were standing together outside the one-way glass window.

"Is this going to work?" she asked.

"Touch and go," he replied. "All we can do is give it our best shot."

"I'm not happy about Platt doing it."

"She insisted on being involved, as you know, ma'am."

"Yes. I've approved your recommendation of a gong for her."

"She deserves it. Which one?"

"Not my call," the DCC replied, nodding at the window. "They've started."

Inside, Inspector Mary Platt sat at the table with Sergeant Alan Cosgrove, a file at her elbow. On the opposite side were Naomi Porter and her solicitor. The woman looked pale and was wearing no make-up, bearing little resemblance to her image in the photographs that the inspector had seen. There was a spare chair at the end of the table.

Cosgrove switched on the recorder, flipped open his notepad, and formally opened the interview. Then he asked his first question. "Mrs Porter, do you know why you have been arrested?"

She answered quietly, "Yes."

"Do you know that it is a criminal offence if you do not disclose to the police information you have relating to the commission or imminent commission of an act of terrorism?"

Naomi shot a nervous glance at her solicitor. His nod of assent was barely perceptible. She answered "Yes" again.

Platt placed her left hand on Cosgrove's arm. Her right arm was supported by a medical sling. Cosgrove glanced at her and nodded.

Platt opened the file, taking her time. She scanned the top sheet and asked, "Did you conspire to lure Member of Parliament Edmund Lafitte to the restaurant known as 'Doogie's' on the evening of Saturday, twentieth of March this year?"

Naomi leaned towards her legal adviser who whispered something in her ear. She replied, "Yes, but there were mitigating circumstances."

Cosgrove made a note, as the inspector continued. "Did you know the reason why he was required to be in that place at precisely that time?"

The question seemed to make Naomi Porter uncomfortable. She stuttered, "Yes, but – but there were – mitigating circumstances."

Platt stared at the woman for a few moments. Then she said, "We will get around to any possible mitigation later. Let's just confirm that you knew that there was to be an attempt on Mr Lafitte's life?"

It was a few long seconds before the suspect answered with a hesitant, "No."

"So you are saying that you did *not* know, in advance, that somebody would try to kill him? But you have just said that you knew there was a reason for him to be there. If you did not know about the bomber, what was that reason?"

A bleak, miserable expression appeared on Naomi's face. She shook her head, mutely.

Platt waited for several seconds. Then she said, "Mrs Porter has not answered."

At that point there was a double knock on the door. The constable in attendance opened it and then stood aside.

Sergeant Cosgrove said, "For the record, Commander Bennett has entered the room."

Bennett came forward and drew back the vacant chair. He put a file on the table and sat down, saying, "Commander Richard Bennett, attending at ten forty-six. Please continue."

Again, Inspector Platt took her time. She said, "You say you did not know that there was to be an attempt to kill Mr. Lafitte outside the restaurant, but you have not told us why you conspired to get him there at that time. Just tell us why."

Naomi Porter's face was ashen. Again she did not reply.

Bennett intervened, using a quiet, moderate tone. "Were you under orders? Acting under duress, perhaps?"

Naomi turned to look at her solicitor. They brought their heads together briefly for a whispered exchange. Then the man said, "My client declines to answer that question."

Bennett made it clear that he was still in charge. He smiled and said, "Very well, Mrs Porter, let's leave that for a moment. He opened his file.

"When you learned from Mr Lafitte that he was to be moved temporarily to the narrow boat at Collier basin," he paused to stare directly at Naomi, "who did you tell?"

The effect of the question on Naomi Porter's face was dramatic. Her mouth fell open; she appeared stunned. She swivelled her head to look at her legal adviser, as if expecting him to get her out of trouble. He frowned and shrugged slightly.

She turned back to answer, "I... nobody. I didn't tell anyone."

Bennett sat back and brought his hands together, locking the fingers. "That's odd, Mrs Porter. You see, apart from the police, you are the *only* person who knew that in advance. Yet only a day later, another attempt was made on his life. Can you explain that?"

She did not answer. A leaden silence followed. Mary Platt was impressed but not surprised at witnessing again Bennett's clever, subtle interviewing technique. She knew the suspect was cornered. What would her boss do next?

Bennett leaned forward again, placing his elbows on the table. He took his time, apparently scanning a document in his file. Then he closed the file, looked up and smiled at Naomi. Using a moderate and conciliatory tone, he said, "It's not all bad news." Mary Platt could see that he had the full attention of all present as he went on. "Actually, it isn't you we're after." He leaned forward. "That incident at the marina cost four lives, one of them that of a dedicated police officer. The whole mess has definitely moved up a notch."

Naomi Porter sank her head into her hands. Bennett said, quietly, "There may be a way in which your 'mitigating circumstances' can kick in to make a big difference to your position."

CHAPTER FORTY-FOUR

The place they had chosen was an unfussy Anglo-French restaurant popular with local office workers at lunchtime and it was filling up fast. Naomi Porter sat alone, nursing a glass of red wine.

The man she was waiting for was late again. No surprise there, but this would be the last time. As for surprises, she had one for him. A big one. She would at least draw immense satisfaction from that.

Seated in a corner well away from Naomi, Richard Bennett had a good view of her table and of the front door. He picked up his wine bottle and glanced at the label, before pouring some wine into the two glasses on the table.

"A Margaux, nothing better for a celebration. But worth it, despite the price tag."

Across the table, DCC Helen Aylmer said, "I'll agree if it works. I'm not convinced that Porter's strong enough to see it through. The man's a ruthless bully."

"Oh, she'll get him all right. She won't fold."

"Hmm, we shall see." She took a sip of the Bordeaux. "Good choice, this."

"So was hers. Either a twenty-year stretch or with luck and a charitable view of her cooperation, maybe as little as three or four. A no-brainer, really."

Javid Nasir, immaculately turned out in a smart charcoal grey pinstripe suit, strolled in through the door. He looked around briefly before catching Naomi's eye, turning on the faux smile and sauntering over.

"Hi, sweetheart," was his greeting as he leaned over to kiss her.

Naomi turned her face aside. Better a brief contact on the cheek than something more unpleasant on her lips. "Hello," she answered.

He drew his chair out and sat down. "Ordered yet?" he asked, picking up the menu.

"Only the wine. It's Beaujolais."

He frowned. "You know I prefer Bordeaux."

"Sorry, my mistake." She resisted the urge to smile.

The waiter came over and they placed their orders. Nasir picked up the wine bottle, examining the label critically before pouring some into his glass.

"Oh well, it'll do, for once." He put the bottle down and looked up. "You said it was urgent? What's so urgent that you couldn't tell me on the phone?"

"It's sensitive, it has to be face-to-face."

His eyebrows arched. "Sensitive? OK, sweetheart. Go ahead, I'm here."

"I won't be doing any more special jobs for you. Not now, not ever again."

He threw his hands up. "Not that again." His tone changed and he lowered his voice. "You do what I want, when I want, and exactly as I want it, or..."

The waiter had arrived with their first courses. Nasir stopped speaking as they leaned back to let the man put the dishes down.

He left them, saying "Bon appetite," mispronouncing the word.

Naomi asked, "Or what?"

Nasir smirked. "Or you'll need surgery. Do I have to spell it out for you?" He snorted, "I come all this way for that? We've been through this before, so what's new?"

Naomi was ready for this, choosing her words carefully. "Twice I've delivered the lamb and both times you and your lot have failed to slaughter him. I want to stop before your IS people's incompetence does me worse damage than your threats. You killed four people at that fiasco. I'm telling you, I've had enough."

"Keep your voice down," he hissed, raising his own more than he may have intended.

She looked at him evenly. "You know, there was a time I thought we really had something good going for us. Then you got in deeper with them and now it's gone way beyond that. I can't deal with it anymore. Not unless things change." She picked up her cutlery and started on the light first course. He had not replied so she went on, speaking softly. "I'm keeping my voice down. We both have successful careers. Now would be a good time to cut your ties with IS and get a life. A real life, with me."

The man's face darkened. Naomi held her breath. Had she pressed the right button? He wiped his mouth with his napkin and spoke slowly, speaking so quietly that she could barely hear him.

"You fucking bitch. Who do you think you are? You don't get it, do you? I'm *proud* to work for the State of Islam in this shit country of yours and I will never change that. I don't give up. The next operation that I plan will fix

Lafitte for good. Next time, I won't be using amateurs." He sat back, breathing heavily.

Naomi's eyes rounded. *It worked*! As calmly as she could, she said, "OK, I get it. And I don't need to keep my voice down. Neither do you. But we have to get the lip sync right."

His brow furrowed. "Lip sync? What the fuck...?"

"All around us," she waved her fork in an arc, "there are policemen with cameras on us."

Nasir looked as if he had been struck by a rock. His eyes widened in a look of sheer horror.

She added, "To make certain that they get the synch right on your commentary. I'm wearing a wire, *sweetheart*." Stressing that last word gave her a delicious buzz.

Nasir's face betrayed instant, uncontrolled fury. He leapt up, tipping his chair back. "*Bitch!*" he screamed, moving to attack her. He was immediately grabbed by two beefy men, who wrestled him to the ground.

CHAPTER FORTY-FIVE

Stella did not know why Hector Walford had asked her to go to his office. The room reeked of stale cigar smoke, with a tinge of the more pleasant and familiar musty odour of books. It was a corner room with views over the town's main shopping centre. Stella hoped that the senior partner would be giving her the good news that she had been expecting for months, confirmation of her elevation to partnership in the firm. The five weeks since the funeral had been a difficult time and she had thrown herself into her work. Keeping busy helped. She might never get over the shock of losing Edmund and although nothing could even begin to compensate for her loss, the promotion would help ease the pain.

He was a good boss on the whole but when it suited him, Walford liked to adopt an avuncular manner that could be a tad patronizing. He was doing it now, as he settled back in his expensive leather chair behind the enormous oak desk. He raised his bushy grey eyebrows, starting with a fatuous question.

"How are you getting on, Stella?" he asked. "I mean, at home."

"I'm managing, Hector."

The senior partner sat forward, placing his elbows on the desk and steepling his fingers. "Good, good." Stella said nothing, waiting for him to get to the point. Walford turned on a smile. "I have some good news for you."

Stella perked up. *Was it really going to happen?* She did not reply, so he continued. "I've had a call from the Cameron Farquhar partnership. Do you know them?"

"The Edinburgh law firm?" Heavyweights in the legal world. Stella wondered where this was heading.

"One of the oldest in the city."

Stella could not recall having any contact with them, certainly not recently. "What's the good news? Who's our client?"

Walford smiled, genuinely this time, it seemed. "Not ours, theirs. Your great aunt Esther Stewart."

Stella frowned. "What great aunt? Stewart? I've never heard of her."

Walford seemed to be enjoying himself. "I'm not too surprised. They did say that they'd had to trace you. Esther Stewart, formerly MacGregor, has passed away and it appears that you are the only known living relative."

"Are you serious? Is this about a legacy, then? I knew that we had some MacGregors in our family somewhere, but I've never had any contact with any of them."

"Yes. It appears she's left you a property. A cottage near Moreston." He picked up an envelope that was on the desk and handed it to her. "This is for you. They were going to send it but decided that it would be better if I gave it to you."

Stella turned it over, scanning the label on the front. It was addressed to her. "Why?"

"You'll need some time off, you need to go to Scotland."

"Do I have to? I'm too busy to take time off."

Walford leaned back. "Is it such a bad idea? You could

do with a break and this seems like the perfect opportunity. There's nothing on your work schedule that can't wait a couple of weeks. I had a call from George Hewitt, senior partner at Camerons. He's keen to meet you, handling the matter himself."

Stella could not understand that. "Why? It can't be that important to them."

Walford inclined his head. "Maybe it's because you're better known than you think." He put his hands, palms down, on the desk. "Anyway, that's all I know. There's a letter in there with all the details." He stood up. "Just a couple of things I'd like to add. First, take the time off, Stella. Go to Scotland, the break will do you good." He smiled again. "After that, your partnership in the firm will be here, if you still want it."

On her way back to her office, Stella was enjoying the feeling of elation that came with confirmation of the promotion. Well, she deserved it. Years of hard work and unswerving loyalty to the firm had brought their just reward, finally. But what did he mean by 'if you still want it'? The welcome but unexpected acquisition of a cottage in Scotland was hardly likely to be a good enough reason for not taking the promotion.

On the express train approaching Edinburgh the following Monday morning, Stella had time to reflect. She felt that she didn't need a holiday, so there really was no need for her to be in Scotland. The letter had changed her mind. It was signed by George Hewitt himself and it was he who was to meet her at Edinburgh Waverley Station shortly. Then she would change trains and go on to Moreston, where she would board a local to her destination, a place called Auchterdern.

She had enjoyed the luxury of a first class sleeper compartment on the overnight Caledonian Express, all paid for. By whom? She would know soon enough. Much better than flying and more convenient for her meeting with Hewitt.

She was intrigued. Why would the senior partner of such a prestigious law firm take the trouble to meet her? At seven-twenty in the morning! She did not believe it was because of the brief time she'd been in the news. Perhaps it was something to do with her mysterious deceased aunt? She checked her watch. Nearly seven-forty. The train was running late and she was due to meet Hewitt at the entrance to Coffee Heaven. The letter said that it was in the main complex, not difficult to find.

"No, please, let me." George Hewitt insisted on paying the bill.

"Thank you." Stella picked up her breakfast tray and followed Hewitt to the table where she had deposited her suitcase a few minutes before.

He said, "Coffee and croissants, a good choice." He was having the same.

She looked across at him. She had expected him to be in his late sixties, perhaps even older, but he could not be much over fifty, she thought. He was of average height, with a full head of hair, greying at the edges. He was wearing lightweight rimless spectacles.

"This is convenient," she declared. "I skipped breakfast on the train."

"We've time enough, although it could be close. Your train was twenty minutes late arriving. The Moreston express departs at eight thirty-two, Platform Sixteen. It's about a five minute walk, allow ten. So we have around twenty minutes." His tone was measured, with only a trace of the Scottish accent that she had expected.

"And I have a hundred questions. Are you sure we have enough time?"

He smiled, his eyes twinkling. "Och, I couldn't possibly manage that. About ninety would be the limit, if you keep them short. Ask away."

Stella was munching. She swallowed, smiled and said, "For a start, why would the senior partner in your firm be the one to meet me? My modest legacy is not important enough, surely?"

"A loaded question, Mrs Tudor. If I agree that the matter is unimportant, I run the risk of upsetting you. Every client's need is important to us. But if I say that it is, I would be uncomfortable because actually that is not the case."

Stella's smile widened. What a charmer. "It's Stella, please. And if I may say so, that's a lawyer's response. So it isn't too important? In that case, you haven't answered my question."

"Well, Stella, you're right. It's not hugely important, but that does not mean that it's a trivial issue. Quite the contrary." He was looking down, stirring his coffee. "Fact is, I have an apartment in Drummond Place, less than a mile away, so it was no problem for me to get here, even at a time when I would normally be taking a good breakfast." He looked up. "The reason why it's not a trivial matter will be revealed to you by Mr Brown at Auchter. Like I said in the letter, he's the estate agent up there. More I cannot say."

"You can't say? Why not?"

"Those are another two questions." His eyes twinkled again. "At this rate, you could get close to the ninety. Mr Brown's the one who'll explain, I promise. He'll be there at the station to meet you."

"How will I know him?"

"I cannot describe the man, I've not met him. But Auchter's a request stop, on a branch line out of Moreston, a feeder that terminates at the stop after Auchterdern, to give the place its full name. Trains run only on Mondays and Fridays, one in each direction. If you happen to be waiting at one of the stations for an oncoming train, you have to hail it by raising your hand and waving so that the driver can see you."

"Are you serious?"

"Totally, I assure you. So Brown will be there and it's quite possible that there will be no one else around. If so, he'll be the one waving, to make sure that the train stops." He looked at his watch. "Now, I think we'd better make a move. If you miss this train there'll be others going to Moreston, but none that will get you there in time for you to make your connection."

It was not until Stella had boarded that she realized that she was no wiser; she still had no idea of what was going on.

CHAPTER FORTY-SIX

Moreston to Auchterdern. The last lap, Stella mused, savouring the exceptional beauty of the rolling hills and shallow, verdant valleys unfolding. A perfect setting for a holiday cottage. That said, did she really need it? Somewhere so remote that it would take more than a day to get to? And if she decided to rent it out, there would be costs involved in managing and maintaining the place. Perhaps best if she just sold it. She had been given no idea as to its value, but doubtless the man she was to meet would have some answers.

She had boarded the single-carriage train at Moreston with about a dozen or so others, all of whom seemed to know each other. Hardly a train. It was more a sort of bus on rails, with all the passengers in one cabin. She was greeted politely by every one of them and was included in the goodbyes by all who disembarked at the intermediate stop. Rural Scottish hospitality, a refreshing change from the impersonal, cold indifference that was the norm when travelling in the south.

There were just two couples remaining, seated near the front, several rows ahead of her. They had been chatting amiably with one another.

"Auchter in five minutes, ladies and gentlemen." The voice of the driver rattled mechanically through a grille on

the bulkhead that isolated him from the passengers. *"If Wullie's asleep again, you gi'e him a nudge, Paula."*

All four chuckled and Stella smiled. Yes, a refreshing change. Could she consider living here? The thought was dismissed as soon as it came to her. Impossible. She had to make a living.

The train slowed as it approached Auchter. The place seemed little more than a hamlet, with houses and bungalows in neat rows. The station was deserted, its sole structure a wooden building that bore more than a passing resemblance to a large garden shed that needed a fresh coat of varnish. A painted metal sign above the exit declared it to be Auchterdern.

Stella stayed in her seat while the other four passengers stood by the door, waiting to alight. None had any luggage. She collected her holdall and wheeled suitcase and stood up.

"You're getting off here, Miss?" one of the men asked.

"Yes, I am."

"Will ye be needing transport?"

The carriage wheels squealed in protest as the brakes took hold and the train lurched to a stop, its diesel engine throbbing rhythmically.

Stella replied, "I'm being met, thank you."

"Ah." The others stepped out, but he stood aside to let Stella off. She nodded her thanks and stepped onto the platform with her luggage. He followed and moved to join his companions, who were heading for the exit. "Then I'll bid ye good day, Miss."

Stella looked around. The place was deserted, nobody around except for one person. A man dressed in a sports jacket and jeans standing at the other end of the platform, about fifty metres away. Mr Brown, she presumed. He was wearing a tartan peaked cap, beneath which his face was adorned by a full brown beard. Heavy dark-rimmed spectacles perched on his nose. As he started to walk towards her, Stella moved forward to meet him, until they were only yards apart.

The train began to pull away, gathering speed. To Stella's surprise, the man stopped and turned his back, apparently gazing into the distance. She took another step forward.

"Mr Brown?" she asked. "Are you Mr Brown?"

He spun around to face her. "I am now."

"Good God!" The shock of hearing Edmund's voice was more than Stella could handle. Blood drained from her face and she felt her head getting lighter. Her grip on the holdall slackened and it fell to the ground. A split second before she lost consciousness she became aware of his arms around her, strong, supporting and comforting.

"Better now?" Stella heard as she came round. She opened her eyes to see Edmund's bearded face just inches from her own. They were sitting on a wooden bench, her head cradled in the crook of his arm.

She blinked. "Edmund?"

"Hello, sweetie. Yes, it's me. Only now it's Edward."

Stella put a hand to her face. "Uh, I passed out. Sorry."

He smiled. "You're allowed to faint when you see a ghost."

She sat up. "Some ghost. A *beard*?"

This time he grinned. "You don't like it?"

"No."

"I can trim it down, if you like."

"Anything's better than that hedge."

He was looking at her. "God, how I've missed you." He cupped her face in his hands and kissed her tenderly. Then he broke away and stood up. "Come on, time to get you home."

Home? Her world had just been turned around and her head was spinning. Far too soon to make assumptions; time enough for explanations later.

Stella had a head full of questions that needed answers. Where to start? They had been on the road in his Range Rover for a few minutes. She had said nothing, she was still reeling from the shock of seeing him. In the flesh! She took a long look at the man who was driving. He had taken off the cap and glasses. Yes, it was her Edmund. He needed a haircut and there was that unkempt beard, but otherwise he looked well. Her feelings now were a curious mixture of relief and joy; her initial anger at being deceived had abated. He swivelled his head to smile at her.

"A penny for your thoughts?"

She replied, her tone icy calm. "Since you ask, I think you're an arrogant, self-centred, thoughtless bastard."

His eyebrows arched, his eyes rounded. He seemed about to speak but checked, his lips curling into a crooked smile. "Hmm, unreserved praise, then."

"Well, what the hell did you expect? Flags and bunting? A brass band? Have you *any* idea what you've put me through?"

"Actually, yes." His tone was no longer flippant. "But I had no choice. Surely you realize that, sweetheart?" He glanced at her again. "You've never been out of my thoughts. I've been thinking about you and this day, for weeks."

Stella was looking out through the side window, taking in the beauty of the scenery. Yes, he had no choice; she accepted that. But the whole mess was his fault in the first place.

"Who else knew?" she asked.

"Apart from the spooks, nobody. They told you the plan, but not the bit about me being topped. It was their idea to keep that from you." He glanced at her. "So that you would react as expected."

"It worked. Bastards!"

"I'm really sorry, sweetie, but they insisted."

Moments later she asked, "Hector? Was he in on it?" She wondered briefly whether her promotion had been triggered finally by sympathy. Surely not? She'd earned it by her own hard work.

"They had to tell him, to get you the time off with a credible reason."

"So there wasn't a deceased aunt? She never existed?"

"Only in the sense that she lived in a cottage that doesn't exist either."

She was starting to get annoyed again. "It isn't funny, Ed."

"No, you're right. Sorry. I can't help myself, I'm just so happy, delighted that you're really here."

"So nobody else knew, apart from the spooks and Hector?"

"And George Hewitt in Edinburgh, of course."

"So that's why he was so vague. And Hector's a devious

sod." She shook her head. "I can't believe I've been so gullible."

He was grinning. "As you said, it worked." Before she could reply he added, "I think you'll lighten up when you see the house."

She knew he'd deliberately changed the subject. To her own surprise, she realized that she didn't mind. "Is it far?"

He nodded forwards. "About ten miles. It's called Tully Lodge. Six bedrooms on three acres, with stables at the back. It's on the side of a hill and the views of Rannoch Loch are stunning."

Stella had begun to relax. Stables? Wow! She'd always loved horses. Maybe it would be all right, perhaps even worth giving up her job for. Food for thought. There was still so much that she needed to find out. It was her turn to change the subject.

"What will you do now?"

"Do?"

She made a face. "I mean, for a living. A job, not that you actually need to make a living like the rest of us."

"I'm writing. Or rather, Edward Brown is. I've done lots of stuff for magazines, articles in newspapers, that sort of thing. I was once offered a column in a Sunday paper."

"Were you now? I didn't know that."

He gestured. "I turned it down. Didn't have time for that sort of commitment."

"You'll have plenty of time now. What will you be writing?"

"Novels. I read a lot, especially thrillers. Having a go at novels appeals. I've made a start, got a good plot that I'm working on."

She was intrigued. "What's it about?"

"An MP whose life is threatened by jihadists." He grinned. "All I need is a good ending."

She shook her head lightly. "No chance. No one would believe that!"

"As you say, I have plenty of time now. Writing could keep me busy for the rest of my life, and this is the perfect place for it."

Yes, Stella thought, *that's something that he could do for the rest of his life*. That reminded her of another question.

"Tell me something," she said. "What about that coffin?"

His brow furrowed. "Coffin?"

"A perfectly good coffin. Solid oak, they said. Expensive, with fancy brass fittings. Cost me a small fortune. All just firewood?"

"Ah, the coffin. Nothing we could do about that. You'd have needed to buy one anyway."

"Are you saying it was empty? Is that why it was sealed?"

"No, there was a real body in there. Fortunately not mine." He smiled again. "And dead, of course. An unfortunate consequence of losing his head."

This time she laughed. "OK, I buy that."

"I mean it. It was really lost, not in the coffin at all."

"Then what...?"

The car drew up at a junction. Edmund turned to say, "The head? By now, probably melted down to make candles."

Author's Note

Thank you for reading this book. If you enjoyed it, please leave a review on Amazon.com, Amazon.co.uk or on my website: www.chriscalder.com

I try never to lose sight of the fact that nothing ever written cannot be improved. So I welcome all feedback and value readers' opinions. I am particularly keen to hear your views and respond to all emails that I receive.

Chris Calder